BRILLIANT

BRILLIANT

MARNE DAVIS KELLOGG

ST. MARTIN'S PRESS   NEW YORK

www.stmartins.com

Library of Congress Cataloging-in-Publication Data

Kellogg, Marne Davis.
    Brilliant / Marne Davis Kellogg.—1st ed.
       p. cm.
    ISBN 0-312-30347-5
    1. Americans—England—Fiction. 2. Women art dealers—Fiction. 3. Middle-aged women—Fiction. 4. Provence (France)—Fiction. 5. Women—England—Fiction. 6. London (England)—Fiction. 7. Auctioneers—Fiction. I. Title.

PS3561.E39253B75 2003
813'.54—dc21

                                                         2003041586

10   9   8   7   6   5   4   3   2

For Peter, my dearest darling

ACKNOWLEDGMENTS

Every time I sit down to write a book or tell a story, I'm reminded that I'm the luckiest person in the world, getting to do what I love best. In the case of *Brilliant*, not only was I surrounded and supported by my family and friends, but I got to write about jewelry, fraud, theft, good food, and fine wines—what a delicious combination. It was heaven.

My thanks for guidance in the beautiful world of gems, jewelry, and jewelry-making go first and foremost to Bob Gibson at Raymond C. Yard, Inc., in New York, and Brien Foster, Foster & Son, Denver. Both gentlemen were extremely generous with their time, knowledge, and expertise, and any mistakes that have been made are mine. Thank you also to master jeweler Salvador Vargas, who taught me the basics of making fine jewelry; Henry Baker of Oscar Heyman, Inc., New York; and Lana Lee of Neiman-Marcus Precious Jewels, Denver, who gave me a professional jeweler's loupe, which I treasure. I also appreciated the courtesy with which I was greeted and given behind-the-scenes tours at Van Cleef & Arpels, Place Vendôme, Paris, and Harry Winston, Beverly Hills.

Thank you to Jacqueline Fay and the Sotheby's jewelry department for the opportunity to observe an auction of important jewelry from the inside. Kick Keswick's skill at stealing jewelry from Ballantine & Company Auctioneers is fictitious and has absolutely nothing to do with Sotheby's or anything I learned or observed at Sotheby's.

When it came to selecting the wines for the meals in *Brilliant*, Dorothy Gaiter and John Brecher, who write the *Wine Journal* for the Friday edition of the *Wall Street Journal* and are the authors of *Love by the Glass*, made exquisite choices. I'm indebted to them for sharing their time and vast knowledge.

There are not enough words of thanks for my agent, Robert Gottlieb, president and CEO of Trident Media Group; Kimberly Whalen, director of Foreign Rights; and former Foreign Rights director Maya Perez, for guiding and representing me so well and landing me at St. Martin's Press. Sally Richardson, publisher, St. Martin's Press, and Matthew Shear, senior vice president and publisher of St. Martin's Paperbacks, are outstanding to work with and I am very grateful for their enthusiasm about my work. My editor, Jennifer Enderlin, associate publisher and executive editor, is a total visionary and genius. Working on a regular basis with her and her assistant, Kimberly Cardascia, has been one of my most delightful experiences, ever.

What would I do without our friends? Mary and Richard, who read early manuscripts and have bottomless bottles of rum and scotch; and Marcy and Bruce, who not only have thrown spectacular launch parties at the Denver Public Library, but also provided research materials and access essential to the completion of this book. Delores and Stephen, for introducing us to Provence. Thanks also to Pam and Bill, Mary Lou and Randy, Judith, Mita, and the Norfolk book ladies.

My family is so great—they are all fun and funny and they amaze me: my parents with their strength, courage, and steadfast observation of the five-o'clock cocktail hour no matter the obstacles; my brother John, with his encyclopedic knowledge; my brother Drew, with his business expertise and culinary nerve; Hunter, Courtney, Duncan, and Delaney, for their energy and beauty and for making the tremendous sacrifices required to be in the Marine Corps; Pete and Bede, for their independence, talent, good humor, and creativity; our wire fox terrier, Kick, for keeping our world in a constant chaotic roil, and, of course, my husband, Peter, who, like fine wine, just gets better and better and better—cowboy boots and all!

BRILLIANT

ONE

I've reached the point in my life where the thrill of my job is generally vastly more thrilling and interesting to me than the thrill of sex. I'm really into dependability these days.

Especially now, with the incessant buyout negotiations over. Our lives had taken on the heady, sexually charged atmosphere of a political campaign—late-night meetings, secret phone calls, and passwords—all of which masked the fear and apprehension of the reality, of how our lives would be changed. We—and by "we" I mean me, Sir Benjamin, and a handful of old-timers, specialists, and experts, who have been with the firm for dozens of years—were busily pretending the so-called merger would have only a good side. We pretended that if we kept up our façade of charm and fair play, there would be no downside; they would let us keep doing everything the way we always had, with the notable exception being that they would have delivered us from the bondage of financial jeopardy. We would become the crowning jewel in Brace International's already dazzling charm bracelet of luxury goods manufacturers. They would keep the wolf away from our door.

Who were we kidding?

They *were* the wolf. We were Little Red Riding Hood, and we'd pretended they weren't going to gobble us up; that Ballantine & Company Auctioneer, Ltd.'s proud, almost three-hundred-year history as a family-owned firm wouldn't be sucked under and obliterated by a high-rolling, high-style American buccaneer and his legendary overdrive life that seemed to use *"W," People,* and *Vanity Fair* magazines as his personal diaries. Oh, my, yes. We were about to have sex kittens, haute couture, fast cars, and scandals out the old wazoo.

We had no choice. Sell out ("merge," as all involved insisted upon calling it) or sink. Without bubbles. Just slide under and vanish. As anxious and sad as I was about the company's future, I have to admit that from a strictly business point of view, the push and pull of the takeover had been exhilarating. If you *really* want to know the truth: It was *better* than sex.

But now we had reality. Every day, Sir Benjamin Ballantine's ongoing humiliation grew into a heavier and heavier burden. Sometimes, it was so crushing, I felt I couldn't breathe. So, when the phone rang at three-forty-five in the morning, I knew it wasn't going to be anything fun. I knew who it would be and why he was calling.

"Kick." Sir Benjamin's jammy accent echoed through his speakerphone as cleanly as though he were talking to me from the other side of the room. He said my name as a statement, no question, no apology for calling in the middle of the night. He said it as though we'd already been in the middle of a conversation and he'd just had a new thought. I knew him like a book. Just as I knew that Silvia, his angry, anorexic, aristocratic wife, her lips locked perpetually in a bloodless line of disappointment, slumbered fitfully upstairs, one eye on the clock gauging how much longer until the next sleeping pill.

Tonight, he sounded slightly different, a little more off, a little drunker. His tone was wan. It sounded parched, empty, and tired. Thank God, I thought, he's getting as sick of this as I am.

"Yes, Benjamin," I answered. "What is it?"

"I just wanted to hear your voice"—he paused for effect—"one last time."

"For heaven's sake, don't start all this suicide business again. I can't take it."

Truthfully? I wished with all my heart that he would follow through on his threats: just get a gun and go out in the backyard and shoot himself. Put himself and the rest of us out of this drenching misery.

Occasionally, I thought about shooting him myself.

"Wait a minute," I said. "Wait a minute. Let me get a little squared away here."

"But . . . ," he began.

"Hold on, hold on. Just give me a second."

"*Goddamn it, Kick, don't put down the phone. Please . . . ,*" he sobbed.

But it didn't move me. I laid the receiver on the table—I used to lay it down gently and soundlessly; but now, I just put it there, if the receiver hitting the tabletop made a clatter into his ears, well, it did. I pushed myself up against the headboard and snapped on my bed lamp, turning my pink-and-champagne paisley room into a comforting and serene friend. I tugged my satin nightgown loose from around my legs. Then I got all my covers neatly arranged, combed my fingers through my streaky blond hair, and lit a cigarette. I always have to have everything in place before I can do anything properly—listen, cook, take a note, really anything at all—but once I'm set, I'm set. There isn't anybody more rapt than I, when the situation demands it. This one did not.

As I reached for the phone, I spotted a stash of chocolate mint wafers under the curved edge of the ashtray and slipped one of the luscious little square green-and-brown sandwiches into my mouth, where it began to melt almost immediately. A creamy little bite with the mind-clearing snap of mint—the ideal remedy for the situation at hand.

"Back," I said. All I could hear was the sound of him struggling for composure. My tongue forced the soft chocolate into the roof of my mouth until it formed an even coating. I ate another.

"I can't do it anymore, Kick."

"Oh?" I didn't even try to keep the boredom out of my voice. I tucked the receiver under my chin, reached for the new issue of *Country Life* I'd brought home from the office, and flipped through it, looking for our ad. There it was—Mrs. Baker's glorious ruby cabochon and round diamond necklace—shining from the page like a bonfire, scheduled to be auctioned after the first of the year. What a magnificent piece it was, a true work of art with each pea-sized cabochon fashioned as a blossom resting in diamond petals. I hoped some very lucky lady got it, not some heartless dealer who would break it down for the stones and melt the platinum and gold to use for something else.

"God, I hate all of this," Benjamin wailed. "I hate him. I hate his tight Italian suits and those god-awful cheesy diamond cuff links and shiny ties. I hate that goddamned slicked-back hair and his whore of a wife. I hate his commonness, his lack of class. I hate the way he hates me. The contempt on his face when I'm speaking. I want to slap him, teach him some respect."

"Benjamin, please." I yawned. "Let's talk about the future. Why don't you retire? Become chairman emeritus?" I noticed a little snag on my embroidered silk coverlet, retrieved a small pair of sewing scissors out of the bed table drawer, and clipped it. "There's no shame in that. You can get a little place in the country and get away from everyone. Stop the fight. It's destroying you. It's not worth it."

"I'll die before I quit."

I didn't say a word. I took a last drag of my cigarette and puffed out a chain of smoke rings, a singularly unbecoming skill no lady should perform in public, and believe me, I don't; but at the moment, there wasn't much else to do.

"I even feel you pulling away from me. It's written all over your face. That's all right. I don't blame you. But you know I can't retire and leave the House of Ballantine in the hands of an outsider. Especially an *Irishman*." The concept of the Irishman threw him into a new fit of sobbing—as far as he was concerned, he might as well have sold to Satan himself.

I flipped two more pages—Good, our ad was much better than Sotheby's. Better piece of jewelry. Better layout and lighting. Better photography.

"There's been a Ballantine at the helm since 1740—the burden of

260 years of family tradition coming to end on my watch is more than I can bear. I don't know what else to do. I can't see any way to win." He sounded lost and far away.

The words had already formed themselves inside my mouth to say, "For heaven's sake, Benjamin, get a goddamned hold of yourself. Act like a man for a change." But the explosion reverberated into my ear as unexpectedly as a car crash. I never heard or saw it coming.

Then, there was nothing but echoing silence.

I held the silent receiver for I'm not sure how long, my mind a complete blank, until I heard Silvia's shrill voice trumpeting down the stairs, so piercing it was scarcely muffled by the closed library doors. "Benjamin? Benjamin? What are you doing now? You woke me up out of a dead sleep. Benjamin! Answer me!" I heard the deep rumble of the heavy pocket doors sliding open. "Benjamin, do you have any idea what time it is? Oh, my God."

My breathing was shallow, tentative. I hung up the phone. It was over.

I was free.

T W O

I suppose I was in shock, but I felt surprisingly calm. And happy. No, not happy. Relieved. I leaned against the headboard and lit another cigarette and had another chocolate and just looked around, knowing that for the first time in my life, I was in control of my life. The lightness was amazing. I was floating. It's just me.

When the merger had been completed and Owen Brace had taken over, it took less than seventy-two hours to see how completely unworkable the arrangement was between him and Benjamin. The two men could scarcely bear the sight of one another. While not terribly far apart in age, when it came to vision and energy, Owen was waxing at fifty-four and Benjamin waning at sixty-five. The men were polar opposites.

Owen Brace, a self-made man, Irish-American, one of the most successful international takeover artists in the history of business, was a high-speed adrenaline addict and a notorious slash-and-burn specialist. The energy and power he exuded were so tangible, he seemed to suck all the oxygen from the air around him. Regardless of Benjamin's jealous accusations that Brace was cheesy and common, both of which applied to a significant degree, he was also dashing and debonair. And dangerous. If he were a sportsman, I think he would have been a fencing master, but as far as I could tell, the only sport he loved was business. Oh, and sex. If he wasn't on the phone or in a meeting, he was in a bed.

Well-born Sir Benjamin Ballantine, on the other hand, an Englishman through and through, was polite, patrician, a gentleman, duty-bound by his mother's archaic Victorian upbringing. His low-key, amicable style that lured clients to Ballantine & Company, his self-deprecating sense of humor, and workmanlike talent on the auction floor had not withstood the test of time. They belonged to another world, dust was piled on their shoulders. He was unable to make the leap to accommodate what twenty-first-century customers required. His stubborn refusal to grow or adapt pushed him deeper and deeper into depression and dragged the company and its demoralized staff down with him.

The only thing that kept Owen and Benjamin from coming to blows was me: their senior executive assistant, caught literally in the middle of the *ancien* and *noveau régimes*. Fortunately for all of us, I'm more stable than most people. I can carry a lot on my broad shoulders.

Because I'd been with the firm for what was now decades, and become a mother figure to Benjamin (although I was significantly younger), it was justifiable to see why my loyalties had lain with him. But finally, my battle standard flagged. He robbed me of my sleep every night. I was exhausted. My tiredness grew in direct proportion to his tiresomeness. He'd become excruciating and infuriating, making me regret my pledge to his father—my late, beloved, deus ex machina, Sir Cramner Ballantine—that I would keep an eye on his aging, ineffectual son, not to let him stray off into troubled waters. Even more importantly, I'd sworn not to let him run Ballantine & Company into the ground, which, in spite of my efforts, he had. I was sick of the whole arrangement, unfulfilled by my obstinate loyalty.

I was still angry at Sir Cramner for dying, even if he had been ninety-two by the time he left. I missed him so deeply, I couldn't seem to get the light turned back on in my life. He'd been gone for almost three years, but not a single day passed that I didn't think about him, and how much I still loved him. I wanted him to come back to me, even if it was just long enough to kiss his sweet, laughing lips one more time.

But, as the days and months and years passed, and I didn't seem to be getting any closer to my own demise, I knew I needed to get back on course. I was tired of being alone. There was no one to talk to.

I wanted to go to my little farm in Provence and lie in the sun, smell the lavender, listen to the bees. Have lunch with my friends. To spend the second half of my life with people who enjoyed the same things I did. But the problem is, with my past, it's just not that simple.

THREE

My life began the afternoon of my eighteenth birthday when Sir Cramner Ballantine, then a dashing sixty-one, had his driver pull over and offer me a ride in a rainstorm as I made my soggy way, wobbling and weeping, down Carnaby Street in a silly little pink-and-champagne paisley minidress and high-heeled boots to which I was patently missuited, physically and emotionally. I wasn't a Mary Quant–Carnaby Street thing. I was a chubby little farm girl—vastly more Hey-There-Georgy-Girl than Twiggy—from Oklahoma, for heaven's sake, in Europe on a thirty-day, twenty-city, marathon tour from Oklahoma State University, which I attended on a geology scholarship studying absolutely nothing of any value, waiting for I knew not what to happen.

The realization that I'd made a serious and costly fashion mistake that had taken all my spending money for the rest of the trip had triggered something in me. It had plunged me into loneliness and despair, and forced me to admit certain things to myself. I was walking down a strange street in a strange city in a foreign country in a downpour having an epiphany, a nervous breakdown, a catharsis. My life was a dead end. *I* was a dead end. I was damaged goods—everything I'd said was true about myself was false. Everything. I was so desperate to fit in at college, I'd created an entire persona, a fleshed-out history, including a loving family who were tragically, (and conveniently), all killed in a house fire on our big dairy farm up near Cleo Springs.

"Maybe you remember reading about it," I'd say to my sorority sisters. "Our whole farm burned to the ground. It was in all the papers—I was the only one to escape. It was horrible."

"Oh, yes," they'd answer sympathetically. "I do remember hearing about that—what a nightmare."

They were just being kind, of course. They were nice girls from nice families. They couldn't remember the fire—it never happened. But it also never would have occurred to them that someone as sweet, sweet as powdered sugar icing on a coconut cake, and plump, plump as a luscious plum, and unassuming as a choirgirl as I would make up such a gruesome story. They didn't know they were talking to a world-class liar.

For starters, I wasn't a farm girl. I was oil-field trash. I never knew my father, and my mother lived at the bottom of a Four Roses bottle in a grungy trailer, which was as squalid and perfume-drenched as you'd expect an Oklahoma oil-field-camp-follower whore's trailer would be.

Only my cubbyhole of a bedroom was clean and neat, and I was the only one who could get in—there was a dead bolt on my door. I possessed the only key, not that there was anything worth stealing.

I was fifteen and a half when I had a baby. I gave it up to strangers without even peeking at its face. I didn't even know if it was a boy or a girl. I didn't even know who its father was. All I remember is lying in my bed at the Florence Crittenden Home—a series of charity-supported residences across the country where girls "in trouble" (as opposed to "troubled" girls, which I later became), went to have their babies and give them up—in Omaha, and crying for two days straight, feeling emptier than I'd ever imagined was possible.

I can pinpoint it to that exact time when my heart hardened into an impenetrable block of ice, impervious to anything but the most superficial scratch, leaving me able to shed an occasional tear at the melodrama of others' lives, but otherwise permanently embedded in emotional permafrost. My heart had been hermetically sealed against deeper cuts.

Lying there in that clean, white bed, I realized nobody on the face of the earth knew who I was or where I was, and furthermore, nobody cared. I also somehow had the grace to understand I could look at that as either a tragedy or an opportunity.

I made the decision I was going to have a nice life. I wasn't sure exactly what that meant, or how I was going to go about getting it. I only knew I had a bigger plan for myself than following in my mother's footsteps. I wanted to make something of myself, to be somebody.

I left the Crittenden Home with a reference to the personnel manager at the May Company department store in Tulsa and within a few weeks I'd begun to make a fairly decent living as a salesgirl in Men's Accessories. I supplemented those earnings by shoplifting.

After a while, I was able to move from the boardinghouse to my own little studio apartment. I'd stand in front of my bathroom mirror for hours, listening to the Beatles and the Supremes on the radio and trying every single beauty tip in *Seventeen* magazine—I bought tweezers, pumice stones, razors, every eye shadow color on earth, pale lipsticks and nail polish and hair falls. I spent a fortune on my skin. But, because I was a big girl—I think I was born carrying an extra twenty-five pounds—I never had the courage or confidence to wear any of this glamour in public. In spite of what people would say about how pretty I was, I saw myself as fat and unattractive and concentrated on being wallpaper. In a sad sort of way, that's what let me excel at my avocation because, unfortunately for us, large girls are basically invisible if we want to be, which most of us do. Or did. Things are different now.

Twice, I got caught and locked up overnight in juvenile detention. In those days, juvenile detention in Oklahoma more resembled foster care and the "cell" they held me in was actually a bedroom in the judge's house with bars on the window and a lock on the door. The house always smelled of Lysol and bacon grease, and the food tasted the same way. The judge's cook, who sang hymns and praised Jesus all day long, brought my trays resentfully. She looked down on me as white trash, a soul not worth saving, and I guess she was probably right, except it certainly wasn't a very Christian way for her to act.

The arrests didn't deter me. I simply became more careful as I continued to steal. I pawned all the goods for cash and for my sixteenth birthday, bought myself a little yellow Corvair convertible. I never saw my mother again.

I became very skilled at disguise and sleight of hand, which I practiced diligently every night with marbles, which are harder to manipulate than quarters because they're round and slippery. They're also about the same size as many pieces of jewelry.

On Wednesdays, my day off from the May Company, I dressed in my other "work" clothes. My favorite was the green plaid skirt, white blouse with a Peter Pan collar, green cardigan sweater, and saddle shoes that were the uniform of Tulsa Country Day School. Sometimes I'd braid my hair, or put on a pair of thick glasses, perch a little beret on my head, and wait nearby whatever shop I'd reconnoitered.

The multistate chain of Mallory's Jewelry Stores had the nicest merchandise and were the easiest and most satisfying to rob. I had applied for a job as a stock girl with Mr. Homer Mallory, who had a Confederate flag behind his desk and a picture of John F. Kennedy on his wall. At the end of the brief interview he told me what an asset I'd be to Mallory's and I'd hear from him when the next opening occurred. But I was no more than out of his office and out of what he believed to be earshot, when I heard him say to his secretary, "Can you imagine putting a girl like that in front of our customers? She's got no class. We'd go out of business." It gave them both a good laugh. I wanted to crawl under a rock. This unnecessary cruelty by a redneck, two-faced, overweight ignoramus with boils and body odor launched and justified my crusade. To be sure, my code of ethics became more defined and refined as time went on. But at that point, robbing Mr. Mallory made me feel I was doing something worthwhile and commendable. I was exacting restitution, claiming costly revenge on behalf of all downtrodden people everywhere.

So, I'd hang around near a Mallory's and as soon as a well-dressed man or woman approached the entrance, I'd drop into their wake and slouch in after them. The clerk always assumed I was the daughter, a pathetic, hangdog girl with a defeated attitude, bad skin, and a thyroid condition. I could drop earrings, charms, lavalieres, brooches, rings, watches, and bracelets into my overgrown bosom quicker than greased lightning, and then I'd say something like, "I'm going outside for some air," and the clerk would say, "That's fine, dear. Would you like a soda?" "No, thank you," I'd say. And then the customer would think I was the clerk's daughter, and I'd be back home in my tidy little apartment before anyone figured out what was what.

Well, I wasn't quite as clever as I thought. On what was going to be my biggest caper—the Mother's Day sale at Homer Mallory's newest store, his pride and joy in Oklahoma City—I was spotted by a sharp-eyed clerk who'd worked for one of my previous targets. She recognized me and went into the back room and called the police before I was even all the way through the front door. I was apprehended and since, by then, my rap sheet was pretty extensive, I was incarcerated for twelve miserable months in a different sort of girl's "home." One for "troubled" girls, with sturdy bars on the windows, where I gave as good as I got. I could scratch an eye, pull out a handful of hair, and throw a punch with the best of them. But, truthfully? I took no pride in that. Any knucklehead can learn to hit.

My dream for a good life, to make something worthwhile of myself, had been seriously derailed, and I'd look around the lunchroom, and think, Is this really how you want your life to be? Is this really what you, personally, want to be: a second-rate, petty thief? Are these the kinds of people you want to associate with: common criminals? No. I was special. I had taste and was getting what I thought was class. I was a *jewel* thief—these girls stole *hubcaps*. I was smart and pretty and as strong as steel. All these girls wanted was to get married and have babies and have someone take care of them, even if they did get slapped around by their husbands every now and then. I decided that would never be my life. My life would be great, comfortable, rich. And furthermore, I'd get it by, and for, myself.

I would become the greatest jewel thief in the history of the world.

I had the big picture, but the nuts and bolts still eluded me, until one Saturday night.

Saturday night at the Girls Home was movie night. They'd escort us all into the auditorium and show some boring movie no one watched, we'd all just sit and talk and smoke through the whole thing. But one night, they showed *Pillow Talk*. Everybody else thought it was stupid, but for me it was transforming. Doris Day was everything I wanted to be: She was beautiful. She had beautiful clothes and a beautiful apartment and rich men after her. But more than that: *She worked!* She was self-sustaining. Self-sufficient. She had a great attitude and never lost her bearings. Doris became my heroine, my role model, my beacon in the dark. She gave me hope and showed me the possibilities of what life could be. That was it. I would become like Doris Day. I made a solemn pledge that as soon as I got out of the reformatory, I'd work smarter.

Incredibly, it never occurred to me to reform.

When my sentence was up, because I'd been a juvenile, my records were sealed and a private scholarship fund volunteered to pay my college tuition—regular attendance was part of my probation requirement.

"We're giving you the opportunity to turn your life around, Miss Keswick," the scholarship lady told me.

"I certainly appreciate it. I won't let you down," I said, and I meant it. But I hated college. It was horrible. As far as I was concerned, I was still doing time. I was bored out of my mind. I was meant for something more than this: I had goals and aspirations. But with no one but a distant Doris up there on the big screen to guide me, it was hard to find my way.

FOUR

So there I was in London, England, as far from Oklahoma as I could get, wanting to escape. To disappear and start over. And so what did I do? I ditched the college tour group who'd gone to see Shakespeare's stupid girlfriend's house on some stupid river, and spent all my money on this stupid dress. Dumb.

"Oooo, you look a regular cream puff," the shopgirl with her platinum hair, black-rimmed eyes, and white lips (possibly the most glamorous person I'd ever seen in my life) had cooed in her wonderful accent, which had me seduced.

"Don't you think it's kind of short?" My eyes watered from the incense sticks that smoldered around the shop. I squinted at my rear view in the large mirror. "Aren't my panties showing?"

"Well, you aren't going to be wanting to bend over, are you?" Ha. Ha. Ha. "Do you want to try the boots? We've been showing them with this frock."

Frock! *Frock!* Do you have any idea how many "frocks" we had in Oklahoma? Zero. We had housecoats, suits, dresses, blue jeans, and even cocktail dresses, but frocks? You must be kidding. So naturally, I had to have the boots, the hot pink, shiny vinyl, high-heeled boots.

What in the hell did I know about fashion? Or anything, for that matter, I cried as the rain soaked me. Even after all I'd been through, this was unquestionably the lowest point of my life. I wasn't Doris Day. I was eighteen years old, and I was still nobody. Obviously too stupid to have an umbrella, at least that's what the other people on the street were thinking. Look at that stupid fat girl from Oklahoma, she's too stupid to come in out of the rain. The dress stuck to me like a bathing suit.

That's when the pearl gray Rolls Royce Silver Cloud pulled over and a man's voice called to me from the backseat. He looked and sounded like Cary Grant in *That Touch of Mink* trying to cajole an insulted Doris into his car. "Get in here, miss," he said authoritatively. He leaned over and opened the door. "Get out of the rain."

I stepped through the looking glass.

The Rolls Royce smelled like spice and had little glass vases with real roses.

"Miserable weather," the man said, and draped his raincoat around me. He did it gallantly without groping me or making any cracks about my almost naked appearance. His driver took us to Claridge's, which I thought was his house, the way they all greeted him by name. He guided me gently, and directly, to the waiting elevator.

Forty-eight hours later, Sir Cramner and I were still in the suite at Claridge's, rosy and pink with love, champagne, laughter, happiness, and nonstop room service. I'd never seen nor eaten such beautiful food in my life. Nor been in such a beautiful suite of rooms. I had no idea such places even existed. My bathroom at Claridge's (our suite had two!) was bigger than my whole apartment in Tulsa.

"Always insist on your own bathroom," Sir Cramner said. "That way, the romance stays alive."

This was the man for me.

My prayers had been answered. I think it was the pink vinyl boots, which I wore for two days. I finally had to cut them off with my fingernail scissors.

He offered me a job as the mail room girl for the executive suite of Ballantine & Company, bought me a proper wardrobe, and set me up in a spacious three-room flat in Belgravia in quiet, leafy, Eaton

Square, home to embassies and people who lived private, sedate, lives behind picture-perfect Edwardian façades.

I had no idea that people could be so nice.

I consider those days at Claridge's as when my real life began. I might have been slightly street savvy—well, as street savvy as someone from Oklahoma can be—but when it came to social or cultural awareness or refinement? I was a virgin, a blank canvas. I was as green as a person can get. I was also smart enough to know it and wanted to learn. I became a giant sponge that absorbed every drop of information it came into contact with. I studied the women who worked in the auction house as well as the women who attended the auctions—how they dressed and carried themselves. How they modulated their voices. I noticed that none of them—at least the ones with style, class, and power, not the mistresses or tarts—wore colored eye shadow or white lipstick or flashy clothes. I devoured books on manners and etiquette, learned the value of discretion and the virtue of keeping my mouth shut and the essential nature of confidentiality and trustworthiness.

When it came to the material things—paintings, furniture, jewelry, porcelains, textiles—I was lucky enough to be working in the greatest school in the world. Whatever came through the doors of Ballantine & Company—whether they were the real thing or fakes—was fuel for my insatiable desire for knowledge. And because my interest and enthusiasm were genuine, the firm's experts were generous with their knowledge and expertise. Over the years, my eye has become as good as, if not in some cases better than, theirs.

Because I enjoyed my circumstances so much, and the security Sir Cramner provided me, I was able to become secure with myself as well, and accept myself, all of me. My size didn't mean I was less of a girl. I began to see my shapeliness as an asset, and why shouldn't I? All the men around me seemed to see it that way. I drew them like flies.

I stopped buying cotton underpants and Cross-Your-Heart Extra-

Support Bras that, in spite of their promises and best efforts, turned my bustline into something resembling a low-slung watermelon, and started buying lingerie—silk and satin panties and slips and lacy low-cut French bras. I bought well-cut and well-made suits and dresses that fit me properly.

Jewelry continued to be my passion and occasionally I'd mention certain pieces that were coming up for auction to Sir Cramner and he'd buy them for me, and I'd wear them in the evenings in one of my custom-made peignoirs. After a particularly successful series of sales, he surprised me with the *Pasha of St. Petersburg,* a twenty-five carat, brilliant-cut diamond pendant. From the moment he draped the thin platinum chain around my neck, I've never taken it off. Sir Cramner and I loved nothing more than a good scotch and a quiet evening in my flat watching the news—with me in my negligée, loaded up with bijoux, the quarter-sized *Pasha* winking from my décolletage. We'd have Indian or Chinese food delivered from around the corner, or I'd fix his favorite dinner of a cheese soufflé and tomato bisque with a dollop or two of sherry. It was a comfortable and cozy existence.

Did I mind that he was married and had a family and a family life? That he only came to call an evening or two a week? Or that he would never marry me? Well, I'd be lying if I said that I never occasionally longed for a life in the full light of polite society. At first, I couldn't help but be resentful of my geishalike existence but after a while, I took up a hobby: learning to make fine jewelry, and it filled my evenings. From time to time, I'd meet a man and think, This is the kind of man I want. I could settle down with him. But the fact is, they were all just like Sir Cramner. Kind, good-natured, funny. Married. As the years passed, I made a conscious decision to get over my desire for a traditional marriage and family and settled into the comfort and pleasure of who I was and what I had.

Sir Cramner and Ballantine & Company Auctioneers became my life. I loved him, the company, and the business. I loved the person I'd become. I was elegant. I was refined. I was a lady.

My life of crime continued, but on a much more elegant scale. In the beginning, my financial security was most definitely a factor, but not the only one. As I got older, I saw more and more completely unnecessary injustices inflicted on total innocents by those who had so much and still felt the need to take advantage of others. I'd been able to leave my childhood neglect behind me long ago, gotten over it, landed on my feet and flourished through my own sheer will, determination, and opportunities presented by Sir Cramner. But not everyone's got the same grit, and legitimate victims do exist, and when I see a person of wealth and means inflict cruelty or abuse on a defenseless creature, two- or four-legged, if it is within my abilities, I will not let it pass unpunished. People who have money should be grateful for what they've got because the fact is, money *can* solve most of one's problems and there is absolutely no excuse for a rich person to cause pain and suffering for a poor one. So, in my own little way, I do what I can. I steal what I hope they love.

I'm not trying to make myself sound saintly or like Robin Hood or a do-gooder, because I'm not. I do give away at least 10 percent of everything to charity but I keep the rest for myself. Tax-free.

I know if anyone knew my secrets, they would be surprised. Who am I kidding? They would be beyond surprised. They would be thunderstruck. But, there's nothing I can do about it—it's just who I am and what I do. What I've always done, and as I set out to be all those years ago: I'm one of the best in the world.

Just to add a touch of class to my residential burglaries, a little bouquet of shamrocks tied with an ivory satin ribbon replaces the goods. A signal to the target that the bad news is they've been robbed, but the good news is they can take pride in knowing they were robbed by London's best: the Shamrock Burglar.

FIVE

And now tonight, just like that, with Sir Benjamin's single shot to his muddled head, my world had changed again. My debt to Sir Cramner and Ballantine & Company was discharged, paid-in-full.

I rolled out of bed, slid into my robe and mules, padded into my pink, mirrored dressing room, and looked in the dressing table mirror. I was as pale as a ghost. I frowned at myself. I didn't know what to think. It was as though I were looking at someone else.

The clock said four-thirty—too early to go to work, too late to go back to sleep. I went into the kitchen and switched on the lights in my ivy-walled garden. Icy rain struck the windows, and for a while, I sat in the dark at the kitchen table with a steaming mug of coffee and watched it cascade off the lattices and splash on the bricks. The garden lights illuminated the trunks of the potted fruit trees, making them shine like black patent. My mind spun. I thought about everything and nothing. My stomach growled.

What I needed was an omelette.

With a flip of the light switch the rain receded into the distance and my old-fashioned, professional chef's kitchen blazed into view. The heavy white enamel appliances, chrome knobs and handles, and glazed tile surfaces glittered and gleamed like an ad in a cooking magazine. I took kitchen scissors and clipped shoots of chervil, parsley, chives, and tarragon from my indoor herb garden along the kitchen windows. The outdoor freshness of their fragrance calmed me. The omelette pan came off its hook, and fresh eggs, a chunk of aged Gruyere, and butter came from the refrigerator.

I grated a handful of cheese and then, as I cracked the eggs into a glass bowl, I began, seriously, to examine my options.

All right, then. What should I do first? Quit? I could. I had plenty of money, and I still had my looks. I was good-sized. Not obese or any-thing, I just have never really denied myself much in the way of food or drink. I'd say I look *healthy*, toothsome, fine-figured. Sir Cramner once described me as a sort of full-bodied Catherine Deneuve, and it's a pleasing, and I think fairly accurate, comparison. A little work's been done to tighten up my jawline and take the bags out from under my eyes. People have given up trying to figure out how old I am, and I don't tell.

I turned a burner onto HIGH, and whipped the eggs with a fork until they were just blended. A nice hunk of butter went into the cold pan, which I placed on the hot flame and rolled until the pan was coated and the butter melted completely and released its creamy bouquet. The eggs slid from the bowl and burbled in the sizzling heat. I gave them a couple of seconds to begin to form and then grasped the han-dle of the omelette pan, tilted it up and began to jerk it toward me roughly. Julia Child says, "You must have the courage to be *rough* with the eggs or they won't loosen themselves from the bottom of the pan." Mine loosened nicely and the eggs began to curl over on themselves a little more with each pull. I sprinkled in the herbs and cheese.

"What do you think, old boy?" I said aloud to Sir Cramner's spirit.

"It's time," he answered.

"I miss you."

"Move forward. It's time," he said again. "But whatever you do, don't liquidate the Trust."

Those had been among his dying words. The KDK Trust. My secret weapon.

———————

"What's your whole name, Kick?" Sir Cramner asked one day. By then he'd promoted me to being his executive secretary and assistant.

"Kathleen," I answered.

"No, I mean your whole given name."

"Oh, given name," I said knowledgeably. Given my mother's condition, I think I was pretty lucky to have any name at all, but I knew what he meant. Whole three name, name. "Kathleen Day Keswick." I had picked "Day" ages ago, of course, because of Doris.

That's how the KDK Trust, LLC, came into existence.

"I'm not going to live forever," Sir Cramner said. "And I don't ever want you to worry about your independence. No one can find out who is behind the KDK Trust, the bank will manage it. Don't ever tell anyone what I've done."

And then, with a stroke of his pen, he gave me 15 percent of Ballantine & Company.

To this day, no one knows who's behind the KDK Trust, not even our new owner, Mr. Owen Brace, with all his megamillions and high-powered lawyers. The trust and my control of it were shielded by England's strict banking laws regarding confidentiality. It had frustrated and infuriated him when my bank continued to reject his offers to buy my shares, especially when the offers had been so lucrative. The entire Ballantine family finally relented and surrendered all their holdings, leaving me as the only outstanding shareholder. Fifteen percent is enough to make a difference. Brace knew it, and I knew it, and it drove him nuts. Too bad.

My omelette slid onto a warm plate, and I skimmed the top of it with a film of butter and a sprinkling of more cheese. I carried the plate to the table, sat down, and picked up my fork and knife. The first bite was as delicious as I knew it would be and filled me with a sense of well-being. Warm, almost hot. Creamy and tangy. Rich and satisfying. I took a deep breath and inhaled all the fragrances. I think it was the best omelette I'd ever made.

Then I got out the calendar. November 1—a good day for my new life to begin. I would give my notice on December 1, and leave at the end of the year.

At six o'clock, I got into the shower and by seven, my hair was dried and pulled into a knot, my makeup applied. I stepped into a black Chanel suit, sheer stockings, low-heeled pumps, and a triple string of pearls. I looked simple and elegant. And respectful. After all, I was about to find out, officially, that I had a funeral to arrange.

SIX

TWO WEEKS LATER

"We wish you luck, Mr. Brace," Mr. Radcliffe said, getting to his feet. He was as tall as a stork. "But we've decided to accept Sotheby's offer."

"May I ask why?" Owen concealed his surprise well. This was his first opportunity to try to close a major piece of business for the house. He'd assumed that the highly prized and pursued Radcliffe Collection would fall into his lap based sheerly on his personal celebrity. "Would you like to discuss the commission further? I'm willing to negotiate."

"No, no. Both houses have made identical offers, and I know there's negotiating room."

"Is it the publicity package? Do you think it should be increased?"

Color had crept up Mr. Radcliffe's neck, and his wife's lips were so tightly clamped, they had almost disappeared into her mouth.

"Please tell me, sir," Owen pressed, "so I don't make the same mistake again."

"All right, young man, I will tell you because you've asked me. The fact is, I'm sorry to say, I just can't relate to a man who wears as much jewelry as you do. We wish you good day." With that, the Radcliffes left.

Whoa. The words were almost incomprehensible to a man whose fortune had been built on high fashion, to whom the concept of less-is-more was impossible to grasp. At Brace International, understatement was practically a firing offense. And suddenly, wham, a cold fish right in the face from a member of that upper-class club Owen was so anxious to join. One succinctly cutting phrase forced Owen to acknowledge that his flashy hundred-thousand-dollar, multi–time zone, calendar watch and the Boucheron gold-and-diamond cuff links had just cost the house several million dollars in commissions. Dollars he desperately needed.

I felt sorry for him. A flush of embarrassment darkened his face and reddened his eyes, which, as best as I could tell, were as close to indigo as eyes can get.

I closed the office door. "If I may, sir," I ventured.

"What is it, Kick?"

"Well"—I sought to be tactful—"in the auction business, appearances are everything."

"Appearances are everything in every business. What's your point?"

I persevered. I had nothing to lose. "There are a few realities you need to hear if you're going to get anywhere . . ."

Why did I care if he got anywhere? Well, there was just something about him that intrigued me, in spite of his harsh bullyboy manner, rough edges, and absence of Golden Rule ethics. Or maybe it was because of those things. I'd never met anyone like him in my life.

I couldn't wait for the next installment in the daily soap opera of his fourteen-month-long marriage to movie star Tina Romero, and the way she bamboozled him, as only a twenty-two-year-old, Puerto Rican, sexpot bombshell can bamboozle a fifty-four-year-old man. She was a tempestuous, spoiled, completely immature, stacked, keg of nitroglycerin. A glamour-puss with a Charo-type accent who would sweep into the office, unannounced, dressed in clothes that could only be described as "missing," or "transparent," or "extreme." These were the kind of clothes that were held in place with double-stick tape. Surefire, front-page attire for an international movie star at the Academy Awards or the Cannes Film

Festival, but not the sort of image an auction house seeking its survival ought to present to well-heeled potential clients. I mean, if Mr. Radcliffe thought Owen's accessories were flashy, I truly cannot even begin to imagine what he would have thought if he'd gotten a look at Tina.

And she adored Owen. She climbed all over him like a monkey, like a little girl on a favorite uncle, like a woman-child on a sugar daddy, which was fine in private, but she pawed him no matter who was watching. And Owen couldn't or wouldn't stop her. It was pretty amazing. She called him Daddy.

I was astounded by the parade of famous models and movie stars who called him, or whom he called, constantly, and with whom he had quick flings. By quick, I mean like between courses at lunch. Whatever it was he did to them, they liked it. They kept coming back for more. He was some sort of human animal sex magnet.

He counted on me to keep these ladies straight with his schedule, and then right out of the blue, he'd instruct me to break off an affair.

"Forgive me for being impertinent," I said to him one time, "but I don't think you can exactly call this an 'affair.'"

"Excuse me?"

"These are not affairs, or even liaisons. I think an affair connotes a relationship where the two parties have met more than three times."

"Excuse me?"

"I just don't think you should call these little get-togethers 'affairs.' I'd call them 'proceedings.' Or 'incidents.' That would be more appropriate."

He studied me like I was an idiot. I didn't care. He needed to know these things. "Very well," he finally said. "Would you be so kind as to break off the 'proceeding' with Letitia."

"Of course, sir. Consider it done."

Then I would call the girl with a last-minute cancellation and a heartfelt apology, which would be immediately followed with the delivery of a gift from one of Brace International's manufacturers of luxury goods—a pashmina cashmere shawl from the Cesarina Mittando fashion house, or a crocodile handbag from Percoco Leather, or sometimes a combination of the two. It was the least I could do. I only sent liquor from Lividia Spirits, Nottingham Whiskey, or Père Patrice Champagne to business associates. No former girlfriend had received a car from the Panther Automobile Company, or a yacht from Geo Shipbuilding.

In spite of my disdain, I felt myself being seduced by Owen's charm, or charmed by his seductions, I'm not sure which, but I was being pulled inexorably onto his team. I found myself wanting him to succeed because I truly enjoyed fielding calls from the world's richest people and most powerful leaders—heads of state, companies, and banks, who sometimes sought, sometimes offered, advice or money. Some of them were beginning to learn my name.

At the bottom of all this, though, was the money. I was transfixed by the money. Not only by how Owen was pouring it into Ballantine & Company, buying top experts by raiding other houses and offering exorbitant salaries, freshening up certain aspects of our fusty image, and restoring and renovating our three-hundred-year-old building, which still had hundred-year-old plumbing and wiring; but also by how he juggled the finances among all his companies, constantly shifting funds among them to maintain solvency. Every single one of them—clothing, luggage, wine and spirits, cars and yachts—was in a Code Blue financial situation. They were the highest-end, highest-quality goods available, but unfortunately, the size of their institutional marketing budgets generally equaled the size of their sales. It was a textbook, business school example of how paying to keep up an image can be a self-canceling exercise to the bottom line.

The interest and principal payment demands from the banks were courteous but constant, demands Owen met by playing a high-stakes shell game that hinged on his ability to demonstrate to his stockholders and bankers a strong balance sheet of the parent corporation, Brace International. Fortunately the corporation had a highly profitable real estate holding company with numerous properties in key retail locations all over the world. This particular enterprise charged exorbitant rents to its tenants, thus providing a large and predictable enough cash flow to offset any losses by the subsidiary firms.

The point is: It was all a giant fraud. The high-rent tenants were the selfsame, money-losing subsidiaries, which, if they hadn't had to pay such steep rents, might have been able to turn small profits. The holding company owned the land under all the corporation's factories, office buildings, and shops. This was a closely held secret, known really only to four people: Owen; his attorney, David de Menuil; Gil Garrett, the president of Panther Automobiles; and me, although I'm sure he didn't think I had the sophistication to understand what was going on. It was a high-wire act like nothing you could imagine. His composure and sangfroid were astounding. He worked autonomously. I never once heard him consult a board member, although he had several. I don't know how he took the pressure.

Initially, I was outraged by how he operated, putting our beloved company in an even more precarious position. I couldn't understand why he would want to own Ballantine & Company, but then I saw how it could work. An auction house, a successful one at any rate, generates a huge amount of cash flow, much of which can go straight to the bottom line. Brace International and Ballantine's were each other's last hope. And I had a front-row seat.

I succumbed to his energy and antics. I couldn't wait to see what was going to happen next. Now that I could leave whenever I wanted, I couldn't wait to get to work in the morning.

Okay, I'll admit it: I was starting to find Owen Brace unbelievably attractive.

". . . because appearances in the auction business are the opposite of all your other enterprises," I explained, the Radcliffes now just a memory. "We don't want to be trendsetters. We're guardians of the past. You need to look good, look solid. You can't go around looking much better-off than the clients, even though, in most instances, you probably are. Or at least, they *think* you are. They're trusting you with their most treasured family possessions, things they love and usually don't want to give up. You should view yourself the way you would look at a funeral director—you can't afford to appear as though you'll be disrespectful or cavalier with their goods. That's why Ballantine's has always had a dress code, which you are making a mistake to ignore."

He listened to me carefully. His dark eyes glittering like glass.

"I know the backstage of this business is not anything you expected." I shrugged my shoulders and crossed my arms across my chest. "But, that's the mystique of it, and if you're really committed to getting this old girl off the ground, which you seem to be, judging by the amount of cash you're shoveling into her, and attracting the sorts of high-visibility clientele you need, well, sir, you can't go around dressed like a gigolo."

I might as well have whacked him on the side of his head with a frying pan. He stared at me for two full beats, and I returned his look without blinking. "How long have you been with Ballantine & Company?"

"Much, much longer than you," I answered.

"Are you always so honest?"

"Yes, sir. I am."

He grinned at me. "You know what, Kick?"

"No, sir. What?"

"You are pretty goddamned cool."

Something fizzy buzzed up my spine—like the tingle from the first sip of champagne.

The next morning tailors from Gieves & Hawkes arrived at eight sharp. Within days, Owen and the rest of the staff were in dark pin-stripes, starched, white, Egyptian cotton shirts, and banker's ties and shoes.

A more fitting, new era had begun. More fitting-*looking*, at any rate.

I delayed submitting my resignation indefinitely—Provence would always be there—but Owen seemed so sincere, so diligent in his efforts, I began to feel an obligation to help him get the company stabilized.

SEVEN

"Kick," Owen called through his open office door. "Come in here."

"Excuse me, sir?" I pretended not to hear.

"Come in here . . . please."

Better.

Benjamin Ballantine had been in the ground for ten weeks and basically, except for the dress code, all three hundred years of propriety had exited the executive offices. We were now under the command of a more modern regime, a cadre of Brace International's youthful staffers, who, if they'd had any inkling that Mr. Brace's entire empire was on the verge of toppling, falling right off the cliff, might not have been so cavalier.

"Kick," Owen called again. "What are you doing?"

I picked up my book. "On my way, sir." Just as I stood up, the top of Tina's peroxided head crested the staircase. Then the whole kit 'n' caboodle of Owen's child bride roared into view. She was moving fast on long slim legs that shot out from her full-length lynx coat like hurdler pistons and pounded up the stairs two at a time. The coat that matched her hair flew open to reveal her running bra, bike shorts, and sneakers. White-rimmed dark glasses covered her big brown eyes, which had lashes like Bambi's. One hand held her omnipresent bottle of Evian water—what on earth she needed all that water for, I'll never understand. Security, I suppose. Just the same as she "needed" the 250,000-dollar coat. Her other hand wielded a large manila envelope rolled up and borne aloft like an

Olympic torch. Because I'd arranged for its delivery, I knew the envelope contained divorce papers.

Owen realized that if he was going to save the business, and turn himself into a respectable gentleman, he had to stop living his life on the front page of the tabloids, which meant Tina had to go. As far as I could tell, the decision hadn't appeared to cause him any particular brain damage—he'd handled it with the same offhand attitude as ordering up his barber. But I guess when you're on your third or fourth marriage and divorce, it all takes on a rhythm of its own.

"Get David on the phone, please," he'd said. "I've got to get a divorce."

The separation had been carefully and efficiently orchestrated by my office and David de Menuil, Owen's on-call round-the-clock attorney who seemed to have no life but Owen, and implemented around Tina's schedule of publicity appearances for her new movie.

"Theoretically, this timing should make it easier on Tina," David explained. "Sort of a good news–bad news approach. Bad news: Your husband's divorcing you. Good news—your public needs you— you're the star. She'll get over it in a hurry."

I'd had Owen's new Savile Row wardrobe, papers, and important works of art—all items Tina probably had never noticed since they were neither cell phones nor mirrored—removed from the town house and installed in a residential suite at the Dukes Hotel down the street from the office. The items in his residential safes, mostly U.S. dollars, gold bullion, jewelry, and handguns, all of which spoke volumes about Owen's murky roots, were transferred to the wall safe in his office. The only personal items left behind at his former home were his former wardrobe and the gifts Tina had given him, the majority of which were either sexual or sparkling.

"Good morning, Miss Romero," I began.

"I know." She flew toward and then past me. "He's 'in conference,' he's 'not available at the moment.' Well, for once he's 'in' for me. He can't do this to me. You should call the police right now, because I'm going to kill the fucking son of a bitch."

"Should I call your agent, as well?" I asked. "And your publicist?"

"Sure." Then she threw open the door to Owen's office so hard, the frame cracked, and I watched her virtually launch herself across the desk at his throat. They both crashed to the floor.

The invective was impressive—an unlikely, but effective, assemblage of dockhand language in English and Spanish.

"Should I call security, sir?" I asked. By then he had Tina on her knees, her arm wrapped up behind her back and was on the verge of breaking her wrist. He had a quartet of mean-looking gashes on his cheek from her fingernails.

"No. Just close the door."

Moments later, she evidently broke out of his hold, because for quite a while, the sounds of screaming and things breaking reverberated throughout the executive office reception area. We were used to it. None of the executives even bothered to stick their heads out of their offices. I heard the set of ceremonial Wedgwood plates, made to celebrate and record King Edward's coronation, whistle across the room like Frisbees until they met up, head-on, with the antique burled walnut paneling.

Then, the sobbing started. Then, silence. Then caterwauling exclamations of ecstasy that went on until we were all exhausted, nervous wrecks. Finally, the door opened and Tina emerged. Her face was splotchy from crying. "I'm sorry I cut your face. I promise I'll never do it again. Just don't do this to me. I'll do anything if you'll keep me. Please. Anything."

Owen stood in the door, a handkerchief pressed to his cheek. He had his suit coat off. His fitted white shirt was as crisp as a cracker, and he had on a red-and-navy regimental tie, something I imagine he'd often made fun of in the past as the sort of tie only a fuddy-duddy would wear. He certainly didn't look like he'd been making wild passionate love. "Believe me, Tina. I'm only doing this for you.

For your sake. You can't have your career always living under my shadow."

She began to cry again. "But what will I do without you? You're my whole world."

I admit I felt sorry for her as she passed my desk. She was just a child, a dejected and rejected and totally misguided child. "Is there anything I can get you, Miss Romero?" I asked.

She shook her downcast head.

I told her I was sorry.

"To hell with you," she said. "This is all your fault. Owen was never snooty until you showed up."

I reached out to touch her arm, but by then she'd put on her dark glasses and started down the stairs. Each step seemed to straighten her spine and by the time she reached the front door, her famous red-lipped Latina smile was back in place, and she was ready for her permanent entourage of bodyguards and paparazzi.

I went into Owen's office. "Oh, dear," I said. Two lamps were smashed to bits, as was a glass tabletop.

"Goddamn crazy fucking bitch," he swore.

"Are you all right, sir? Would you like me to look at that?"

He pulled the linen square away and examined it. "No, thanks. I think it's stopped bleeding. Well," he said as he crossed back to his desk and righted his computer screen, "that's over."

"Do you think she'll be all right?" I asked. "I mean, she won't do anything crazy will she?"

"What are you talking about? All she does are crazy things. Who cares what she does. She's no longer my problem."

"She sure can scream," I said. "We're talking Academy Award winners."

"Actresses," he said. "All sizzle, no steak. They're all complete idiots. If you don't write out their scripts, they're totally lost. What time is the Carstairs meeting?"

"Eleven o'clock."

"What time is it now?"

"Nine-fifty-five."

"Is Bertram ready?"

"I think so, but I'll double-check."

"I want him in the car by the time I get there. We'll leave in five minutes. Did you look at the figures from Panther?" He studied the latest sales projections on the monitor.

"I did."

"Talk about another goddamn mess—I'm up to my nuts in them today. Did you know this corporation's had six different owners in the last eighteen years?"

I nodded.

"I've decided owning Panther is like being married to Elizabeth Taylor or Zsa Zsa Gabor. First year's the honeymoon. Second year: daily sessions with a shrink: Can we make this marriage work? Knowing deep down that you don't really think it can. And third year: How do I get the hell out of this mess with some of my assets still intact?"

"It's definitely a mess."

Owen shook his head and tapped his finger on the glowing red numbers. "There's no light at the end of the tunnel."

"I'm sorry to hear that. Are you certain?"

"Yeah. It's the classic conundrum: As long as the cars are manufactured in England, by hand, it's unworkable. But . . . that's part of the car's magic, its attraction. It's what keeps the waiting list ten years long."

"They're so beautiful."

"Not to mention it's the sweetest car on the road to drive. It's a real heartbreaker. And I'm just as much of a sucker as the owners before me and whoever owns the company after me. Frankly, for me, the prestige of corporate proprietorship has diminished with each quarterly report—sort of like living with Tina and her implants. The thrill is gone. Get Gil on the phone. Please."

"Yes, sir."

Gil Garrett, Owen's best friend, if a yard dog can have a best friend, was president of the Panther Automobile Company. The two men had been in a number of deals together, and they'd both known going in that Panther's future was on the line since day one. They sometimes spoke hourly. The deal was now in day #475: heavy relationship counseling.

"And close the door."

"Yes, sir."

I returned to my desk and unwrapped a marshmallow caramel and sank my teeth into it. As the sugar dissolved on my tongue, I couldn't help but wonder what all he'd done that had gotten her calmed down so quickly. My imagination ran so wild, I think I was blushing. I popped the rest of the chewy little morsel into my mouth and got my papers, purse, and gloves together in preparation for our imminent departure for Carstairs Manor, Lady Melody Carstairs's Richmond estate.

EIGHT

"Give me the latest, Bertram," Owen said as the company's gleaming new $265,000 dollar Bentley limousine pulled away from the curb in front of our St. James headquarters.

We left right on schedule. I sat on the backseat with Owen. Bertram Taylor, our ballyhooed new president, sat sideways on one of the jump seats, a sheaf of papers on his lap.

"How many times do I have to tell you, Michael? Close the goddamn window," Owen shouted at his driver/bodyguard, a musclebound thug who'd driven for him for several years, and who looked completely out-of-place in his formal black livery. I'm fairly positive he'd been called Mickey until Owen bought Ballantine & Company and upgraded him, too.

Michael gave me the creeps. Bertram and I looked quickly at each other and then away. Owen's rudeness was embarrassing and unnecessary.

"Sorry, boss," Michael mumbled.

The privacy screen rose silently as we turned onto Piccadilly and sped through misty drizzle past the Ritz Hotel and along Green Park.

"I've worked the numbers down as far as I can, possibly farther than I should, and I think we can make a very competitive offer," Bertram answered.

Bertram Taylor was one of the, if not *the*, world's top antique furniture experts and auctioneers. His smoothly parted grayish hair and bright blue eyes lent him a jovial, boyish, dashing air, especially when he went to work on the podium, and his hair would flop in his face and his eyes would flash with challenge and derring-do. He was fluent in six languages and had "the touch" when it came to working a room of high rollers—he could squeeze the proverbial blood from a turnip, raising the competitive temperature in the saleroom to dizzying heights and putting buyers on the edges of their seats. He could take the sins of envy, greed, and covetousness and transform them into irresistible, even desirable, virtues.

Bertram's family background—he was an Eton and Oxford man— and body of knowledge provided him with uncrackable confidence and unprecedented carte blanche access to potential clients. His deference to his new chief, Owen, more resembled respectful camaraderie than subordination. He could do more for Brace than Brace could do for him, and they both knew it. Adding Bertram's name to the letterhead as president and chief auctioneer was not only Brace's first significant management acquisition and public declaration that he meant business, but also provided blue-ribbon credibility to the leadership team.

Owen lured him away from Christie's by offering a doubled salary and a larger cut of the action. People were stunned when Bertram jumped the monolithic mother ship and signed on with the buccaneer. But, like me, he was drawn by Brace's proven success in other fields, not to mention his prowess. Owen was fearless, he ate risk for breakfast. Everyone in the business, loyalists and skeptics alike, was curious to see if he could pull it off—resuscitate Ballantine's and move it into the big leagues—and if he could, how he would do it. In the auction world, it was the insider's opportunity of a lifetime. If you had the guts.

He and Bertram started slashing sellers' commissions, which threw the other houses into even greater uproar. The risk was unprecedented, foolhardy, and the possibility that his strategy would work was pooh-poohed.

"It's a great way to go broke," an unnamed official was quoted in the paper. "We wish Mr. Brace all the success he so richly deserves."

Another article questioned Owen's integrity. It didn't faze him a bit.

"That's their problem," he responded. "They wouldn't know integrity if it sat on their heads. My responsibilities are Brace International's bank account and happy shareholders. In that order."

What an incredibly gritty and cold-blooded attitude, I thought. Especially when his bank account was in the red and the hapless shareholders were in the dark! It was like working for the devil!

The trick required to turn around Ballantine & Company was not only to make sure goods were auctioned for exorbitant prices—for which we needed exorbitant, sought-after estates—but also to jimmy around the buyers' and sellers' commissions—shaving a little here, adding a little there—which was where the house made its money.

Auction house commissions are based on a fairly complicated, sliding-scale formula, but a good rule of thumb is that the seller's commission, that which is paid to the house as a fee for selling one's estate, is 10 percent; while the buyer's commission, that which is paid to the house by the person buying the goods, is 17 percent. Therefore, if the house has *sold* your aunt Mary's sterling silver tea set for one hundred dollars, you will receive ninety dollars: one hundred dollars less 10 percent. And if you're the one who *bought* Aunt Mary's tea set at auction for one hundred dollars, you'll pay one hundred seventeen dollars: One hundred dollars plus 17 percent. So, from the hundred-dollar sale, the house made twenty-seven dollars. A respectable markup of 27 percent.

"Carstairs Manor is a gold mine," Bertram continued. "Here's another batch of photos." He pulled a thick packet out of his briefcase. "They're not the best, there's so little light in most of the house—but look at the marquetry and veneer on this seventeenth-century sideboard. I've seldom seen such intricate craftsmanship, and it's in perfect condition."

Owen studied the top photo carefully through his glasses and whistled under his breath. "Sweet." He drew the word out as though he were admiring a girl on a street corner.

"That piece alone could bring over 8 million," Bertram told him. "The place is packed with goods similar to and even better than this. We've had such inadequate time to assess it all. The Christie's and Sotheby's people were there for over a month—we've only gotten to the paintings and furniture. Nothing's been done on the jewelry, porcelains, or real estate. But, on balance, I have the advantage of knowing how those firms put together their proposals. I think we can guarantee over 400 million dollars for the lot at auction." He had Owen's full attention.

"Break it down."

Bertram spoke quickly and succinctly. "If you cut the seller's commission to seven and a half percent—the other two houses won't go lower than eight, if even that, I've never heard of either one of them going below eight and a half—I'm confident we can get the account. Lady Melody is notoriously tight. That percentage point equals four million in her pocket—she'll like it."

"That's 30 million in seller's fees." Owen smiled. "And if we increase the buyer's commissions two and a half points to nineteen and a half percent, that's almost another 80 million—over 110 million to the house for the sale. What will we net out of that?"

"I would say between 90 and 95 million." Bertram handed him a sheet of paper. "Here are the options."

"Do you think the buyers would pay nineteen and a half?"

"I think they'd pay twenty-five percent just to own something of Lady Melody's. She's bigger than Jackie Onassis. The only estate bigger than this would be Princess Arianna's."

"Well, then, let's put it at twenty-five."

Bertram shook his head. "You could get away with twenty, but twenty-five looks greedy. I think the public would resent it. I recommend nineteen and a half."

"Done."

Bertram had every quality I valued in a man. He was bright and funny, with a generous spirit, and when he looked at me, he saw me, our eyes met, we connected. But it was a professional connection— mutual respect but no affection. He was married, of course. Weren't they all?

N I N E

The beautiful Richmond countryside unrolled outside. Whenever I drive through Richmond, I think of Elizabeth I, then eight-year-old little Princess Elizabeth, waiting alone and confused with only her household servants as company, in the beautiful palace alongside the Thames. Waiting and waiting for her father to send word, invite her home. It never happened. He tried to poison her instead. No wonder she was so tough and had such serious relationship issues.

"I wish I knew a little more about her background," Owen was saying. "I mean, I've met her, and I know she's a famous author, and I know Carstairs Manor is supposed to be one of England's top privately owned residences but . . ."

"If I may, sir," I spoke. "I know quite a lot about her."

Bertram raised his eyebrows and grinned.

"Shoot," Owen said.

"Well, Lady Melody Carstairs hasn't always been a 'Lady.' It was a title bestowed upon her by the Queen for services rendered to the Empire. Melody Carstairs isn't even Melody Carstairs. It's a pen name she adopted when she was in her twenties, sixty-some years ago. Her real name, as well as her true history, have been lost to time. She has approximately a billion copies of her six-hundred-plus books in print. She's never married, although when she was in her early thirties, she had the only major romance of her life, but he was killed in a climbing accident on the Matterhorn—fell to his death—or something equally dramatic, and she's never loved again."

By now Bertram and Owen looked like they were both about to throw up.

"Hey," I said. "Do you want to know or not?"

"Keep going," Owen said.

"All her books are really about her search for another perfect man, and in the end she always finds him. It's quite touching, actually. And now, according to the London *Sunday Mirror*, the reason she's decided to make arrangements for herself and liquidate her estate and give it away to charity is because she doesn't want any of her relatives, none of whom is even a little bit close to her, or a direct connection for that matter, most especially her nephew twice removed, who goes around making his living off being her relative, to wrangle for her money over her coffin."

"How do you know all this?"

"I'm a fan." I might have been blushing a little. "I've read every single one of her books, and . . ." what-the-hell, I thought, tell it all, ". . . this is a typical take-charge move. Her heroines are always self-sufficient, take-charge girls."

"Rather like you, I gather." Bertram laughed.

"Exactly like me."

If I do say so myself, all three of us were charmed and amused by my girlishness. Owen laughed and shook his head. "Thanks, Kick."

"My pleasure." I paused. "There is a bit of a dark side."

"Oh?"

"It's been gossiped about for years, and probably is just gossip, but it was a huge scandal back in the sixties. A woman claimed Lady Melody was her mother, which naturally Lady Melody denied vehemently—her virgin image has always been protected at all costs. At any rate, the woman had a strong case, but Lady Melody had more money and could afford better solicitors, who basically decimated and crushed this woman in court and smeared her in the media. She ended up committing suicide."

"I remember that incident," Bertram added. "It was a tragedy. I'd forgotten all about it."

"That's no accident. Lady Melody's public relations machine went into overdrive to make us forget."

"Do you think she was her mother?"

I nodded. "I do. And I think it's too bad Lady Melody acted the way she did. She should have acknowledged the woman as her daughter and just gotten on with it. People would have accepted it and forgiven her."

"Sad," said Bertram.

"Can we all put our hankies away now and move on to the real world?" Owen asked.

Mickey's, or rather Michael's, foot was even more leaden than his personality, and we fishtailed on the gravel at the entrance to Carstairs Manor, ricocheting a spray of stones off the iron gates. We were ten minutes ahead of schedule.

"Hey!" Owen put the privacy screen down and yelled. "Take it easy—you chip the paint on this car it comes out of your paycheck. Slow down."

"Sorry," Michael mumbled, and proceeded at a more suitable pace down the tree-lined lane toward the distant manor house, which had evolved over the centuries from a rustic hunting lodge into a majestic limestone pile in a private park. The rain stopped and the sky was clearing. Sunlight filtered through the canopy of bare branches.

"Here's how this'll work, Bertram. You and I will meet with Lady Melody—you'll tell her how you got to the 400 million. Then I'll give you the high sign, and you'll excuse yourself and I'll discuss the commissions with her. I'm going to start at eight and a half percent and see how she reacts."

"Be careful, Owen," he warned. "She's a very canny, decisive woman, and she keeps her cards close. That's most likely what she's negotiated at least one of the others down to. If she senses you're trying to manipulate her, you'll be out the door before your tea's cool enough to sip. Don't play games with her, don't underestimate her, and don't let her shut us out for half a percent. We have to get this estate. Start at eight."

"Okay. Eight. Kick, you stay close to the car and keep the lid on any emergencies. You're in charge. I don't want to be interrupted."

"Yes, sir."

The red enamel front doors opened.

"Okay," Owen said, and cracked his knuckles. "Showtime."

Dear God.

Bertram looked out the window, pretending he hadn't heard.

I jammed the tip of my pen into his thigh. "Listen to me," I muttered under my breath. "Do not crack your knuckles ever, ever again."

I swear to God, it was like trying to do a makeover on a Beastie Boy.

After Bertram had left the car, I put my hand on Owen's arm. "Sir."

"What?" He looked petulant.

"Rein it in a little," I warned. "And don't forget, Lady Melody writes romance novels—even though she's eighty-seven, she still considers herself a young and desirable woman."

"I know." He winked. "How do you think I convinced her to let us bid on this project in the first place?"

"Give it a rest, sir. Sex is not the answer to every question."

"That's what you think."

Lady Melody herself appeared through the doors. From where I sat, she looked *exactly* like her pictures: white hair held back with a black ribbon, perfect makeup, a sweet, kind old-lady smile on her lips. Owen took her hand and kissed it and guided her through the front door into the shadows of the manor. I watched her put her fingers delicately on the scratches on his cheek, a look of concern on her face. I could almost hear her purring. Talk about an Iron Maiden.

TEN

I called the office to see what was going on.

"Tina has called a press conference for three o'clock," our lawyer, David de Menuil, said.

"I'll tell Owen when I see him, but I don't think we'll be back by then."

"Don't worry about it. If she says anything worth responding to, I'll handle it."

"Poor girl. I think she really does love him—she's so dependent on him."

"I think she's got Owen confused with her father. She needs to grow up. I'll let you know if anything develops."

I placed a few more calls, covered all the bases, then fiddled around with Owen's calendars for a few minutes. They were complicated. Every company had a different color ink: Panther Automobiles was burgundy, which came out of the printer looking more like dried blood. Ballantine's was green, signaling hope, I hoped. The schedule was always so jammed with meetings it looked as though a child had scribbled all over the page with seven different colors of crayon.

Then, with a few quiet moments facing me, I decided to see what was what.

"Call me if you need me," I told Michael, who was leaning against the car smoking and listening to music through his headset. "And do me a favor, pick up your cigarette butts. This is Carstairs—not Asbury—Park."

The entrance of Carstairs Manor was laid out predictably, and smelled predictably old and damp. A small, severe foyer, almost like a church lobby, was followed by a slightly larger, equally severe room where a worn limestone staircase curved upward into the turret off to the left. Beyond lay a cavernous reception hall, which had an ancient and massive, smoke-marked, fireplace. The floor was stone blocks, worn smooth by centuries of use. This was the original great hall of the lodge, and it was easy to envision drunken lords with grease-stained leather jerkins, bad teeth (if they were lucky enough to have any teeth left at all), and dirty, food-packed beards, home from a day of stag or wild boar hunting, slouching around the fire and gnawing on bones while the womenfolk in their big aprons, wooden shoes, caps tied tightly beneath their sagging chins, silently refilled their tankards and tried not to arouse the dozing, ill-tempered dogs.

In spite of Lady Melody's feminine touches, such as three golden harps on the hearth, chintz-covered furniture, and the world's largest private collection of Rubens paintings, the room was too big, too cold, and too ill suited to life in the twenty-first century. Its only real function was as a conduit to the dining room, a cheerful eighteenth-century addition with mullioned windows and gleaming heaps of silver, and the library opposite, where the meeting was taking place behind closed doors. There was no noise, except for a phone ringing far away that was quickly answered.

I checked my watch and slipped into the shadows of the cavelike passageway beneath the stairs, confident what I was looking for lay behind one of the three heavy, oak doors, each a masterpiece of seventeenth-century hand carving. The first turned out to be a closet, jam-packed with coats and rubber boots.

The second, which I had to wrench open, hid a winding back staircase, probably one of six or seven in a house this old, intended for the servants. It smelled of mildew and damp plaster as though it hadn't been used for centuries. I stepped in and closed the door behind me. It was pitch-black, not a hint of light anywhere. I always carry a tiny squeeze light in my pocket—you never know when you'll need a little pinprick of light to help you get your key in the lock late at night. Or crack a recalcitrant safe. I began a careful ascent. The wall felt chilly and moist beneath my fingers, the silence as absolute as a tomb. Even with the little beam, I couldn't see more than the next step, but finally, a small band of light from beneath a door illuminated a landing at the second floor. I leaned against the wall, gasping for breath. I was giddy with excitement, and my heart was pounding so hard it was all I could hear. I shouldn't be doing this. I should have gone into the kitchen and asked where the powder room was, but the thought of seeing Lady Melody's bedroom drew me like a magnet.

Thanks to fan magazines, I knew everything there was to know about her. She did all her writing in her bed, leaning against dozens of lace-trimmed bolsters and pillows. I'd seen hundreds of pictures of her in newspapers and magazines, and read how every morning of her life, before she went to work, she fixed her hair and her makeup and put on jewelry from her extensive collection. She chooses the jewelry based on the character she's working on that day. She sits there in bed, fingers and wrists dripping with gems, bed jacket fluffed around her (according to an article in *Woman's Review*, she has almost a *thousand* bed jackets) while she writes long-hand on a lap desk.

All right, Kick, I told myself, if you're going to do it, do it. My pulse had returned to normal. I took a breath and put my hand on the cold brass doorknob and turned. It made only the quietest, well-oiled click. I pushed the door open an imperceptible fraction and checked my watch—I'd been gone for less than two minutes. There was no noise in the hallway. No sound of cleaning or dusting. I opened the door farther and poked my head out and looked around. Because of an article in the Sunday *London Times Magazine*, I knew

Lady Melody's bedroom was the one with the open double doors at the top of the stairs. It would be a good-sized room with a rounded wall of windows that opened onto the park. Sunlight streamed out invitingly.

I listened again, more acutely this time, still no sounds. I stepped into the hallway, leaving the door slightly ajar, and dashed across to the inner sanctum.

Her bed, a golden boat with a pink satin canopy, was unmade. It was said to have been Marie Antoinette's, but if you'd been in the auction business as long as I have, you'd soon discover that if everything that people claimed had been Marie Antoinette's had been, she would have needed ten palaces the size of Versailles to house it all. The delicate antique coverlet and down puff were tossed aside, half-on and half-off the bed. All those famous pillows? Nowhere to be seen. In the middle of the bed, on top of the morning papers, next to an open laptop computer that appeared to be on-line to CNN-FN, sat a breakfast tray with dried-out scrambled eggs and toast crumbs, which were being consumed by a fat gray cat who scarcely gave me a look before he continued his leisurely breakfast. A dinner tray stuck out from under the bed. The tail of another cat twitched the bed-skirt. The room had an uncomfortable, cat-urine-tinged, peach-air-freshener smell. One of the mullioned windows in that big bowed nook needed opening.

Books and magazines littered the floor. Mail-order catalogues with folded-down pages were all over the place. Along one wall, twenty or thirty postal service boxes overflowed with unopened fan mail, and I felt a sting of humiliation for those whose gushing missives had been treated so contemptuously. There were sterling silver champagne buckets on almost every table, maybe eight or ten of them, each with a bottle of Dom Pérignon floating in melted ice. Most of the bottles had been opened and used flutes sat here and there. But the real corker, the pièce de résistance, was above the fireplace: an enormous (and very famous) Gainesborough portrait of a young woman in a pink dress smiled placidly over the mess. Incredibly, someone, maybe it was Lady Melody herself after a few belts of champagne, had painted a huge black mustache on the girl. I almost gasped out loud. It was one of the most insolent things I'd ever seen. Someone had been having one hell of a party.

ELEVEN

I moved quickly into her dressing room. It was dirty and smelled of stale perfume. I wasn't a bit surprised to find the real-life Lady Melody bore little resemblance to the public one. She'd done a bad thing, disavowing her daughter all those years ago, and the guilt had rotted her from the inside out. If my long-abandoned son or daughter walked into my life today, a herd of wild horses couldn't trample my joy at meeting and showing off him or her. But then, who am I to throw stones or cast aspersions? Me, the Queen of the Double Life.

Dozens of scarves—everything from large silk Hermès squares to cotton pocket handkerchiefs to fringed shawls—lay piled and draped about. Atomizers, powder puffs, hair ornaments, tons of makeup, piles of jewelry, coins, and stacks of pound notes in every denomination covered the surface of the dressing table. I would have liked to have had that table in my dressing room—it had a pink tulle skirt covered with sparkles and faced an antique gilt-framed mirror bolted to the wall by little flower-shaped mirrors. Yellow sticky notes were pasted everywhere. I went over and looked more closely.

Although I'm a jewelry expert, it wouldn't take one to see that some of Lady Carstairs's pieces were much better than others. I glanced at my watch: four minutes gone. I sifted rapidly through the assortment, then spotted a diamond bracelet, approximately one and a half inches wide, set with maybe sixty stones. I dug my jeweler's glass out of my pocket. On cursory study, the diamonds looked to be of stunning color and quality, possibly D but most probably E or F, there were so many of them, approximately two carats each.

I recognized the piece instantly as the one the beautiful spy, Lucinda, had worn to the ball to identify herself in *Kiss the Stranger*, five or six novels ago. It was modeled on the bracelet Queen Victoria had made by Garrard Crown Jewelers in 1850 to wear with the King George III Fringe Tiara. More recently, both the bracelet and tiara had been owned by the Queen Mother, who had loaned them out to family princesses to wear at their weddings. The pieces are well-known and easily recognizable to people who pay attention to such things. Such as I. This bracelet seemed to be a fairly good copy.

The tiara and the bracelet were first seen together in 1851 in Winterhalter's painting, *The First of May*, in which a dewy Queen Victoria has her arm around her seventh child (out of a total of nine), baby Prince Arthur, later the duke of Connaught, while his godfather, the duke of Wellington, who has his white hair brushed forward to cover his balding head, presents him with a gold box studded with dime-sized emeralds and rubies. Victoria, who was thirty-two at the time of the painting, has on a pink-and-silver skirt I'd kill for. Baby Prince Arthur is balanced on the green velvet arm of a sofa, a spray of lilies of the valley clutched in his little fist, while his father, the long-suffering Prince Albert, stands behind them. He seems preoccupied, or to be talking to someone offstage. He looks like he's late for a meeting.

Depending on the stones in Lady Melody's replica, the breakdown value of the piece could be around 3 million.

I slipped it into my bra.

A cushion-cut diamond engagement-type ring—the model for all the engagement rings in all Lady Melody's books—sat in a little bone china dish, among various and sundry other junk. It was maybe seven carats and on quick examination appeared to be a D Colorless Flawless stone. Remarkable fire. It looked alive. Just the way she'd described it.

It joined the bracelet in my mighty bosom.

Was that a noise? I froze and stood still as a statue to listen. No. It was nothing. Six minutes gone. I'd better get going.

But an art deco diamond-and-sapphire Cartier watch caught my eye. I picked it up and was trying to untangle a cheap, clip earring from its thin platinum chain, when voices entered the bedroom. I laid the piece back on the dressing table, exactly where it had been, just in case anyone was keeping track, which I seriously doubted, and stepped into the darkness of the sour closet.

Through a crack in the door, I watched two maids, one young, one old, both dressed in old-fashioned gray cotton uniforms with white aprons and caps, bustle into Lady Melody's bedroom.

"I don't see how she can live like this," the girl said. She placed the computer gently on the bed table and gathered up the newspapers, while the other woman lifted the cat off the pillows and set him on the floor, stacked up the breakfast and dinner trays and put them in the hall, then returned to help make the bed.

"It's what makes her happy. It's not our place to judge."

"Do you think she'd mind if I just arranged a couple of those stacks?"

"I'm not going to tell you again, Jane. Don't touch them," the woman snapped. "She knows exactly where everything is. Now go replace the towels and bring her laundry hamper while I refill the ice buckets and we're done."

"How much of that bubbly do you think she drinks a day?"

"I haven't a clue."

"Well, I think she drinks three or four whole bottles. Sometimes five. Don't you think that's a little strange?" The girl pressed. "Drinking by yourself all day?"

"Jane."

The warning tone certainly was clear enough to me. Come on, Jane, I thought, get with the program here. Get your stuff done and get out.

"Yes, ma'am."

The girl passed within two inches of me—close enough for me to smell her Jean Naté splash, which I'm allergic to. I squeezed my eyes closed and held my nose, praying I wouldn't sneeze. She took her time picking the wet towels up off the floor and stuffing them in the hamper. She took fresh ones from the shelf, hung them over the gold-plated racks. She draped one of the scarves around her shoulders and pirouetted to admire herself in the mirror, and then sorted through the heaps on the dressing table, inches from where I hid, until she found a pair of matching fake diamond drop earrings that she held up to her ears and admired, giving herself a coy smile in the mirror. My sneeze was building steam. Damn her and her Jean Naté. I pinched my nostrils closed as tightly as I could.

"What are you doing in there?" the older maid called. "Come on. We have work to do."

"Coming, ma'am." The girl put the earrings back quickly, picked up her hamper, and was gone.

"What do you think you're doing in that scarf?"

"Oh, sorry, ma'am." She darted in and threw it on the stool just as the sneeze erupted behind my flat hand and pinched nose and almost exploded my eardrums. The diamond ring and bracelet were burning holes in my skin.

TWELVE

I didn't move until I heard a door close at the far end of the hall, then I raced through the partially restored bedroom to the small door at the top of the secret stair. I'd been gone way too long—nine minutes had elapsed—and it frightened me. What if Owen was looking for me? What if the meeting was over and they were waiting in the car? I took my phone out of my pocket and turned it on—no calls— pulled off my shoes, and went down the steps as quietly and quickly as I could and peeked out. It was as silent as it had been when I left.

I dashed through the third door in the vestibule which turned out to be, as I'd hoped, the powder room. I locked the door and leaned back to catch my breath and found myself in a surprisingly cheerful, frilly, little confection for such a dour entry. The wallpaper, yellow and green and covered with soaring blue birds, brightened the walls, and instead of a typical bathroom sink and counter, a shallow basin had been carved into a pure white marble slab, supported by white marble dolphins as legs. The antique mirror above was framed by fat, gilt dolphins, as well. The fixtures were golden swans. A delight-ful series of hand-colored fashion etchings of eighteenth-century ladies' hats in thin gold frames covered the wall. I wished I had time to study them and decided to do the same thing in my dressing room. Actually, I wished I had time to steal them.

Outside the tiny leaded window, our car sat unattended.

I pulled off my black suit jacket and hung it on the doorknob and unbuttoned and removed my white silk blouse. I glanced at myself in the mirror. As I knew I would, I looked exhilarated. My cheeks were pink and healthy and my eyes glowed with happiness. I took the two pieces of jewelry out of my bra and laid them gently on the counter—this seemed to be an exceptionally nice score. Then I took off my bra and turned it inside out. On the bottom of each cup was a small pouch stitched along the underwire, each with a narrow Velcro closure. I ripped the pockets open and tucked the bracelet in one, and the ring in the other, pressed the Velcro back into place and got quickly re-dressed. I ran cold water over my wrists, powdered my nose and put on fresh lipstick. By the time I got back outside, I looked completely normal.

A couple of minutes later, Michael appeared from around the side of the house. He appeared to be arranging himself and walked with the swagger of a little boy who'd been relieving himself in Lady Melody's hydrangeas.

"Where have you been?" I asked.

"Nowhere."

"Go around to the kitchen and tell them you'd like to wash your hands."

"I don't work for you."

"Shall I tell Mr. Brace you've been watering Lady Carstairs's flowers?"

Michael considered for a second, then hung his head and headed toward the other end of the house.

"I didn't think so," I said.

Shortly, Bertram emerged. His expression was unreadable. I was in the backseat with the door open, reading a magazine and eating my lunch.

"How did it go?"

"I don't think we have a snowball's chance in hell. That looks good." He indicated my sandwich. "Do you have any more? I'm ravenous."

I handed him a section. "Tell me, what's going on in there?"

Bertram took a bite and leaned against the car, tilting his face into the wintry sun. "He doesn't have the slightest idea what he's doing, or what would be involved in a sale this big."

"I don't think that's entirely fair," I said, defensively. "I mean, we've been in the auction business for almost three hundred years—we've done major estates before, just not recently."

Bertram regarded me kindly. "Unfortunately, the halcyon days of Sir Cramner are long gone. Everyone in the industry misses him—not just you."

I opened my mouth to speak, but, for a change, no words would come. "I don't know what you mean," I finally blurted.

"Don't be embarrassed, Kick. It's well-known you were his muse and inamorata. But times have changed, and the company hasn't changed with them. You know what I mean—there's more to it than getting the people to come and banging the gavel. We have no depth, expertise, talent. Do you have any idea how many experts we'd have to hire to appraise and catalog this estate? Dozens. Just because he's got me doesn't mean he can turn the place into a world-class competitor overnight." He took another bite of his sandwich.

"It's exciting, isn't it?"

"If you want to know the truth . . ." Bertram squinted down at me, ". . . working for him is the most exciting thing that's ever happened to me, even if we are rearranging the deck chairs on the *Titanic*. I feel like I'm twenty-five years old."

"I know." I laughed. "Do you see any other big prospects out there?"

"Other than this?" He shook his head. "None on the immediate horizon. I know the Fitzgerald Collection's already basically committed to Sotheby's for next spring—that's several million in Impressionists, if the market holds. And then there's the Von Bergen's old masters, but they aren't going to take a chance on a staggering house.

They don't need to—they can write their own ticket at Christie's. I think this is the best sandwich I've ever eaten. What is it?"

"Just cream cheese, apples, and raisins. Nut bread. Pretty simple."

"I'm going to tell my wife to make this. Where do you get the bread?"

"You make it."

"Oh, well that probably won't work around our house."

"Have you heard anything new on Princess Arianna's estate?" I wasn't even slightly interested in having a conversation about Bertram's wife or her culinary abilities.

"You know her sister, Odessa, controls it all, and she's playing the field. Odessa's a master strategist, cunning as a fox. She should make up her mind pretty soon, but she won't choose us. God, if we could just get our hands on one aspect of the princess's estate. The jewelry alone's enough to put us in serious contention. But for the moment, Lady Melody's our only major prospect. Of course, I don't know what I'll do if we get it. Nice problem to have, though."

"What's that?" I said.

"What's what?"

"Listen." The sound of shouting reverberated through the great hall and out the front door.

"My God, it's Brace." Bertram started running.

"Hey! Somebody! Help!" Owen stood in the library doors, shouting at the top of his lungs. "Lady Melody's collapsed."

I saw the figure of her ancient butler shoot across the hall like an Olympic sprinter.

Melody Carstairs hadn't exactly collapsed. She was seated comfortably upright in the corner of a sofa, her eyes and mouth wide-open. She didn't look as though she were breathing. She looked like a doll. Actually, I was sorry to see that up close, her makeup looked a little like Bette Davis's in *What Ever Happened to Baby Jane?* and, she'd had her face lifted a few too many times—her skin was as tight and transparent as Saran Wrap.

"Lady Melody. Lady Melody." The butler repeated her name, then put his hand on her cheek, then on her neck to feel for her pulse. "I believe she's passed," he said, and very gently closed her blind eyes.

"Oh, my God," Owen said quietly. "I can't believe it."

"What happened?" Bertram asked.

Owen took a moment to reconnect. "I can't believe it. We had a great meeting, she'd just signed the contract, and she said, 'Let's have a glass of champagne to celebrate.' My back was to her for only a second to open the bottle and when I turned back around she was like that. Frozen."

Did he say *signed the contract?* We bit our tongues.

I looked at Lady Melody. I'm sorry to speak ill of the dead, but she had spots on her skirt and blouse and she smelled slightly like her bedroom. Her hands were in her lap, nails polished a bright cherry pink. She wore an emerald-and-diamond ring on one hand and a large single pearl ring on the other. A diamond bow brooch was pinned to her bodice—it was a very good replica of the Queen Victoria bow, four loops of diamond ribbon, a melee of large and small stones, gathered to a central diamond cluster with two ties curving daintily out below. Garrard made three of the bows for Queen Victoria in 1858, two large, one small. The large ones had been in the Queen Mother's collection and among her all-time favorite pieces. Her daughter, our Queen Elizabeth II, wore one of them to her mother's funeral with a pearl drop. It was very touching and made me cry.

Lady Melody's version was good-sized, maybe three and a half or four inches across.

She was just sitting there, mouth open in surprise, cheeks pulled taut by her tight skin, black ribbon tied in her hair, diamond ribbons pinned to her chest, ready to go to a party. We all waited for her to say something.

The butler was the first to break the silence. "Might I suggest we leave milady in peace until the concerned parties arrive. I have standing instructions to call the doctor and funeral home in an occurrence such as this—we are forbidden to call for help. Please."

He held out his arm to the door as though he were leading a tour of the house. The show in this room was definitely over, and we filed out, looking, no doubt, as stunned as Lady Melody.

For the first ten minutes of our ride home, no one said a word, and then Owen withdrew the signed document from his briefcase and, as if on cue, we all started laughing. Unfortunately, I'm afraid if someone—other than our in-house gorilla (I'm referring to Michael)—had heard us, we might have sounded a little bit like hyenas.

THIRTEEN

Our return to the office was jubilant. Owen called all the staff together and gave them the good news. What a tonic it was for all of us, too. Not only did it put some much-needed cash into the company, but once Bertram finished giving a rundown of the goods and a description of their superior quality, our experts—sorry, tattered lot that they were—were euphoric. It had been a long, dry season at Ballantine & Company Auctioneers and the Lady Melody Collection was just what the doctor ordered.

Owen left the office at five-thirty. "Have a good weekend, Kick."

"Thank you, sir. You, too. And again, congratulations."

He looked me in the eye, and I could see the relief. "Thanks."

I waited until the housekeepers had finished cleaning his office, then locked it behind me and caught the bus for home. It was already dark out, but the lights along Piccadilly and throughout Knightsbridge, thousands and thousands of tiny white lights around lampposts, windows, and doors, made everything sparkle and shine gaily. The sidewalks were crowded, and I got off the bus in Sloane Square to join the throng and do some marketing. The evening was sharp and cold, and by the time I got home to Eaton Square, my mood was jovial as could be.

My apartment has an extremely elaborate and sophisticated security system—five freestanding lines of defense, actually. Inside the front door is the keypad for the general burglar alarm, which beeps normally like everyone else's and notifies the alarm company it's been set off until it's disarmed. Like many homeowners, I also have motion detectors throughout the place, the difference being that mine are independent of the general system, are invisible, and make no noise in the apartment but go directly to the alarm company and police department. There's a charming little oval-shaped entrance foyer outside my bedroom—beneath the whole area of its rug, as well as beneath my bedroom windows, are pressure-sensitive pads. If any of these pads is activated, a deafening, mind-rattling alarm bell starts ringing, and does not stop until the police arrive—the sound is so excruciating, it is unbearable. There are undetectable miniature video cameras embedded in the walls throughout the apartment and on the front landing. Finally, on the back wall of my closet, on the shelves where I keep shoes and handbags, inside a shoe box that's glued to the shelf, is another alarm keypad.

I can arm and disarm any and all of them either manually, or by using a remote which looks like a cell phone and sits innocuously on my entry hall table when it's not in my pocket or purse. I never disarm them all at the same time, only each as it needs to be done. Every night, I review the day's videotapes, and I'm pleased to say I've never seen anything to indicate someone may be on to me. My housekeeper comes Wednesdays and Thursdays, and on those days, I leave off the motion detectors and pressure pads when I leave for work, and she lets herself in and out with the basic system.

Tonight I was especially glad to be home, especially glad it was Friday. I felt like celebrating. I turned on my favorite Schumann concerto, dropped the bag of groceries in the kitchen, and went into my dressing room, where I hung up my suit and blouse and pulled on a fairly smart-looking, cozy, cashmere warm-up suit I'd bought on the chance I might start actually exercising, over and above an occasional stroll around the square.

Then I went to the back of the closet and entered the alarm code, pushed on the spring latch, and the wall swung forward to reveal my pride and joy: my workroom, with its jeweler's bench and tools, crucibles, molds and rollers, high-powered halogen lights, sound system, and series of video camera screens. Beneath the rug, is a three-foot-by-four-foot floor safe, ten inches deep. It is meticulously organized with metal drawers—similar to safety-deposit boxes—all filled with stones, divided not only by type but also by quality, carat, and cut. At any given time, the safe holds between 3 and 30 million dollars' worth of gems.

I stepped inside, pulled the door closed behind me, and laid Lady Melody's bracelet and ring, each on its own velvet pad, on top of the bench. When the halogen lights hit them, I saw they were very special pieces indeed.

I set them aside for later examination and took out the tray holding my newest project. It was a necklace, designed in the sixties by Cartier. It belonged to the estate of the late Mrs. Baker of Galveston, Texas, who shot up her injured Preakness winner with buterol so he could run in the Belmont Stakes, during which he collapsed and ended up having to be destroyed. Her necklace had eleven cushion-shaped Kashmir sapphires, each between seven and eleven carats, free-floating in pairs of curved rows of baguettes, each frame connected by a cluster of perfect round diamonds. When the necklace lay flat, the sapphires were almost flush with their surrounds, but as the piece curved around the neck, the sapphires emerged, thrusting themselves forward like powerful blue, blue eyes.

Kashmir sapphires, the most rare, beautiful, and precious on earth, have a distinctive and hypnotic electric color, and when you've seen one, you never forget it. They can never be confused with the brilliant, paler blue of Ceylon sapphires, the second most precious of these stones, which themselves are extremely rare, valuable, and expensive, but still are only worth about one-tenth of a Kashmir; or the haunting dark, inky blue of their poorer Burmese sisters.

There are only two ways a Kashmir can even begin to be duplicated. One way is by heat-treating a Ceylon. When this process is properly done, it is almost impossible, unless you are a true expert, to tell them apart, but it's very time-consuming, and the cutting and faceting have to be identical to the stone you're trying to replicate.

The other way is to call your supplier in Zurich who manufactures synthetic stones and order exactly what you need, which is the route I chose. The synthetic Kashmirs in my copy would be indistinguishable from the original stones in carat, color, and cut.

The necklace was scheduled to be auctioned in two weeks, and this was one of those pieces I was confident would be bought by an individual, not a dealer, because it was so exceptional. It would go for between 5 and 6 million pounds. I had eight color picture blowups of the real thing, each taken from a different angle by our in-house photographer for the sale catalogue, pasted above the bench. The photographic detail was minute.

My copy, which I would swap for the original the second Bertram's gavel fell on its sale, was progressing well. I planned to finish all eleven of the curved pairs by the end of the weekend. Their connecting diamond clusters were already complete.

I considered sitting down, putting on my light visor and going right to work, but it was dinnertime, and the day's excitement had made me hungry. Actually, I was starving to death.

My refrigerator is a work of art—always filled with fresh ingredients, a selection of well-roasted meats, cheeses, and delicacies, ranging from Beluga caviar to white Italian truffles. A double-wide, under-the-counter wine cabinet holds an outstanding selection of red and white wines and champagnes. I love wine and spend what some might consider an inordinate amount of time and money selecting vintages for myself. I don't care. It brings me great pleasure. This evening, I picked out a beautiful Chablis, a 1998 Grand Cru "Blanchot" Domaine Vocoret, poured myself a hefty glass, turned on the lights in the garden, switched on the TV set to hear the evening news, opened my favorite Delia Smith cookbook to Fillets of Sole

Véronique—poached sole with cream sauce and grapes—and went to work.

I stirred a third of a cup of rice into a cup of water to leach out some of the extra starch. Although many cooks disagree, I think in the long run, if you soak your rice and change the water at least twice before cooking, it ends up being much fluffier (certainly less starchy, but probably not enough to make any big difference). While the rice soaked, I peeled the outer leaves off a handful of Brussels sprouts and scored their bottoms.

"It's a sad day for all Britons," the reporter said. "But particularly all *romantic* Britons. Eighty-seven-year-old Lady Melody Carstairs died at her home, Carstairs Manor, this afternoon. She leaves a legacy of literary romance unequalled in the history of British letters—668 novels, translated into a dozen languages, almost a billion copies of her books in print."

I put the rice and vegetables on to cook and unwrapped the two small Dover sole fillets, which I cut in half, salted and peppered, rolled up into one-inch-tall pinwheels, skin-side out, and placed in a buttered skillet.

Pictures of a younger Lady Melody flashed across the screen, but she looked the same in all of them, no matter her age. I wished I didn't know what I knew about her.

I poured in a half cup of vermouth, added a little tarragon, turned on the heat, and assembled the ingredients for a roux. Unfortunately, I was so concentrated on making the roux—you can't take your eyes off a roux, or the butter and flour will burn and ruin the whole affair—I wasn't paying any attention to the news, so when I looked up, I only saw a split second of Tina Romero, Owen's soon-to-be ex-Mrs. Brace, holding her three eeny-weeny Chihuahuas and crying, then the timer for the rice went off and when I turned back, she was gone and the anchor girl was on to football.

I'd completely forgotten about Tina's press conference. I checked all the other stations and never saw her again and in the meantime, of course, the roux burned and I had to scrub out the pan and start over.

Finally, at about eight, I sat down to dinner with the evening paper. The fish was sweet and tender and the grapes were pleasingly tart. The buttered rice with the cream sauce and delicate fish were comforting and mouth-wateringly delicious. The Brussels sprouts were okay. I ate them at any rate. The wine was excellent, crisp and fresh and just right with the sole, as I knew it would be.

I was about to start the crossword puzzle when a blurb caught my eye: PRICELESS PAINTING TURNS UP AT BAYSWATER POLICE STATION. The story went on to say that a very rare and valuable self-portrait of Rembrandt had been discovered at the Bayswater police station at approximately three-thirty in the morning leaning against the duty officer's high desk. Most probably the work of the Samaritan Burglar.

Whoever the Samaritan Burglar was (and I had my suspicions as to his identity), I admired his style enormously. He stole extremely valuable works from residences and offices and in their place left a calling card that read: "If you are going to own a work of this importance responsibly, you'd best improve your security system." And then, usually before the owner even knew it was missing, it would turn up at a police station in perfect condition.

There was a man who attended many of our fine art auctions, a very dapper fellow I called "David Niven" because he affected the late actor's pencil-thin mustache and jaunty step. He never bought anything, but of the Ballantine-auctioned works that had been stolen by the Samaritan Burglar, this fellow had been at their sales and made a point of congratulating the buyers in a very familiar way if they were present. I got the impression that the buyers never knew who he was but felt they should, he had that familiar kind of look that put them on the spot. He probably said something to the effect of, "Don't you remember we met at that beautiful brunch at Lady Pilfley's last week? So fine to see you again." Or some such thing. Information he could get out of a column. I had no basis in fact to think he was the Samaritan but something in his appearance and manner didn't jibe. He had a wiry, athletic body, lithe and agile as though he were possibly a long-distance runner, but he seemed to take pains to conceal his athleticism with racetrack-clubhouse-style clothing. He was attempting to pass himself off as an aristocrat.

In my opinion, the Samaritan Burglar, whoever he was, should not be considered a burglar at all because he was performing a valuable public service with a great deal of class, style, and panache. I knew and appreciated a master when I saw one, and he was a master. Takes one to know one.

"Nicely done," I said, and turned to the crossword.

FOURTEEN

By ten-thirty, my day was done.

The bathroom glowed with candlelight and my tub, a footed affair, brimmed with bubbles. I sank beneath them and sipped a glass of champagne while Schubert's little String Quintet in C Major played quietly in the background. My magnificent solitaire, the *Pasha of St. Petersburg,* lolled lazily across my breasts reflecting the soft light like a small setting sun, while the bracelet purloined from Lady Melody sparkled from my wrist. Her engagement ring gleamed from my pinkie finger, and a tight fit at that—she must have had tiny hands. Pikaki mist perfumed the air.

I unclasped the bracelet and drew it slowly across my forearm. It was one of the most fastidiously constructed pieces I'd ever seen. It moved as easily as a satin ribbon, every curl flashing and catching fire. The diamonds were among the most perfect, and perfectly matched, I'd ever seen as well. I couldn't stop looking at them through my loupe. Each was D Colorless Flawless. VVV1. In other words: perfect. The oval clasp was the size of a small egg and encrusted with diamonds of various shapes and sizes, known as a melee. I studied it closely and noticed a tiny latch, invisible to the naked eye. I slid the latch down with my nail and the top of the clasp popped open. It was a locket. It concealed a miniature painting. It looked like Prince Albert, his dreamy blue, hound-dog eyes gazing longingly at me. The work had the most exquisite detail, as fine as a colored photograph. It was a masterpiece. The thought crossed my mind that nothing could be so beautiful but the original. But that would be impossible. The Queen Mother had owned that, so this couldn't possibly be the real thing. Or could it?

Now wouldn't that be something?

I put the loupe down and picked up my champagne and considered the possibilities. The late Queen Mother's jewelry collection was among the most valuable and renowned in the world, containing many exquisite pieces, some better known than others. This bracelet, for instance, while not particularly well-known to the public, was a family favorite. But . . . the Queen Mother had liked to gamble. Her racing debts were almost as legendary as her jewelry. Could she have sold the original and hers was actually a replica? She and Lady Melody, while not contemporaries, were close friends. Is it possible she sold it quietly to her pal for a big pile of secret cash? No.

I studied the maker's mark. Garrard, 1850.

I laughed out loud. This was ridiculous. Lady Melody must have paid a fortune to have some disreputable jeweler make such a detailed copy. Garrard would never agree to construct an exact replica—they'd lose their warrants and their reputation.

And if it were the real thing. So what? What difference could that make to me? None. I had no provenance.

Closer examination turned up no personal messages engraved in the setting. It was simply the most beautiful vivid, erotic piece of jewelry I'd ever seen.

The diamond engagement ring was a stunner as well, but on closer examination, the stone, which had superior color and clarity, paled in comparison to the quality of the stones in the bracelet. How good was it? Very, very good. Distinctive? Not really. It was a commercial, retail piece, nothing particularly special or distinguishing in spite of the size and quality of the diamond. It was the sort of item that would be bought at auction by a dealer for the breakdown value. It would be remade. Possibly even recut. The ring bore the maker's mark of Graff, who, if the piece were brought to his attention, could easily identify it and who the original owner was, most likely Lady Melody herself.

So, the question was: Should I sell them through a private dealer or break them down myself and take the stones to my vault in Geneva? I couldn't take my eyes off the bracelet. Anyone who broke it down should be shot. But one of my hard and fast rules was break a piece down or sell it, immediately. I never took the chance of being caught with stolen goods in my possession. This might be an exception.

I studied it and studied it. If I kept it, where would I wear it? My place in Provence where I planned to retire? No. Nobody wore jewelry like this in the country. And exactly when was this retirement going to come around, anyhow? Talk about a moving target. I was now at least two months behind schedule. I loved Provence with all my heart, I was happier there than anywhere. Why didn't I just go there and disappear? It would be so easy.

I'd had my little farm outside of St. Rémy de Provence, near the village of Éygalières, for fifteen years. As far as the United Kingdom is concerned, I'm an ex-pat American national who has her passport renewed at the American Embassy every ten years and who's lived in the same Belgravia residence for thirty-four years, pays British taxes, and flies to her second home outside Marseilles for Christmas, Easter, and August, where she is a taxpaying, land-owning, French visitor in good standing.

That's one reality. The other is that I use false Liechtenstein papers to travel in and out of England on my frequent jewelry-related business trips, portraying me as Léonie Chaise, a dowdy, middle-aged, Geneva-based international executive in the steel industry. Léonie Chaise has a pied-a-terre in Liechtenstein and is on the road all the time. I maintain her identity the whole time I'm traveling because the number of times I go in and out of England would not be possible or feasible for Kick Keswick, and they'd also be nobody's business.

FIFTEEN

The downstairs buzzer rang, and I almost had a heart attack. It was ten-forty-five. I ignored it. But whoever it was, was persistent. It rang again and again. I hefted myself out of the tub, wrapped a towel around me, and instead of reopening the workroom to check the screens, I went to the front hall.

"Yes?" I snapped into the quaint intercom. "Who is it?"

"Kick. It's me."

The voice sounded familiar. "Me, who?"

"Owen Brace."

You've got to be kidding.

"Can I come up?"

"Of course," I answered. "First floor. Flat B."

Presumably he'd forgotten to give me some papers or correspondence or something he needed first thing Monday morning, although I couldn't imagine what. That's what faxes and e-mails are for. By the time I opened my door, I'd put on a thick terrycloth robe and a little lipstick. The bracelet and ring were back in the safe.

Owen was holding on to the neck of a bottle of champagne and seemed slightly tipsy. "I'm sorry to barge in at this hour; I hope I didn't waken you."

"No, no, come in. I thought you were having dinner with Céline."

"I was, but I couldn't take it anymore. She ran into some friends at the bar, and I left her there. I'm sick of conversations with coked-up models who only have first names and no knowledge of life before 1989."

"You mean they studied the Gulf War in history class?"

"Exactly." He laughed. "If they've even heard of the Gulf War. Most of them are illiterate."

He pushed past me and walked down the hall into my sitting room and crossed directly to one of the sets of double doors that opened out onto Eaton Square Garden. He smelled brisk and citrusy, and faintly of tobacco.

"This is nice."

"Yes, thank you," I said. "You sound surprised."

"I suppose I am. Isn't that a Boule desk?"

"Yes, it is. I'm surprised you recognized it. You must have been studying up." The bowlegged console—its gold ormolu bumpers, red enamel, tortoise trim, and brass overlay in perfect condition—sat in front of the windows. I always keep a vase of white flowers—lilies, lilacs, French tulips, hydrangeas—on its corner. Tonight they happened to be roses and jasmine.

"Smells like a whorehouse in here."

"Thank you very much."

"Just kidding." He shrugged out of his raincoat and tossed it on the sofa. I picked it up and hung it on the rack in the hall.

I'd worked hard to get my apartment just the way I wanted it, carefully collected its contents, until it resembled, overall, a three-room jewel box. My own Demi-Parure, if you will, to use an archaic jewelry industry term that describes three matching pieces: a brooch, earrings, and necklace. A Parure, itself, has five, including a tiara and a bracelet.

"What can I do for you, Owen? I'm sure you're here for a reason, other than adult conversation."

He held up the bottle. "Do you have any glasses?"

"No."

"You don't have any glasses?"

"Of course I have glasses, Owen."

He followed me into the kitchen and sat on one of the stools. "Did you see Tina's press conference? David left me a message that I should watch—said he's got it all covered, whatever that means. It's supposed to be on again at eleven. He sent a video to the hotel, but I didn't have time to watch." I set two flutes on the counter. "Do you have anything to eat?"

"Sure. Wait till I get some clothes on. I'll be right back."

Well now, wasn't this a situation? Naturally, it was nothing like my nocturnal visits from Sir Cramner, and I certainly didn't plan to slip into a negligee. Owen Brace and I were contemporaries, and although he wasn't aware of it, I didn't need his approval or his money. I opted for comfort, and pulled on the cashmere warm-up suit.

It was startling to see a man in my kitchen again, especially such a handsome, vigorous one who looked so totally at home. A man with some Sir-Cramner-color in his face unlike the sepulchral Ballantine gray that had matched Benjamin's suits and complexion. Owen's jacket hung on the back of a chair. He'd rolled up the sleeves on his white dress shirt and loosened his tie. His banker's shoes shone, and his suit pants hung straight, held in place by silvery gray damask suspenders with a shadow of pound signs discreetly woven in. Owen was in beautiful condition. He was of medium-tall build, fit and trim, flat stomach, longish hair smoothed back. His eyes moved constantly, like a wolf's, and he had a quick, friendly, disarming smile that he turned in my direction when I walked in. The TV set was on, and he was fixing Brie and cold roast beef sandwiches on sliced baguettes.

"This is great. You can't imagine how great it is to open someone's refrigerator and find some actual food inside. Usually it's just a couple of yogurts and a bottle of Evian. Well"—he picked up his flute— "cheers and thanks."

"My pleasure." My tone was as neutral as my attitude.

"You're quite the gardener." He tilted his head past the breakfast nook in the direction of the terrace garden, which was always in bloom with one sort of thing or other. "What're those things?"

"Sprouts."

"Huh. You didn't strike me as the sprout type."

"Well, I'm full of surprises, aren't I?"

"Yeah, you are." He smiled again. "It's unexpected."

"That's why they're called surprises. Oh, here she is."

Tina's face, mostly hidden behind her white-rimmed, signature dark glasses, filled the screen. Owen punched up the sound.

"We had a terrible row," she said into a bank of microphones on the front steps of their former love nest, Chihuahuas tucked in her arms like little pop-eyed Beanie Babies. "I tried to leave, I've been afraid of him since the day we married. But"—she began to cry—"I couldn't take it anymore, and he got so angry, he hit me." Tina gingerly pulled off the dark glasses to reveal a black eye. "So I threw him out of the house. My heart is broken."

"What in the hell?" Owen choked, spewing champagne across the counter.

I started to laugh.

"She is a complete idiot. I can't even believe it."

"That's obviously what David meant, that he has it covered. We all saw her leave today, and we can all prove she didn't have a black eye."

"I know, but who the hell needs the aggravation."

An updated story on Lady Melody's demise followed, but unfortunately, the firm wasn't mentioned. The news video showed bouquets already starting to pile up at the gates of Carstairs Manor. If I'd known she was going to die, I probably would have grabbed another souvenir or two, like that Cartier watch. Oh, well—never look back.

"Would you like another sandwich?"

"I'd love it."

I fixed us each another—adding a little strong, hot mustard to zap up the Brie and beef, and a little swipe of soft butter on the bread. While I worked, Owen opened us each a bottle of beer and poured it into pilsner glasses. We chatted and got to know each other a little.

SIXTEEN

"Where are you from originally?" I asked.

"Short or long version?"

"Short—it's late."

"Okay," he said between mouthfuls, "short version: I'm from Toledo, Ohio. Dad was a dockworker; Mom, a waitress. Both deceased. I went into the army out of high school, got drafted, did a stint as a supply sergeant in Vietnam. Stayed in the service, did tours of duty in Germany and New Jersey, while I completed my college degree."

"In what?" I asked.

"Well, it's not exactly a college degree, college degree. It's in auto repair. But I worked the whole time in supply, and by the time I got out, I'd already set up a distribution network for my first business venture."

"Which was?"

"Used automobile parts."

"Handy." I assumed most of them had been pilfered from the army motor pool. He'd been married three times—always with bad results.

"My first wife was a beautiful girl from Rhode Island. Linda. We didn't have any money, we both worked all the time. We were always exhausted. She worked the late shift at the Uniroyal plant in Trenton—we lived in base housing at Fort Dix—and one night she fell asleep on the way home and ran off the bridge. Boom. That was it. A few years later, I met Cheryl. By then I'd made some headway in the business and had a little money to spend. Cheryl was everything I ever wanted. Total babe. She was smart, beautiful, a body that wouldn't stop—she could do things to me . . ."

"Hey," I said. "Clean it up. This is not a fraternity house."

"Sorry." He seemed a little thrown by my tone but picked himself up quickly. "Okay, she was a lot of fun to be with. We had a ball. We got married in Las Vegas, one of those Elvis chapels—one of those silly things you do when you're a kid—and went to the Grand Canyon for our honeymoon." Owen stopped and shook his head. "Uh," he cleared his throat. "Never mind. Anyhow, then I end up with Tina, the bad girl from San Juan." He looked at me with a wry smile. "I think I'm pretty much done with marriage. And I'm pretty much done with women under forty. I can't take the dumbness anymore."

"I wouldn't make any big declarations if I were you." I laughed. "I think you'll stick to that plan till about, oh, tomorrow afternoon when some babe will call."

"You're probably right. How old are you?"

"Over forty."

We both laughed.

"Okay, your turn. Where're you from?"

I told him the authorized version of my life's story. I left out basically everything that was true, except the part about being from Oklahoma. "My father was head of North Sea exploration for Phillips Petroleum, and we were transferred to London from Bartlesville when I was sixteen. I just never went back."

"Which way's the head?" he asked when I was done.

"I can tell you've found my personal history absolutely gripping."

He laughed. "You're a real fanatic about manners, aren't you?"

I nodded.

"Don't you ever lighten up?"

I shook my head.

"Okay. That was great, Kick, a real cliff-hanger. Which way's the head?"

"Right down the hall."

It was shortly before midnight.

When he hadn't returned after about five minutes, I went to find him. He was in my bedroom, studying the painting over the mantel, a minor Impressionist. A gift from Sir Cramner.

"This room is beautiful."

"Thank you," I answered.

My bedroom is beautiful, a secure little boudoir wrapped like a gift—top to bottom, head to toe—in salmon pink and champagne paisley, all pulled together in fine pleats to the center of the ceiling and crowned by a Baccarat chandelier with crystal drops the size of hen's eggs. The gentle, calming paisley is everywhere: on the bed, headboard, and lining the two walls of bookcases which flank the room.

Seeing a stranger in my kitchen had startled me, but seeing one in my bedroom caught me completely off guard. Invitations to my bedroom were tougher to come by than invitations to commoners to spend Christmas at Balmoral. Virtually impossible. This would never do.

SEVENTEEN

"This is an impressive painting." He got up close to the canvas and squinted at the signature.

"I wouldn't go that far."

"No, I mean really impressive."

"Well, you haven't exactly been in the business of studying impressive art for long, so I wouldn't categorize you as an expert in much of anything."

Owen studied me quietly. "Huh," he finally said. "I don't impress you much, do I?"

"Well . . . ," I began.

"No, it's okay. It's refreshing."

"Your ego impresses me plenty. Come on, let's go back to the kitchen. This room's not part of the tour."

I was concerned that he would start to investigate the books. The fact is, I have the one of the world's most complete private libraries dedicated to all aspects of jewelry and gems, but I have no interest in anyone stumbling across that fact.

Nobody is even vaguely aware of my interest in the field beyond regular business knowledge, and that's the way it must stay. I don't even want the subject to come up outside of the office because the risk of exposure, accusation, arrest, jail, trial, and incarceration are real. This is not a game to me—I take it seriously and do it with the highest possible professional skill and standards. My life and I teem with secrets—the left hand is hidden from the right. It never occurred to me in my wildest dreams that a total stranger would ever be in my bedroom. The only people who had been in my flat were Sir Cramner and my housekeeper.

I was horrified that Brace might start looking at the books, which covered jewelry from A to Z. The collection has information about gemstones, from precious: diamonds, emeralds, rubies, sapphires, and pearls to name a few; to semiprecious: amethysts, aquamarines, coral, opals, peridots, topazes, tourmalines, turquoises, and so forth.

The volumes were bound in varying muted hues of Moroccan leather and served as a peaceful complement to the paisley. Actually, if you paid close attention and opened one of them, say, *The Three Musketeers*, you'd discover it was actually about emeralds. No matter what the titles said, the bindings were the approximate color of whichever gem the book was about.

I also have histories and biographies of jewelers and their establishments, from Crown Jewelers Garrard & Company and Louis Cartier, to Oscar Heyman, Graff, Verdura, Fabergé, and Raymond Yard.

I've cataloged important, historic, one-of-a-kind pieces, such as the astonishing Cambridge and Delhi Durbar Parure, made for Queen Mary from the Cambridge Emeralds and Cullinan cleavings to wear at her 1911 coronation and subsequent durbar proclaiming her Empress of India. In my opinion, it's the ultimate of the jeweler's art.

I have historical references on famous stones, such as the Koh-I-Noor, the Cullinan, the Star of India, the Hope Diamond, and the DeBeers Millennium Star. On famous missing stones with romantic, mysterious histories—the Great Mogul, the Darya-I-Nûr, the Great Sancy, the English Dresden, and the mythical Braganza, or King of Portugal, the second-largest stone ever found. I have extensive technical works on cutting and faceting. And I keep lengthy records of the provenance and movement of pieces in major collections, including those originally from the estates of Their Royal Majesties, Queens Victoria, Alexandra, and Mary; the Nizam of Hyderabad and Berar; Merle Oberon; Marie Antoinette; Barbara Hutton; the duchess of Windsor; Queen Elizabeth II, the Queen Mother; and now Lady Melody Carstairs; and a score of other ladies still with us whom my respect for confidentiality and my hope they or their heirs will choose our house when the time comes for their collections to be auctioned prohibit me from mentioning.

Owen picked up a thick volume off my bed table. "What's this? Russian?"

"Yes."

"*The Mysterious Missing Romanov Treasury.*" He read the title. "What's up with this?"

"It's just something I've always been interested in." He was starting not only to make me nervous, but also a little self-conscious. Aware that I was standing in my bedroom with a relative stranger who was handling one of my fondest books. It was as unsettling as if he were handling me.

"What about all those jewels that are always going on world tour? I thought those were the Russian crown jewels."

"Those are nothing compared to what's said to exist."

"Seriously?"

"Yes."

"Like what?"

"Look, Owen, let me tell you later. I mean, it's fairly abstruse, and it's almost one o'clock in the morning."

"I can take abstruse. Tell me." Then, *he sat on the edge of my bed*, holding my book. I was shocked. "I'm very interested."

"All right," I began reluctantly, "but let's go back to the kitchen. I'll tell you the story."

"No, tell me here. It's so comfortable in this room." His eyes were inscrutable. On one hand harmless, vulnerable. On the other, he exuded such an intense sexuality, I almost felt as though he were hypnotizing me.

What was this? Some kind of wrestling match? It was as though he knew he had touched an important nerve in me and decided to see how far he could push it, see who was in charge. The air in the room crackled with tension. I found myself unbelievably drawn to him, and angry, and defensive. And he knew it. Well, to hell with this. It was my room, and I wasn't going to let some barbarian with an overload of testosterone turn me into an uncontrollable goofball.

"All right." I took a seat in an armchair. I lit a cigarette.

"May I have one of those?"

"Surely."

He got up off my bed and came over. I handed him a cigarette and held the lighter for him. His hand touched mine. It was like being stroked with warm velvet. And it was not an accident.

It took every ounce of self-control for me not to jump or pull away. I forced myself to be steady. I closed the lighter and set it on the table. "You aren't actually coming on to me, are you, Owen? Because if you are, I have news for you: stop."

He had the grace to laugh. "Sorry. That was pretty stupid, wasn't it. I apologize. There's just something about this room. And you. I feel like I'm talking to Princess Grace or something."

"Get a grip, son. You've had too much champagne."

"I really am interested in the Russians, Kick."

"All right. Then sit down in that chair over there and prepare to be educated."

He ignored me and resumed his place on the bed. All right, suit yourself, I thought. I refuse to be riled.

"According to legend, Dowager Empress Marie Feodorovna— mother of Czar Nicholas, from whom she was estranged because of a dispute with Rasputin—took the lion's share of the monarchy's crown jewels with her to the Crimea, where she stayed for two years, theoretically under the 'protection' of the White Bolsheviks. She and her entourage escaped to England in April 1919, with two large leather-bound trunks, one said to contain her personal jewelry, which was substantial, and the other the treasury of crown jewels. But when she arrived, the trunk with the crown jewels had vanished. The household rumor was that she'd entrusted them to one of her guards, and he'd disappeared with her permission and instructions."

"Where are they now?"

"Nobody knows."

"How do you know?"

"Sir Cramner Ballantine told me. He insisted one day the man would emerge and Ballantine & Company would be auctioneers of the Romanov Treasury."

What I didn't tell Owen was that Sir Cramner had told me this story on that first afternoon in the suite at Claridge's, and the thought of it was so inspirational to him, and captivating to me, we'd pulled the covers over our heads for the umpteenth time. Ballantine & Company was still waiting for that great day, and whatever secret made Sir Cramner confident it would arrive had died with him. But the possible existence of such an extraordinary stockpile waiting somewhere, in a cellar, or attic, or bank vault, lying and waiting for more than eighty-five years, just waiting for the light of day to touch it and set it ablaze, had mesmerized me from that moment forward.

"What do you think made him so sure? And why is it making you blush?"

"What?!" I couldn't help but laugh—the memory of that afternoon so long ago still made me happy. Me in those hot pink patent leather boots amused me so much I almost blurted it all out. "I don't know what made him so sure. Possibly he received a message from the Dowager Empress, or else he made it up. I don't know."

"Thanks for telling me." He closed the book and caressed it, and it was as though I felt his hand on my cheek.

EIGHTEEN

The silence sat heavily on both of us. This was the sort of moment that in the movies, people can't take the pressure anymore and rip each other's clothes off, and go after each other like dogs.

What on earth am I saying?

We waited.

"Cool ceiling," Owen said. He was lying on my pillows, arms crossed behind his head. He was like a schoolboy, a child, trying to get a reaction.

"Thank you."

My bed (I bought the mattress from the Four Seasons Hotel), has six especially soft down pillows and makes me feel like a princess. I wasn't at all pleased to see a fornicating barbarian enjoying them, but I decided to respond with tried-and-true wartime tactics regarding how invadees successfully neutralize invaders: Don't let them see what's important. My face was blank.

"Are you almost done in here, Owen?" It was a schoolteacher's voice.

"Nice carpet."

"It's a rug." A faded Aubusson I'd grabbed for the reserve price from the estate of a Lady covered my bedroom floor.

If anyone were looking, the only out-of-the-ordinary thing they might notice about my bedroom is that there are no family photos, for reasons I've already explained.

Except for one picture, I took it a couple of years ago in St. Rémy at the Café des Alpilles. There was a young man, an American, who looked to be in his early thirties. Happy, well-adjusted, with a young woman who loved him. He was loved. He looked like what my son would look like. If I had a son. That afternoon, I posted myself on all the Internet adoption sites, just in case he or she might need me for some reason, some medical emergency or something. I've never heard anything from anyone.

"Who's this?" Owen picked up the picture.

"My godson."

"Huh." He got to his feet, leaving a deep indentation in my silk satin puff and breaking the spell. "Well, I'm on my way. Thanks for the break. We've got a lot to do starting Monday."

"I know. Again, congratulations. This was an unbelievable coup—obviously meant to be. Sir Benjamin never could have pulled it off."

"Coming from you, that's high praise. It's just the first step, but it was an important one. Now the real work begins." Owen stopped at the front door. "What are you doing this weekend?"

"Going to visit friends in Scotland."

"Really? Where?"

"Outside of Edinburgh."

"Have a good one. See you Monday."

I was so glad he was gone, I thought I was going to faint. I'd had a close call of some sort, but I wasn't quite sure what.

Before I went to bed, I removed the diamond from Lady Melody's engagement ring, dropped its platinum setting into the smelter, where it melted, and returned the stone to the safe. I picked up the bracelet and ran it across my arm one last time. I could feel its history seep into my blood, intoxicating me. I'd never possessed a piece of such importance. I ran it along my cheek, across my lips and down my neck, and across my breasts. I'd never felt such pleasure, or love. The bracelet was mine. From now on, I would call it the Queen's Pet.

The next morning, I checked my e-mail, as I did every Saturday morning, to see if there had been any inquiry from the adoption sites. And, while I waited for the line to connect, my heartbeat stepped up and I held my breath, knowing there would be no message but hoping all the while that I would be wrong. Maybe today would be the day.

It wasn't. I took a breath and signed off. It's okay. I don't know what I'd do if I did hear, and it made me happy to know that my son or daughter was all right. Didn't need to find me. Had no emergencies that needed one of my kidneys or a piece of my liver, or a lung, or my heart. The fact is, I would give any or all of them just for a message. Sometimes I wondered if my child had a child, but I tried not to think about it too much. Not to think about if perhaps I had a whole family out there somewhere wondering about me, too.

I slipped my tiny laptop into my purse, and with my hair tucked under a gray wig, took the Underground to Heathrow and caught the first flight to Geneva, where I deposited several high-quality gemstones, along with Lady Melody's diamond solitaire, in my safe-deposit box. I spent the night in a pretty lakefront room at L'Hôtel du Lac, had a very satisfying cheese fondue for dinner around the corner with a crisp Swiss Riesling, went for a brisk morning walk along the frozen lake, and was back in London in time for lunch, where it was rainy and cold.

The afternoon was spent in my workroom, completing the pairs of curved rows that served as the frame settings for the Kashmir sapphires in the necklace. I turned all the overhead lights on high, switched on the facing pair of high-intensity fluorescent lights on my Meji microscope, which had a magnification power of 45x, and went to work. The room was silent but for the soft hum of the air-conditioning and occasional remarks, encouragements, and observations I made to myself.

Each curved row had eight baguettes of graduated size from roughly a little less than one-quarter carat to approximately three-quarters carat. Every curved row pair was slightly different because the central sapphires were of different sizes—ranging from seven and one-half carats to 11.1 carats. I was working on Frame Number Eight. I took a small platinum ingot and rolled it to two millimeters of thickness. Then I sliced off two, 6.5-millimeter-wide strips, making several steady passes rather than a single deep cut, and very carefully coaxed them into their slightly tapered, curved shape. I measured constantly, and when I was satisfied the shape and proportion were exact, I laid the baguettes in place in their preassigned order. Once they were all properly positioned, I pressed them hard onto their platinum beds, where the culet, or bottom point, of each diamond made its own distinctive imprint.

A jeweler's bench has dozens of implements, many of them appearing to be identical, but in fact each one is specialized to its task. There are buffs and burs for finishing and polishing, pliers, tweezers, and torches, and about fifty different gravers for cutting and shaping. My gravers were the finest available, made of the hardest Swiss steel and, therefore, able to keep their blade longer on platinum, which was the metal I preferred to work in.

The back of a piece of good jewelry should be as beautiful and interesting to look at as the front—that is where quality and workmanship present themselves. The visible area of the stones on the back should be almost as large as the front. The smaller the visible area, the poorer the craftsmanship, and generally the poorer the stones and the metals. Platinum is hard and light, demanding to work with. It requires patience, precision, and talent, and its rewards are multifold in the way it almost invisibly presents and holds stones. Most top jewelers, when they cut through the metal to seat a stone, have a trademark shape—spades, hearts, diamonds, clubs, circles, squares, triangles, ovals, and so forth. Mine was a shamrock. By the time a piece is complete, the original cut-through shape is no longer visible, but if it is subjected to intense expert scrutiny, sometimes, it's said the signature can be identified. I don't believe it.

I turned the first indented bed over and began to cut. The wooden knob handle of the scalpel-sharp knife graver was familiar and solid in my hand. The work was slow and painstaking. Once the cut-throughs were done, the stones were seated and the metal slightly heated and softened and cajoled into making a beautiful, secure bed. Then I folded the sides up and cut off the excess platinum, tucking it down so it formed just the tiniest lip along the girdles of the baguettes, securing them in place. The light that came up through the diamonds, and reflected off them, was magical and mysterious. The workmanship was indistinguishable from the original.

My concentration was absolute, and by evening, I'd completed all the pairs of curved rows. The physical toll that kind of concentration and bright light exacts is painful. My neck and shoulders were practically paralyzed, and my eyes burned so badly, it hurt to blink. I put away the necklace, reracked the tools, and tidied the room. Then, before closing up for the night, I took the Queen's Pet out of the safe and held it to my cheek. It sizzled. I sizzled. Prince Albert and I smiled at each other. It was like having a secret lover. I kissed him good night before tucking the bracelet away.

It was pitch-black and freezing cold in the kitchen, so I turned on the fire, poured myself a huge scotch, made a large bowl of popcorn, wrapped myself up in a cashmere throw and watched TV mindlessly until it was time to go to bed.

NINETEEN

Monday morning rain streamed down the windowpanes when the alarm went off at six o'clock. It was dark outside. Eaton Square was foggy and quiet. I love rain. Maybe that's why I've always loved London so much—we never got any rain to speak of in Oklahoma, and England's droopy weather makes me feel secure, deeply rooted in a long history of stiff-upper-lip endurance. I snuggled under the covers and listened to the news of the day on BBC, gave some serious thought to calling to say I wouldn't be in, but instead got myself together.

I had breakfast on the bus, same thing every day: a hot, sugary, glazed cruller from our little Cliveden Place French bakery, Oriel. I sat in my regular seat, with all the regular people around me, all of us eating our biscuits or croissants and reading our papers, while we splashed down the street. How much would I miss this when I made my final departure for France? Not enough to keep me from going. Whenever that turned out to be.

I'm usually the first one at the office, and this morning was no exception. The ancient porter, Alcott, and I always try to see who can beat the other, but it's a moot game, fixed like games children play with their grandparents, letting their seniors win just so their feelings don't get hurt. He's old and creaky, and even if he gets there before I do, I can always beat him up the stairs, but I don't. This morning, however, there was no sign of him. It was already seven-thirty. Small, candlelike lights burned in the first- and second-floor windows. I pushed open the heavy wrought-iron gate, went up the steps, and let myself in.

"Good morning, Roger," I greeted the senior guard, who sat behind a tall, bulletproof divider, overseeing a bank of airport-type security screening lanes. "Good weekend?"

"There was a lot going on in the paintings and furniture departments—all the experts buzzing about the Carstairs estate, working overtime."

"I'll bet. See you later."

"Have a good day, Miss Kick."

I laid my purse on the X-ray conveyor and passed through the metal detector, greeted the guard—the harebrained, night-shift girl who followed Roger around like a trained dog—and entered the comfortable, serene, mysterious, and magical world of Ballantine & Company Auctioneers.

The huge house was silent. Peaceful. The air redolent of our private brand of cedar-scented furniture wax. Not a sound came from the auction and showrooms off to either side, nor from above, where the second- and third-floor balconies circled the spacious first-floor atrium. I ascended the grand stair to the second floor, where the executive offices were located, and turned on the light on my desk, which sat at the top of those stairs. It was a forbidding battleship of a desk, befitting what could appear to be a forbidding battleship of a woman, and whence I could peer down, with my adopted air of noblesse oblige, on any peon who dared ascend. This was my house.

The front door opened below me and Alcott crept in.

"Good morning, Alcott," I called as I pulled off my gloves and switched on my computer.

"Good morning, Miss Kick." He waved cheerily.

I turned on more lights, and they warmed the reception area, putting a rich glow on the cherry paneling and bringing out the contrasting tones in the antique Persian rug. Little picture lights came on, as well, showing off a set of Picasso drawings on the far wall and a particularly lovely Constable that was hung directly opposite the top of the stairs—neither of these works had met their guarantees at auction and both were now owned by the firm. We had a lot of these sorts of things hanging around at the moment, left over from the last contemporary masterpieces and eighteenth-century English paintings auctions for which Bertram and Owen had made outrageous promises to sellers in the hopes of attracting better works. Well, we obtained a few of the available noteworthy pictures to sell, but fewer buyers than anticipated (or *required,* in case anyone was keeping track of how business was doing), and ended up owning them ourselves. They'd thrown us deeper into debt. But, costly as they were, as far as I was concerned they were a vast visual relief from the tired old hunting prints that Benjamin had favored.

"Good morning . . . *what?*" I heard a man bark, and turned to see Bertram pass through security.

The girl gawked at him.

"'Good morning, *Mr. Taylor,*'" he scolded. "That's what you say. And get to your feet when I come in and get your hair out of your face."

By the time she'd unhooked her feet from her stool and stood up he was already halfway up the stairs. He looked at me and shook his head. "Where do we find these people?"

Every morning it was the same thing, and every morning it made me laugh. "How did the weekend sales go?" I asked, taking his coat.

"Very satisfactory."

"No really, tell me."

"We exceeded the estimates by 20 percent."

"It's starting to happen, isn't it?"

"I wouldn't go that far, but we aren't going backwards at least. You're looking very fit today. Good weekend?"

"Fine, thanks."

"I'll be on the phone with Marchese Cortini for the next hour—no interruptions. Tea. Milk. Two sugars. If you will." He went into his office and closed the door.

I hung my coat, stashed my briefcase, and put on the water for Bertram's morning tea while my e-mail downloaded with the results of the Friday and Saturday sales at our New York branch. Would you believe that pre-Brace, we didn't have e-mail or the Internet at Ballantine? It's pretty incredible. The weekend sales had produced better than expected. I printed out the reports for Owen, who I knew had already checked them himself, then I unlocked the door to his office and flipped on the lights. Something was wrong, disordered. Smelled bad. Smelled horrible, actually. Gaseous and stuffy, as though the heat had been left on over the weekend. I put my hand over my mouth and looked around. Across the room, Tina was stretched out on the couch, one of her long legs on the sofa and the other stretched to the floor. Above her, soft light illuminating a van Gogh (didn't meet its guarantee) glittered off her sparkly cocktail dress and bronzy, high-heeled sandals.

Owen wasn't going to like this.

"Good morning, Miss Romero," I said brightly. "Time to get up. May I bring you a cup of tea or coffee?"

Tina didn't answer. She didn't move. I went closer. "Miss Romero? It's Monday morning." I clapped my hands. She didn't budge. I switched on the side table lamp at the end of the sofa, and it was then I noticed the syringe on the floor, and little flecks of dried blood on her foot, between her toes. Her face was turned toward the sofa back, and when I peered more closely, I saw that her eyes were open, but they looked sort of dried-out. And she was a sickening grayish white color. And the sweetish stuffy smell was coming from her.

"Oh, Jesus," I gagged and gasped for air. "ALCOTT!" I screamed, and ran for the door. "ALCOTT! ROGER! GET UP HERE!" I picked up the phone and dialed the police.

"What it is, Miss?" Alcott, bless his little old heart, puffed up the stairs as fast as he could, while Roger raced past him like a rabbit, his weapon drawn, and charged into Owen's office.

"Oh, my God," I said. "You won't believe it. Tina's in there. She's *dead.*" The emergency operator answered, and I gave her the particulars.

"What do you mean, 'dead'?" Alcott shuffled toward the open door.

"Don't go in there. Go back down and get the door for the police. They'll be here any second."

"Very well, Miss Kick. I thought you wanted me up here." He turned in place, so stiff with old age his body moved as a piece, like a marble statue swiveling on a pedestal, and shuffled back to the stairway. His bony little birdlike hand clutched the handrail. He was about halfway down when the bell started ringing and pounding began on the front door. "Just a moment," he called in his sweet, pale voice. "I'm coming."

God forbid the girl at the X-ray machine could get off her big derriere and go open the door herself.

TWENTY

Alcott had scarcely turned the knob before the door blasted open, practically tossing him to the ground like a little doll. Two muscled firemen, carrying suitcases, dashed past, followed by two uniformed officers. "Where?"

Alcott indicated the stairs, and they flew up, reaching me in record time—they really were in lovely shape, these young men—and raced into Owen's office. There was a momentary flurry of activity until they all realized there wasn't going to be any dramatic rescue of the famous movie star lying on the sofa in the sequined cocktail dress with the needle marks between her puffy, pedicured toes.

A few minutes later, two detectives in wet raincoats followed, taking the stairs one at a time, the junior of the two speaking on his radio, instructing, I assumed, officers outside to close off the area. The older fellow had a slight limp.

I went into the kitchen, started a pot of coffee, returned to my desk, and watched the hullabaloo. The amount of activity was amazing, more and more people arriving every second, the new ones wearing disposable, white, papery overalls—I knew they were paper and disposable from television mystery shows—carrying more and more equipment. Each person was on a cell phone talking to someone else.

"Excuse me." The seniormost detective emerged from Owen's office. "I'm Commander Curtis. And you are?" He looked at me expectantly, pen in hand.

"Kathleen Keswick. Senior executive assistant." I stared at him, he looked so familiar. "Do you know . . ."

"Let me help you: I am not John Thaw resurrected, and I am not Inspector Morse—although I look like him, or them, whichever you prefer. I am, however, a fan of Colin Dexter."

"I just think he's marvelous."

"As do I. But now let's turn our attention to the affairs of the moment, shall we. You are the one who discovered the body?"

"I am."

"Do you know who she is?"

"Yes. She's Tina Romero. Mr. Brace's wife."

"Tina Romero, the actress?"

"Yes."

"And Mr. Brace is?"

"He owns Ballantine & Company."

"Do you know where we might find Mr. Brace?"

"He's living at the Dukes Hotel on St. James's Place." I picked up the phone. "I'll get him for you."

The detective removed the receiver from my hand. "No, thank you, Mrs. Keswick . . ."

He really was most attractive—not in a movie-star, matinee-idol way—his appearance never would stop traffic the way Owen's could. No, I guess maybe it was his demeanor. He seemed serene and reflective, and the way he removed the phone from my hand was gentle, with a firm, authoritative touch. His face was weather-beaten, an old scar curved along his cheek. He had silvery hair and sad, sky-blue eyes that seemed to offer more wisdom than any eyes I'd ever seen. It occurred to me that it must be terrible to be a homicide detective, making your living looking at the raw data of unimaginable gruesomeness and atrocities. His expression was so remorseful, I felt the urge to comfort him.

". . . that won't be necessary." He replaced the receiver in its cradle. "We'll take care of it." He spoke quickly into his cell phone, relaying Owen's name and location. "What time did you find her?"

He turned the eyes back on me. I could tell he found me as interesting and attractive as I found him. Kick Keswick. What on earth are you saying? You're starting to sound like you're turning into some sort of sex nut. Of course he finds you interesting—you're a suspect. He's supposed to study people closely. That's his job. And he's not that attractive. He's actually fairly rumpled. And, he looks as though he's waiting for you to say something.

"Excuse me?" I said.

"Time. What time did you find her?"

"A little after seven-thirty. I was turning on the lights, and there she was."

"Was anyone else in the building?"

"Yes, Roger. Our security guard. And the night-shift scanner girl—she won't know anything, she's dumb as a post. And the early-shift crew in the security headquarters. But I don't think anyone else was here. I was the first one. Alcott arrived a couple of minutes later."

"Alcott?"

"The porter. And then Mr. Taylor came in."

"And Mr. Taylor is?"

"President and chief auctioneer. That's his office." I indicated the closed door. "But he's on an important call, and I'd appreciate it if you wouldn't interrupt him unless it's vital."

"I see. Did you notice anything unusual when you got here?"

"No. Nothing. It was all normal." My intercom line rang. "Excuse me a moment. Yes?" I answered.

"What's all the commotion out there?" It was Bertram. "Can you appreciate how complicated this negotiation is?"

"I'm sorry, Mr. Taylor. But Miss Romero is dead. It's the police."

"Ask them to keep it quiet. You're making it impossible for me to concentrate. And where's my tea?"

"Coming, sir. I'll tell them. Sorry." I hung up. "Mr. Taylor," I explained needlessly. "Excuse me one second, if you will." I motioned to Alcott, who'd taken up his regular position at the top of the stairs, ready to leap into action in any direction. "Mr. Taylor's tea, please, Alcott. If you will."

"Was the office door locked or unlocked?" Commander Curtis continued.

"Locked."

"Is that normal procedure"

"Yes. I'm always the last to leave, and I lock it myself."

"What about the cleaning crew?"

"They start at five-thirty and they always do Mr. Brace's office first so I can be sure it's properly done before I go home."

"And you leave . . . ?"

"Usually about six. And that's when I left on Friday. I went to the market."

His eyes darted up to mine, paused for a moment, then back to his pad. "I see."

Why did I say that? So what if I went to the market.

He nodded and shrugged out of his coat, revealing a slightly rounded, well-used, comfortable-looking body. The pockets on his sport coat were sprung, his tie was stained, and his gray flannel slacks were baggy. But his shoes were shined. Rainwater beaded on the glossy cordovan brogans. "Tell me, Mrs. Keswick, do you happen to have a cup of tea? Or coffee?"

"Both. Which would you prefer?" I popped open the closet door and hung his coat.

"Coffee would be fine. Black. Two sugars."

"Coming right up. And it's *Miss* Keswick." He followed me into the kitchen. "How long do you think Miss Romero has been there?"

"Hard to say without the medical examiner, but I'd say a good couple of days."

"Ick."

"Well put." His eyes twinkled and we both laughed shyly.

TWENTY-ONE

Fifteen minutes later, Owen strode in and took charge. I could tell by the color in his face and the spring in his step that he'd exercised in spite of the rain. He ran seven miles through Hyde Park every morning, looping around the Serpentine and back.

Did I mention I've been trying to go walking on a more regular basis? Nothing to write home about, but as soon as Benjamin died, I decided to live a healthier lifestyle. Besides, I love to walk, especially in France. I made the decision to become a *robuste* walker, to walk five miles every day, rain or shine. To make it a habit. I want to develop the habit of fitness. I was already up to a mile or two every two or three days, or so. I call that progress. A good base.

"You found her, Kick?" Owen said to me, his face expressionless.

I nodded. "About seven-thirty."

"Through here, Mr. Brace," the commander said, directing Owen into his office. "If you could make an official identification." They were back out seconds later. Owen's color had turned about as waxen and whey-faced as Tina's.

"Is there somewhere private I can ask you a few questions?" Commander Curtis asked him. "Just routine."

Owen looked at me. He seemed disoriented.

"The boardroom, sir," I suggested.

"Right." He was looking worse by the second. "Come with me, Kick."

"You might prefer that we talk in private," the inspector said.

Owen shook his head. "I don't have any secrets from Miss Keswick."

No, I thought. Only about 680 million red ones. And that's going by Friday's tally.

Into the boardroom we went. I turned on the lights, and Alcott brought coffee, tea, and warm sticky walnut muffins. Owen had left the portrait of the founding father, the original, bewigged, dew-lapped and whiskey-nosed Sir Ballantine, hanging at the end of the board table above his chair. Before long, I imagined Owen would be claiming him as his own ancestor.

"When was the last time you saw your wife, Mr. Brace?"

"Last Friday morning when she came to the office. She'd just been served with her divorce papers."

"I see. Was she upset?"

"Very. We had a little scrap."

The commander waited.

"A little scrape, in fact." Owen grinned and indicated the four elongated, fading welts on his cheek. "She gave me these. Then she went on TV Friday afternoon and claimed I'd given her a black eye, which I categorically deny."

"A black eye?"

Owen nodded. "You didn't happen to notice if she actually had one, did you?"

"I didn't notice, but I'll make a point of checking."

"Let me save you the trouble: She didn't. It was makeup."

"Did she often use drugs?"

Owen nodded. "Yes, unfortunately. Often."

"Do you know how she got them?"

"No. But I can tell you she didn't get them from me. That business is loaded with groupies and hangers-on, all of whom are more than willing to provide whatever the star wants. It's pathetic."

Oh, please, Owen, I wanted to say. Get over yourself. It's not as though you don't have groupies and hangers-on of your own, willing to provide whatever you want. Okay, so maybe it's not drugs, but sex on demand? Give me a break.

"We don't suspect any foul play, Mr. Brace. This appears to be a straightforward overdose situation—but just so there are no surprises, since she was found in what can be termed 'irregular circumstances,' we are required by law to perform an autopsy. I also need to ask you, sir, where you were this weekend."

"I understand," Owen said. "I spent all day Saturday and Sunday out in Henley, at the plant."

"The plant?"

"The Panther plant. I own it."

"Panther Automobiles?"

Owen nodded.

The inspector was impressed. "Super," he said, making a note. "And did you spend the night in Henley?"

"No, I came back to the city Saturday, but I didn't go out."

"And Friday?"

"I had a dinner engagement Friday evening with Céline—we were at Mark's."

"Céline?"

"She's a model."

"Oh, yes. Céline. I know who you mean. Super-looking girl. Long blond hair. Big eyes."

Owen nodded. "Big . . ."

"Excuse me," I said.

Owen closed his mouth and Commander Curtis bit his lip to keep from smiling. He was obviously enjoying this case, and really, who could blame him, living the grisly life he did. "And Mark is?"

"Mark's. It's a club."

"Ah," the inspector nodded sagely, and took a large bite of his roll, leaving bits of brown sugar at the corners of his mouth that he blotted properly with his napkin instead of licking them off with his tongue, as Owen would have done. "Of course. Mark's. And after dinner?"

"And then I had a late meeting with Miss Keswick at her flat." Owen smiled over at me.

I almost laughed out loud at the expression on the detective's face. Whether or not he'd found me attractive before, now I think he might have been somewhat intrigued. I gave him a very small grin which, if I were younger, I'd say had a little of the coquette in it, but as it was, was simply bright-eyed, guileless, blank, and unforthcoming.

Owen continued, "Tina had held a press conference Friday afternoon. I'd missed it, and I went to Miss Keswick's to watch it on the eleven o'clock news."

"And how late were you there, sir?"

Owen looked at me.

"Until about two," I said, feeling like a naughty teenager. I felt my cheeks color.

"My driver took me back to the hotel, and I went to bed."

"Your regular driver?"

"Yes. Michael. He's out front. At least he's supposed to be out front."

"And then you left for Henley first thing in the morning?"

"Yes, about nine."

"Do you know why Miss Romero would have been in your office?"

"I haven't the slightest idea."

"You didn't arrange to meet her here?"

"No."

"Did she have a key to your private office?"

"Not to my knowledge. I don't have any idea why she was here or how she got in."

"Who has keys to your office?"

"I do. Kick does. The security department, of course. As far as I know, that's it." Owen looked at me for confirmation, and I nodded.

"That should do it, sir." Commander Curtis closed his notebook. "Thank you for your time. And please accept my condolences."

"Can I ask you a question, Inspector?" Owen said. "How long are you going to leave her in there?"

"It should only be another hour or so."

"You can't move her out quicker than that? I've got a lot to do."

Curtis appeared startled by Owen's reaction. "We're moving as quickly as we can, sir. Even after we're done, you'll want to give it a little time for the air to clear."

No kidding. The place smelled worse than the pedestrian underpass from Kensington to Green Park, which is occupied by homeless bums who use no facilities but their pants.

I was so nervous he was going to ask me where *I'd* been over the weekend, I realized I hadn't actually breathed during the entire session, and once he left the room, I gasped for air.

"Are you all right?" Owen said. "You're white as a sheet."

"Fine. It's just sort of a shock."

He shook his head with disgust. "She was a complete loser. What in the hell was she doing in here over the weekend? And how in the hell did she get into my office?"

"Don't look at me. I didn't let her in."

What I didn't mention, and I don't know why, was that there is a private staircase to Owen's office—it leads straight up from what looks to be a welded steel panel in the alley, behind the Dumpsters. It was so old and unused, I wasn't even sure if Owen himself knew about it—I'd never mentioned it or shown it to him. The last person to use it, to my knowledge, had been Sir Cramner, years ago, trying to dodge his wife and her mother. Poor Sir Benjamin never used it—he'd had no one to hide from but himself.

TWENTY-TWO

"I didn't know Tina used drugs," I said to Owen, who'd set up shop in the boardroom while the police wrapped up their work in his office, tucking Tina's moldering corpse into a large black plastic bag and wheeling her onto the rear service elevator and out the back door. "I thought she was such a fitness nut."

"There's a lot you didn't know about Tina. Drugs were just the tip of the iceberg."

I wanted to say, Like what? But Owen didn't volunteer. "Look, Kick," he continued. "About Friday night. I'm sorry if I embarrassed you with my half-assed pass. I won't blame it on the champagne, I meant what I said, but I do apologize." He handed me a section of the morning paper, folded to the daily gossip column. A paragraph was circled in red. "Get me invited to that." His finger jabbed the item. "And get Gil on the phone . . . Please."

The item was about a party to celebrate Mr. Ishmael Winthrop's ninetieth birthday, to be held at his home in Mayfair. This is a side of the auction business that is somewhat unsavory: seeking out and befriending the old and infirm. Correction: The old, *rich*, and infirm. Beneath the industry's veneer of class, and prestige, and privilege, churns a maelstrom of shameless ambulance chasing. It's preferable to get to the prospects and their families before the dearly beloved is departed; therefore, auction house executives and experts spend an inordinate amount of time and money using their connections and wiles to get themselves invited to galas, parties, luncheons, dinners, house parties, and all manner of receptions: weddings, christenings, bar and bat mitzvahs, and funerals, where they will come into direct contact with their targets. Interestingly, this is not as difficult as it sounds. Most auction house experts, associates, and junior associates are from privileged backgrounds, which only makes sense. They are the people who've grown up around the collections and understand and appreciate their history and value. Furthermore, by hiring the scions, the auction house hopes that when their parents or grandparents die, those collections will come to their firm to be sold.

I put in a call to our eighteenth-century British maritime paintings expert, Philadelphia Singer, an attractive woman of about forty who was a grandniece of Mr. Winthrop, and made the request.

"Is it true?" Philadelphia said. "That Miss Romero is dead in Mr. Brace's office?"

"Yes," I said. "Unfortunately, it is."

"I'm so sorry."

"They were separated."

It did sound pretty heartless, but heartless was in these days at Ballantine & Company. In fact, we were beyond heartless. Here in the second-floor executive suite, we were fast approaching take-no-prisoners. Cash was king.

She called back ten minutes later saying how much Mr. Winthrop's family—his two daughters, Sheiglah Fullerton and Beverley Hughes, now both widowed—looked forward to including Mr. Brace and his companion at the soirée, two weeks from Friday.

Sheiglah Fullerton. The name rang a bell, and then I remembered. There had been a magazine piece about her: Her sport of choice was big-game hunting. She paid quadruple the going rate for regular safaris, because she went on ones where she could actually shoot the animals. She had all their heads and hides in a trophy room at her house.

———

"Miss Keswick." Bertram emerged from his office. He'd missed just about the whole show. "What are all these people doing here?"

"I told you, Tina died."

"You mean *here*?"

"Yes."

"Oh, good heavens. This is the kind of publicity we do not need." He shook his head. "Cheap. Cheap. Cheap."

Commander Curtis stepped forward and introduced himself. "I'd like a couple of minutes of your time, if you don't mind."

"By all means, Commander," Bertram said with uncharacteristic warmth. "Come in. I see you're wearing Magdalene colors."

He closed the door behind them. Oxford. Old school ties.

Twenty minutes later, I took Curtis down and introduced him to our chief of security who, with his command post team of four, occupied a room behind the main staircase. Banks of screens monitored every entrance, exit, elevator, saleroom, exhibition room, and storeroom. Even rest room doors had cameras on them.

"This is impressive," the commander observed.

"Tighter security than the Bank of England," the chief boasted. "We can afford to keep our quaint public look because of our advanced security systems. Ms. Keswick makes sure we upgrade them every six months."

They played through the tapes of the whole weekend, starting with five o'clock Friday. Our David-Niven-look-alike customer, who I suspected was the Samaritan Burglar, breezed through the metal detector chatting familiarly the whole time with a well-dressed couple. I could tell by their expressions they were trying to figure out where they knew him from.

"There's Miss Romero," the security chief said. "We had an old masters drawings auction Friday night, including a couple of Fra Bartolommeo studies. Bigger crowd than usual."

"Which one is she?" Curtis studied the flow of blurs that filled the screen.

"You mean you can't tell?" I asked. As far as I was concerned, she might as well have been from Mars she stood out so clearly from our regular customers.

The chief stopped the tape and tapped his finger on the monitor. "There, in the white mink coat and dark glasses coming through the metal detector." He switched to another view of the foyer. "There she is going up the stairs, which wasn't unusual. She usually went up to see Mr. Brace, but of course, he was gone by then. Don't know why we didn't catch this."

The rest of the tapes of the weekend showed just what the guard had said: lots of experts and associates, eager and anxious to get started on the paperwork for the Carstairs estate. But no one, except Bertram, took the stairs to the second floor, and he must have gone up and down ten times on Friday night and Saturday. The rest of the staff used the elevators to the third floor, where their offices and workrooms were located.

Tina never came back down.

Commander Curtis and I told each other good-bye at the front door. He paused, and I knew he was trying to get up the nerve to invite me out. "Miss Keswick," he said. "May I call you?"

"Call me?"

"Yes. Would you be interested in having a cup of coffee, or a drink, or a concert, with me sometime? Some off-duty time?"

"I think that would be lovely."

His face lifted, and I could see the possibilities. A deep kindness resonated in his war-torn eyes. "Good. I'll be in touch."

I hadn't ever been invited out by a police officer, much less a commander, and now probably wasn't the time to start. But, on the other hand, there was something so genuine and fine about this man, if he really did call, I wasn't sure if I'd say no.

"Don't forget you have lunch with Gil," I told Owen later in the morning after the place had cleared out. I'd opened the windows in his office and called a company that specialized in cleanup and fumigating after "unnatural" incidents. I can't imagine making my living in such a business. I shudder to think of the things they must see. "You're meeting him at Mark's."

"Right."

"And Owen, there're lots of media people around, so try to look a little somber. If you go out there looking all happy, it'll be bad for business."

"Right. Maybe I should stay put. Have Gil come here."

"Can if you want to, but people would like a little peek at the grieving widower, especially by our brass sign at the gate."

He looked at me, his mentor, and guide. "Right," he said. I could tell he thought we truly were birds of a feather. But he didn't have a nest egg worth the powder to blow it to hell, and I was getting ready to fly the coop.

Owen left, passing through a flood of flash and television lights, his raincoat draped around his shoulders, no dark glasses. Once he was safely away, I went into his office, locking the door behind me, and over to the secret door that led to the private staircase. If you were searching for it, you could find it. It was simply a section of the paneled wall on an invisible spring catch. A series of prints hung on the panel, and a chair and side table were arranged in front of it. As far as I could tell, the furniture hadn't been moved, the dents in the carpet were where they should be under the chair and table legs. I lifted them aside. The door opened easily, and I clicked on the light switch at the top of the miniscule landing. We all see what we're looking for, but I wasn't sure what that was. As far as I could tell, the door hadn't been opened in years. Or maybe it had been used over the weekend. I had no idea. I closed it up, put the furniture back where it went, and went about my lunch-hour business.

Outdoors, the air was crisp and invigorating, just what I needed to clear my head, and after a brisk, ten-minute, zigzag march, I arrived at Forty-six South Carriage Square, a quiet spot whose grand old mansions front on Park Lane near Stanhope Gate. Number Forty-six happened to be the residence of Sheiglah Winthrop Fullerton, sixty-six-year-old daughter of Ishmael Winthrop. Sheiglah would be out for sure on Friday night two weeks hence, celebrating her father's ninetieth.

I brought along the crossword from the morning paper, a small Thermos of coffee, and a sandwich of Camembert and Delia Smith's fresh date and apple chutney—which is a no-brainer to make and has just enough cayenne bite to keep it interesting—all pressed tightly together on my homemade nut bread. This really is a most delicious combination, very healthful and filling unless you're watching your carbohydrates, and then all you would want to eat would be the Camembert. I chose a bench in Hyde Park across the street with a good view of the house and started to get to know it a little bit.

TWENTY-THREE

It was two weeks after the "Tina Incident," as we'd begun to refer to it. Tina's family had come en force from San Juan to carry her back home, seeking solace amid a constant swarm of television cameras and tears. She'd been their provider, their mater familias, their annuity, and now their only celebrity remained in her farewell. It was sad. Owen had flown over for what turned out to be a state funeral, and that had been that.

The office was back to normal. Ballantine's experts were back at their appraisals and cataloging, the customers were back at buying, inspired by Bertram's exhortations. Owen was back at hustling and juggling the books, although he didn't seem to be whoring around quite as much. Actually, now that I think about it, he didn't seem to be whoring around at all.

Wednesday afternoon, after the stock market closed, the audited third quarter earnings report and sales projections from Panther were announced, and they were miserable. The bad news would suppress the stock further, which would force additional margin calls from approximately eight different banks, with Credit Suisse leading the charge. The pressure would have sent me right off a cliff, but all it seemed to do to Owen was make him tighten up. Anybody who wanted to play chicken with this man needed a set of plutonium ones, to use the vernacular, if you know what I mean.

"Do you want to have dinner tonight?" Owen interrupted his dictation.

"Excuse me?"

"I said, do you want to have dinner tonight?"

"You mean with you?"

"Well, yes. That's the general idea."

"You aren't asking me on a date, are you?"

"Give me a break, Kick. Lighten up. We have a lot going on, and I thought it might be nice to have a change of scenery while we cover some of this stuff instead of staying late at the office."

I considered. "What time?"

"I was thinking we could just go to Caprice from here."

Did I want to have dinner with Owen? Not really, although by Wednesday I was always a little tired of my own cooking and would have had dinner out anyhow. I'd never been to Caprice. It was a St. James's restaurant where all the "in" people from the neighborhood went, including, most especially, Prince Charles.

"I suppose that would be all right," I said.

"You sure do seem excited," Owen said.

"Get over yourself, Owen."

We sat at a side table in the main room, where the power crowd sits, and I had to admit, it really was fun to be out. Sir Cramner had never allowed himself to be seen with me in public, which—from the time I'd arrived in London as a very young woman—was the role I'd basically grown up in, been trained in, and accepted completely. It was just the way my life was. I was fully cognizant of the fact that I was a singular, solitary person with little-to-no experience in the visible, public side of social relations between men and women. I had no really close friends, and the friends I did have were weekend people, like me, in France. I'd never actually "dated" anyone, nor had what could be called a romantic involvement other than with Sir Cramner. It hadn't been from lack of invitations; it was from a complete lack of inclination to get close to anyone. A psychiatrist would probably say I was afraid to love, I avoided it out of fear, fear of attachment, fear of loss. Okay, fine. Whatever. The point is, can you imagine what would have happened to my little empire if I'd spilled the beans for love? For a friendly roll in the hay? The thought gave me chills.

But tonight, with Owen, it was fun. Almost like having a good friend.

We started with vodka martinis, then butter lettuce salad with a light vinaigrette, followed by grilled lamb chops with rosemary-garlic butter, fresh asparagus, and crunchy little potato pancakes. Owen ordered a bottle of Bordeaux, a 1985 Château Le Pin.

"Excellent choice, sir," the sommelier praised him, and why wouldn't he at a thousand pounds a bottle.

"You really do need to expand your horizons," I said after the sommelier had finished decanting the inky black wine and he and Owen had twirled and sipped and oohed and ahhed, and Owen instructed him to let it breathe a bit.

"Excuse me?"

"I don't mean to be rude, but these sort of big showboat wines with their perfunctory decanting performances, I'm sure have the desired effect of impressing your little model girls with your vast oenological expertise." I didn't even try to hide my disdain. "But the fact is, there are ten other, better, more subtle and sophisticated vintages on the list that—if you really want to impress someone who actually knows something about wine—you should learn to select. Besides, Château Le Pin is way, way too big for this meal, and the '85 isn't ready to drink anyway."

"Really."

I nodded.

"Well then, perhaps you'd like to do the ordering."

"It will be my great pleasure. Do you care how much it costs?"

"No."

"Fair enough. This will be a good comparison, because at least the wines are comparably priced." I motioned to the sommelier and asked him to bring a Château Margaux 1961.

Well, the point was, there was no comparison.

"This is incredible," Owen said.

"Now," I said, savoring the wine's velvety taste, "next time, if you really want to show your stuff, you can contemplate the 1995 Margaux—it's said to be the greatest Margaux ever made—but it's still a little young."

I already had four cases in my cellar.

Then we talked about Lady Melody's estate and how the process was coming along. That afternoon, he and Bertram, who'd been locked in what was beginning to resemble a Neo-Greco-Roman wrestling standoff—one of those polite sort of things when both men just lean on each other as hard as they can, but they don't punch or hit, they just lean like bulls forehead to forehead, for hours and hours and hours—agreed to compromise, and scheduled the auction for three months hence. Owen had wanted two. Bertram insisting on six.

"Bertram's right, you know," I said. "It puts a lot of pressure on us. It's a totally inadequate period to inventory, appraise, and catalog the lots, and promote the sale."

"Tough." Owen shrugged. "Anyone who doesn't like it can leave. I know that in the auction business—which as far as I can tell, moves at the speed of the Pleistocene Age—this is hasty, but I don't care. I need the cash."

"I understand."

"Yes, I believe you do. We're a lot alike. Would you like a coffee or a brandy?"

If you ask me, drinking after dinner is for either amateurs or alcoholics, but I didn't want the evening to end and I didn't want a cup of coffee. "A glass of champagne would be just right, thanks."

"Any particular kind?" Owen said to me sarcastically.

"Yes. Pol Roger Brut, please. Nonvintage."

"Make that two."

Once the waiter was gone, Owen continued. "May I ask you a personal question?"

"Sure."

"Why haven't you ever gotten married?"

"Why have you gotten married so often?"

He laughed. "I'm serious."

"All the regular reasons. Right man never came along. I'm now too old and set in my ways. I like my life the way it is."

"Have you ever been in love?"

"Excuse me?" If I'd been a dog, my ruff would have risen.

"Sorry. I didn't mean to pry too much, but I just think you're neat. You're so . . . self-contained. So elegant. I don't understand why you aren't living on some grand estate somewhere and president of the Royal Garden Club."

I frowned. "Please."

"You know what I mean."

"I do. But, strange as it may sound to you, it *is* possible to be happy by yourself. You should try it sometime."

"I think I am." Owen laughed. "Maybe you'll show me how."

"You've completely missed the point."

"Okay. Change of subject. Friday night. The Winthrop party. Will you come with me?"

"You mean as your *date?*"

"What in the hell is your problem, Kick? As my companion. My sister. My aide-de-camp. What the hell difference does it make?"

"None actually. I appreciate the invitation, but I can't. I've got plans. Why don't you take Bertram?"

"He and his wife are going to the museum gala."

"Okay, then, take Céline."

"Very funny. I need someone with some stature and presence. Some maturity and sophistication."

"You're right. You do."

"I need you."

"Owen, what on earth is wrong with you? Are you drunk?"

"No." He shook his head and smiled. He looked almost sheepish. "I have to tell you, Kick. I've never had this happen before, but I can't seem to control myself around you. I'm becoming completely infatuated with you."

A loud buzzing filled my head, similar, I think, to the sound you hear just when you're dying. I put my hand on top of his and looked into his eyes. "Let me tell you what: Forget it. Get back to your babes. I'll just break your heart."

TWENTY-FOUR

Friday dawned. This was going to be a big day: It was the day of the auction of jewelry from the estate of Mrs. Lewis Baker of Galveston, Texas. (The woman who drugged up her racehorse and ran him into the ground.) And this evening would be Mr. Winthrop's ninetieth birthday. I was ready for all of it.

Earlier in the week, I'd FedExed my copy of the Kashmir sapphire-and-diamond necklace to myself at the office which meant it would go through the standard X-ray process and sniff test all our mail was subjected to, but I wouldn't have to try to bring it through our security myself. The FedEx package stayed in the bottom drawer of my desk until Friday morning, when I opened it and tucked the finished piece into my pocket. I had done a great job. My craftsmanship was virtually indistinguishable from the original, and unless it was scrutinized by an expert, no one would ever know the difference. The synthetic stones burned with the feverish zeal of their authentic cousins, the Kashmirs.

We didn't open the doors until ten o'clock, but by eight-thirty customers were lining up outside for the eleven o'clock auction. This was an extremely prestigious sale, Sir Benjamin's only coup in the last year of his tenure. The morning was frigid.

Bertram looked out the side windows at the front door, then turned to his team assembled indoors. "This is even better than I expected. Everybody ready?"

Nods all round.

"Good." He threw open the front door and said loudly enough for the people at the front of the line to hear, "Roger, we must let these poor people in. They're freezing to death."

"Yes, sir," the security chief answered smartly.

"Alcott, would you ask the kitchen to prepare tea and biscuits, if you will."

"Consider it done, sir." Alcott teetered off to the main kitchen, where he'd already alerted the staff to be ready early. Moments later, as the customers streamed in from the cold, the tea, coffee, and hot cocoa tables materialized, loaded with giant silver urns and china cups and saucers emblazoned with the Ballantine & Company Auctioneers emblem. Large sterling silver trays of sweet rolls, muffins, and biscuits were positioned alongside the urns. By eight-forty-five, the main lobby was packed with beautifully dressed women, well-tailored men, trophy wives with their rich, aged husbands, and numerous dealers, most of them Hassidic Jews in their black suits and side curls. The decibels rose. The place resembled a convivial meeting of the Ladies Aid Society.

At nine, Bertram climbed a few steps of the main staircase and clapped his hands. "Ladies and gentlemen, if I may have a moment, please."

The crowd quieted quickly.

"I'm Bertram Taylor, president and chief auctioneer." He paused for a flurry of appreciative recognition. "Thank you. Thank you." He managed to eke out a little color in his apple cheeks. He was such a superb showman. "Welcome to Ballantine & Company—hopefully you're all getting thawed out—we want warm happy customers, not a freezing, screaming mob." Laughs and applause all round. "As you know, the exhibition rooms don't officially open for another hour, but we have a much larger than expected turnout, and I've instructed the jewelry department to set up as quickly as possible so you can have a few extra minutes to look over these pieces, many of which are quite remarkable. If you haven't already had an opportunity to see the collection in person, you won't believe it. We're delighted you're here, and we're going to have a great sale today. Enjoy yourselves."

Bertram gaveled the auction into session at eleven o'clock sharp. All the phone girls were in place, each with her customer on the line, and the private rooms, similar to sky boxes, were filled with Saudis and sultans. There were sixty lots, about an hour and a half worth. My Kashmir sapphire-and-diamond necklace was the last item—the show's crowning jewel, if you will. Photographs of each item flashed on big screens around the auction room.

Once the sale began, the Jewelry Ladies, as they're known, immediately started breaking down the exhibit, returning the jewels to the rolling safes, which were armored stacks of velvet-lined drawers, each with two armed guards assigned to it. I always make a point of assisting the Jewelry Ladies, whether I have a personal stake in the auction or not, and as we worked together, laughing and talking, we all half listened and half watched Bertram on the monitor mounted over the door.

Every now and then one of the ladies would say, "Did you hear that?" And we'd all pause and watch Bertram's final gavel. The sale was proceeding much better than expected, everything was going for at least twice, and sometimes three times, the amounts of the estimates—one of my benchmarks for whether to make a switch or not. Another benchmark is who's doing the buying—private individual or dealer. When the ruby cabochon and diamond suite was bought by an individual, not a dealer, for almost three times its estimate—I knew I was set, because it meant someone willing to spend a great deal of money had just gotten shut out. The buying fever soared.

The time had come to make the switch.

Now is when the rubber hits the road. When we separate the women from the girls. Now is when and why I earn the big bucks.

With my left hand I reached into my pocket and with my right into the case and at the same time, I said, "What did Bertram just say?"

It made all of us, myself included, pause and cock our ears and turn our eyes to look up at the screen, just long enough, only a split second, for me to withdraw the copy from my pocket and thrust the original into my blouse.

"It's just marvelous," the Jewelry Lady next to me said. "I think he said that diamond bracelet brought a million pounds."

"Bertram's so, so talented," said another.

"He's the best," I agreed.

As am I.

Early afternoon, I received a call.

"Miss Keswick? Thomas Curtis here."

"Thomas Curtis?"

"Yes, Commander Curtis with Scotland Yard."

"Oh!" I laughed. "I'm sorry, Commander—I don't think I knew your first name. How are you? I imagine you're calling with Miss Romero's autopsy results."

"No actually, this is a social call."

"Oh?" I sat up a little straighter.

"Have you seen the Singer exhibit at the Tate?"

"About ten times. I can't seem to get enough of it."

"Same here. I've got tomorrow afternoon off and hoped you might join me for a stroll through the gallery—I'd love to hear what you think about some of the paintings, and that way we'll get some culture in and won't feel so guilty about having a good lunch."

What a nice surprise. And actually, one of the nicest invitations I've ever received. So much better than a movie or some sort of a sporting event. The Tate on a Saturday afternoon and lunch? It made me sick to decline.

"I can't do it. I have to go to Henley for a meeting in the morning and I don't know when I'll be back. Please promise you'll ask me again."

"I will," he answered. "If I ever get another Saturday off."

"Are you *positive* you can't come to Mr. Winthrop's birthday party to-night?" Owen repeated.

The "infatuation" subject hadn't come up again. But I'd be lying if I said it hadn't affected me. My relationship with Owen was unlike any experience I'd had before. The more we worked together, got to know each other, the more fun and interesting it became. There was laughter, polite resistance, tug-and-pull, and a sexual, sensuous, at-mosphere of derring-do. He reminded me of a terrier who wouldn't give up. He'd taken the time to try to peek behind my ice-queen door, and I was letting him. God help me. I was having fun. I needed to get out of here.

"For the last time, I cannot. Give it up, Owen. I still have the same plans I had on Wednesday." To wit: Tonight was the night I knew Sheiglah Fullerton, big-game huntress extraordinaire, would be out all evening.

"Change them."

"No. I can't. I won't."

"Do you have a sweetheart?"

"Is that really any of your business?"

"No. But I'd like to know."

"What you mean is, do I have a life? We've covered this before, and the answer still is, yes."

"Okay. Okay. I'll see you at nine tomorrow."

"I'll look forward to it."

I went home from work and disassembled Mrs. Baker's sapphire-and-diamond necklace, liquefying the platinum. I couldn't believe that I possessed eleven, large, Kashmir sapphires—it was unheard of. I cupped them in my hands and rolled them around where they made a joyful clicking sound and sparkled like deep water. They were so beautiful, I wanted to eat them, take them into myself, become part of them, make them part of me. Reluctantly, I folded each one into its diamond paper *briefke,* arranged them in order by cut and carats, and locked them away.

There was no time to sit and congratulate myself. For two and a half weeks, I'd studied Number Forty-six South Carriage Square from a variety of angles, at a variety of times, in a variety of guises, and by the time evening rolled around, I was prepared.

TWENTY-FIVE

It was dark when I left home, but the streets were still busy, and by the time I climbed to street level from my first Underground stop, if anyone had noticed me, they would have supposed I was someone's housekeeper going home from a long day. I blended easily into the foot traffic, innocuous in my tan Burberry, my eyes behind a large beige-rimmed pair of glasses, my hair tucked under a brown wig and a tan rain cap. My grocery basket rattled along behind me, my tools hidden beneath a tall bouquet of leeks, a couple of purple cabbages, a roll of paper towels. I made three different Tube/bus changes to get to South Carriage Square, turning what would generally be a ten-minute walk into an hour's journey. I switched my hat twice.

At about eight-fifteen, I disappeared into the dark of the mews behind Mrs. Fullerton's town house and slid behind the trash shed, where I shrugged out of my coat, and traded my walking shoes for soft-bottomed rubber slip-ons.

My surveillance had revealed that the security system the Fullertons installed in the mid-1980s had never been updated. It might have been state-of-the-art then, but technology waits for no one, particularly successful burglars. At Ballantine & Company, we upgrade our entire system every six months, and redigitize the electronic combinations on our safes biweekly. I do my home every eighteen months.

One of the reasons I've succeeded for so many years is I never sacrifice professionalism for expediency. The precautions I take may seem excessive, but when you get cavalier, you get caught.

I snapped on skintight, latex gloves, put night-vision goggles over my eyes, turning my world an eerie green, and went to work.

The lock on Mrs. Fullerton's back gate was old and easily jimmied. I'd been through it a number of times during the past couple of weeks. I crept in and closed it silently behind me, then crossed the garden and climbed the stairs to the terrace that ran the width of the house. I knew as long as someone was in the house, the alarm system would not be activated because the house was not zoned. They couldn't set the perimeter without arming the whole property—what an incredibly costly and shortsighted mistake. Twice, I'd watched through the garden-level kitchen window as the butler activated the system once the household was in bed, which also meant there were no motion detectors. The system was out of the dark ages.

Tonight, bright lights shone from the kitchen. From the sounds of the television set and the conversation blaring through the windows, the household staff was taking full advantage of Mrs. Fullerton's evening out.

Sets of French doors to the formal drawing room and dining room opened onto the terrace. A few dim lights burned in the drawing room, but the dining room was in complete darkness. Working quickly, I removed a precut sheet of contact paper from my pocket, peeled off the adhesive backing, and smoothed it onto the pane of glass adjacent to the door latch, leaving a good deep ridge running the center length of the piece to serve as a handle. The paper adhered easily. Then, I pulled my little black matte, hard-rubber, ball peen hammer out of my pocket and tapped around the edges, hard enough to shatter the glass. The broken pane came out as a piece on the sticky paper, just like removing the lid from a pot. I folded it up and tucked it into my pocket.

The rest was simple.

Because Mrs. Fullerton, nee Sheiglah Winthrop, had moved into this house as a bride, and it had been Mr. Fullerton's family home for generations, I made a few assumptions. I assumed the main safe in the house would be in the library and would be the original piece of equipment, a beautiful relic installed by one of Mr. Fullerton's long-gone ancestors to safeguard his shares in the East India Company, or some such thing. I also assumed that, at some later time, either by an earlier Mrs. Fullerton, or by Sheiglah herself, a second safe had been added to the master bedroom, or dressing room, to hold the lady's jewelry.

These assumptions were based on experience. The only question—and it really didn't make much difference—was: Would it be the original combination-dial safe, or had Mrs. Fullerton had the foresight to replace it with a new electronic model?

In the mid-1990s, when electronic safes became available for residential use, I replaced my standard combination-lock safe with one that has an electronic-locking mechanism. At that time they were considered crack-proof, and essentially they still are, unless you're in the "business," and know what you're doing. If you don't, then you get three tries at an electronic lock before it freezes for a minimum of fifteen minutes, sometimes more—an eternity in the life of a jewel thief. You can rip off the keypad, but it doesn't make any difference—the brains of the mechanism are sealed between layers of armor at the top of the box, cooked in there like a little pancake—they're nowhere near the keypad. You can try a blowtorch, but the second the vault feels the heat, the locking bars seal up and jam themselves, so even if you cut an opening big enough to reach in and try to open the safe from the inside, it won't do any good. You just have to try to cut a hole big enough to remove the goods through it. If you do all this stuff, you have an awful lot of time on your hands. Or, if you're a true, state-of-the-art professional, you go to EKM Elektronika in Zurich, and for about twenty thousand dollars you get yourself a high-speed digital scanner and pop the thing open in about two seconds.

I found Mrs. Fullerton's jewelry safe sitting behind a row of musty evening clothes in the late Mr. Fullerton's closet. It was a good-sized vault, maybe three feet high and eighteen or twenty inches deep. A beautiful, shiny black, custom-made affair, with a late-twentieth-century combination-dial lock. The most unusual part of it was, it had a deposit window in its front above the door, like an after-hours bank drop. So, if Mrs. Fullerton came in late, or tipsy, she could just take off her jewelry and drop it through the night depository, and not have to fuss around with the combination. What a great idea.

I knelt on the floor and fitted a notched magnetic ring around the combination dial. Then, toward the upper left-hand corner of the door, I pushed on a small suction cup from which stuck a short stiff wire that served as a distance gauge to the magnetic ring's ridges. I moved my shoulders and neck around to loosen them up and settled in, turning the dial, feeling for the tiny hesitations. It took about five minutes to identify the three numbers that made up the combination, and another six to work out their sequence. The lock was a typical four-three-two-one setup, so after a total of eleven minutes, the dial locked itself into place. It's really enough to make you sick—it really should take longer, be harder, make the thief sweat a little more, or even sweat at all!, to get into such a sophisticated vault. Sadly, if you have age, experience, and the right equipment, it shouldn't take more than ten to fifteen minutes. As I moved the lever down, I could hear the bars retracting, sliding free, and Mrs. Fullerton's fine safe pushed itself open with a very satisfying, solid, welcome-to-my-world, click.

It was like a store inside. The shelves were jam-packed with velvet boxes and bags. I didn't have time to evaluate the goods—just started opening cases and dumping their contents into my pack, scooping soft jewelry sacks in along with them. There was an inordinate amount of jewelry, but within ninety seconds the vault was empty. I shoved the empty containers into the blackness of the back of the safe, with the exception of those that had already been empty, which I assumed were for the jewelry Mrs. Fullerton was wearing to-

night. I laid them just as I'd found them, on the front part of the second shelf. I wondered, because of her night deposit drop, how long
it would be before she discovered the theft.

On the top shelf, I tenderly placed my calling card: a small bouquet of shamrocks tied with an ivory satin ribbon. Owen was right—
I'm not a sprout kind of girl. Those were shamrocks I was growing
outside my breakfast room. I guess he wasn't as much of an Irishman
as I thought.

It was probably because my adrenaline was pumping at such a pitch
and my senses were so heightened that, just as I was about to close
the safe, I was able to hear the other sound. Or sense the presence. I
don't know which came first, but my hair stood on end as though I
were about to be hit by lightning, and I knew someone else was
nearby. I flattened myself against the closet wall.

TWENTY-SIX

A strong, pinpoint flashlight beam cut around the master bedroom, finally settling on what looked like a Renoir hanging over the fireplace. I watched a figure, dressed all in black, approach it. He, or she—even with my night goggles I couldn't tell which—balanced the adjustable torch on the mantel, directing the beam at the center of the painting, reached up, and removed it from the wall. Whoever this was, he moved with the assurance of a pro. My heart thudded like a freight train. He leaned the stolen painting very carefully against the chair, pulled something out of his pocket, and laid it on the mantel. It was the Samaritan Burglar. He then picked up the picture, carrying it almost tenderly, and headed toward the door. I let my breath out. He stopped. He'd heard me.

I watched him approach the closet, and I pressed myself farther into the wall, seeing everything as though it were in slow motion. He pushed the door open, casting the beam all around until it fell on the open safe. I had no choice. My arm flew up and then down, cracking him on the back of the head with my little rubber hammer. He dropped like a rock.

After that, I moved fast. My insides had turned to jelly. I tried to calm my heart and control my breathing, but I was terrified. Nothing like this had ever happened to me before. I stepped over the body—please dear God, don't let him be dead, but I didn't touch him to find out—and closed the vault door, heard the bolts run themselves home, twirled the dial, rearranged the clothes back around the safe, and flew out, certain all the lights in the house would be thrown on as I dashed down the stairs to the dining room and that I would be caught with what I was pretty sure was going to turn out to be millions in jewels, if they were all real. But there was no sign of any life in the house, outside of the noise in the kitchen. No shadows, no sense of alarm on the part of the staff, no sign of where the other burglar entered. I decided right then and there, this was my last heist. I thought I was probably going to have a heart attack.

At the Pimlico station, the last stop of my long, circuitous, Underground voyage home, I went into the ladies' room and locked myself into a stall. I had calmed down, and now felt only waves of relief. I was amazed at my own foolhardiness and grateful for dumb luck. I pulled off the wig and glasses and stuffed them into a plastic shopping bag. My hair was soaked and pasted to my head and I opened the roll of paper towels that was part of my grocery camouflage and dried my hair as best I could before pulling it up into its customary twist. I put on some lipstick and blush and by the time I exited the Pimlico ladies' room at a little before ten o'clock and stepped onto the train home, I looked myself.

No, that's not quite right. I looked better than myself. I looked exhilarated. Awestruck. Young and exuberant. I'd just dodged the biggest bullet of my life and I was safe. And I was never going to do it again. Every inch of my body complained from tension. All I could think about was how good my bathtub was going to feel. Steaming hot, pikaki bubbles, Schubert, and champagne.

I sailed through Sloane Square, my shopping basket bouncing along behind, down a side street past all my familiar neighborhood spots, all tidied up and closed for the night, the cleaner, the baker, the greengrocer, the café, the bookshop. I thanked God for every single one of them. They were my touchstones. I went faster and faster, so anxious to get home, I was practically running by the time I rounded the corner into Eaton Square. Tears filled my eyes and streamed down my cheeks.

So, it was a miracle I saw it in time: the Ballantine & Company Bentley was parked at my front door. Owen was in the backseat, watching out the window, waiting for me to come home.

I swerved into the shadowy protection of the front staircase of a neighboring town house, and peered out. My God, it was lucky I'd seen him before he saw me. I waited. Shortly, the Bentley purred away and turned the corner. I waited a few more minutes to be certain he was gone, then circled back into the dark mews and let myself into my sleeping building.

TWENTY-SEVEN

"Knew you'd want a report about how the Winthrop affair went," Owen's message came over the speakerphone in my kitchen as I tugged off my clothes, which were completely drenched, and shoved them into the washing machine. "Made contact, not only with him and his daughters, man . . . talk about a couple of bowwows . . ."

"Oh, that's nice, Owen," I talked to the machine.

". . . but also ran into Odessa Niandros."

I stopped what I was doing. Odessa Niandros could secure our future. She was the sister of the late Princess Arianna, and controlled her estate, which had been estimated at over a billion dollars. The curators of her late sister's collections were still making their final inventories before Odessa decided on their disposition, whether to sell, donate, or maintain them. A few minutes of face time with Odessa, especially for Owen, was invaluable.

"Tried to come by and tell you in person, but you're still out on your date or whatever you want to call it. It's about ten-fifteen. See you at nine. Sweet dreams."

I'd almost forgotten, we were going to the Panther plant on Saturday morning for a meeting with Gil.

As I'd suspected it would be, based on the sheer volume of merchandise, the Fullerton Haul was worth the aggravation. Sheiglah Fullerton had been generous to herself in her widowhood. I knew she'd bought the jewelry for herself. No Englishman, no matter how much money he had, would ever give his wife such daring or big stones in such contemporary settings.

As the lucre came tumbling out of my pack onto the blue velvet padded bench in my workroom and was hit by the high-intensity lights, I realized I was not looking at the payoff of my career, after all. There were dozens of large, nicely matched colored stones, easily sold, including a few colored diamonds—very rare, expensive, highly prized, and generally the domain of collectors, mistresses, or bored, rich, young couples, such as overnight billionaires or professional athletes—all set in platinum or gold. In spite of their good, not great, quality, from my point of view and for my purposes, none of the pieces was worth keeping intact. They were too commercial and too contemporary. Nothing tempting. Except for one suite: The necklace contained forty, two-and-a-half-carat, emerald-cut, white diamonds—not D Colorless Flawless like my bracelet, or even excellent such as E, F, or G, but nice quality: H, I, J, perfectly acceptable. The stones lay tucked closely, side by side, in the invisible setting technique developed by Van Cleef. It was a work of art, easily recognizable as the handiwork of master jeweler Lucien Bragond; undoubtedly one-of-a-kind. Variously shaped silver-dollar-sized clusters of pale pink diamonds were placed unevenly along the band like exploding fireworks. This was probably a 10-million-dollar piece of jewelry. And there were earrings to match. I apologized to Monsieur Bragond as I popped the stones free into velvet-lined holding trays and slid their settings into the platinum smelter, where they surrendered like meringue dissolving in heavy syrup.

I then quickly removed all the stones from all the other pieces, deposited their settings in one of the smelters—platinum, 18-ct. gold, 24-ct. gold, and white gold—and made an inventory.

By the time I closed it, my safe looked like it belonged at Graff on Old Bond Street.

Just before I turned off the lights, I quickly scanned the day's security tapes of my flat. Nothing at all until the company limousine pulled up at my front door at nine-fifty. Owen got out and rang my bell. Waited and rang again. He turned toward the car and waved and Michael got out. I shouldn't have been surprised at what happened next, but I was. Michael jimmied the lock on the front door of my building. Actually, I was shocked. He stood back and let Owen pass and followed him up the stairs to my flat where Owen knocked and rang the bell some more. There is no audio with my system, but it was clear that Michael made an enthusiastic offer to break into my place. Owen told him no. They returned to the car and waited another twenty minutes before leaving.

TWENTY-EIGHT

Saturday morning.

I made a large cup of hot cocoa, two slices of buttery cinnamon toast, and after indulging myself in those pleasures, went into the workroom for my weekly torture session.

I pulled my tiny, titanium laptop out of the safe and checked my personal e-mail. I felt particularly optimistic. I don't know if it was because of the successful switch—the necklace had finally gone for 5 million pounds, and I had all its precious, priceless Kashmirs in my vault—or the huge haul of stones from Mrs. Fullerton's safe. Or the lucky escapes. I wondered how the Samaritan Burglar was feeling. There hadn't been anything on the news about any robberies or murders, so thankfully I must not have killed him and he must have gotten away before she got home. But there also wasn't any story about a Renoir showing up at any police precinct, so maybe it wasn't really him. Maybe it was just a common criminal. Finding Owen waiting at my front door certainly caught me up short, and watching Michael break into my building so quickly and professionally not only gave me the creeps but also disturbed me because he was a thug in livery and would have no compunction about breaking into my apartment as well. So actually, based on that, there was no good reason why I should have felt so happy this morning, but I did. I wakened feeling today would be a special one.

As the phone found the satellite, and the satellite found the server, and it all hummed along at high speed, I knew something big was going to happen—I could *feel* it. I drummed my fingers on my lips and waited impatiently.

What was I going to do when I got the message? What would it say? Hello? Are you my mother? Would I immediately pick up the phone? Would I faint? Or cry? I didn't really know what a mother would do, since mine never did anything but get drunk and lock me out of the trailer. Now I know she was nothing but a kid herself. It was a thousand years and an entire lifetime ago. I was a different person. The Kick Keswick I was born as no longer existed. I couldn't even remember how she felt about things, or what she looked like. I couldn't stir up any anger, passion, or even curiosity. I'd read about how mothers should act and feel, seen movies and TV shows. So, if I were to get an e-mail from some long-abandoned child, I wondered if I'd automatically know what to do, or if my actions and emotions would be copied, counterfeit. Ah, finally, the connection was made. I clicked the e-mail button.

"Come on. Come on," I muttered. It seemed to take forever.

No new messages.

Hell.

I blinked my eyes a few times, cleared my throat, signed off, and tucked the whole affair away in my jam-packed vault.

I couldn't get out of the workroom fast enough, and as soon as I had the door locked behind me and walked into my bedroom, my attitude improved. Sunlight spread across my golden yellow satin bedcover, giving it a comforting glow, and sparkled off the embossed bindings of my books. I decided to feel lively and happy in spite of my disappointment. So what if I didn't have a message, I hadn't ever gotten one before. It wasn't going to wreck my day. Know why? Today was going to be special because I had *plans*. So what if it was a business meeting. It was Saturday, and the sun was shining, and I was going to do something more than my London-based Saturday routine of errands, which I love, but this was an unaccustomed break. I hated even the slightest hint someone could affect my patterns, but I had to admit, I was looking forward to the drive to the country. Okay, maybe I was a little bit looking forward to seeing Owen, too. He was becoming a flame I couldn't resist.

TWENTY-NINE

"Ready?" He shouted through the intercom.

"Ready. I'll be right there."

"Bring a jacket, I've got the top down."

"Right."

As far as I can tell, most females—young girls, young women, grown women, and so forth—daydream from time to time about the same sorts of things, mostly revolving around romance, revenge, money, and power. There seems to be a kind of sequence, depending on the age of the dreamer.

When you're young, say from sixteen to thirty or so, there's the romance/revenge dream: a beautiful wedding, *your* beautiful wedding to be specific, to a dashing, rich fellow, the big catch who kept slipping the loop. But in your dream, you're the one who gets him because you're the only one who didn't need him, and now you're the center of attention and can give the bird to all the boyfriends who dumped you, and all the girls who stole your boyfriends away right from under your nose using every low-down, underhanded female trick in the book, and now the big man everyone wanted is waiting for *you* at the far end of the aisle. And Vera Wang made your dress.

And there's the professional, career-oriented dream that has more to do with power and revenge than romance. It takes place at a board of directors meeting, for instance, where, after a quick, vicious, *masterful*, political battle, you're elected chairman and

CEO, beating out all the men, most of whom you promptly fire, and the rest of whom you simply force to stay and suffer. Maybe you even kick them in the shins occasionally. And your Armani suit fits like a glove and you have a professional gym installed in the empty office next to yours, empty because you fired the creep whose office it used to be who tried to make your life miserable and who's now selling timeshares at some second-rate, Bulgarian ski resort.

Now that I'm older, the third kind of fantasy—the power, romance, money version—has become my particular favorite. It goes something like this: You drive your Panther V-12 Madrigan convertible to the train station to pick up the guy (possibly the same guy who could have been, but wasn't, waiting at the far end of the aisle twenty years ago) who's arriving to spend an afternoon, or the day, or a weekend, whatever, at your country house. You seduce each other on a cashmere blanket under a flowering apple tree on your farm, in your orchard, before, during, and after a couple of nicely chilled bottles of Le Montrachet and some cold chicken sandwiches which your cook has prepared with creamy homemade mayonnaise and the crusts cut off. After which, he gives you a lovely brooch. Then he takes a nap in his room and you take a nap in yours and you don't see each other again until the cocktail hour.

Well, this morning when I got downstairs, it certainly wasn't that dream, but it wasn't bad. Owen held the door of his black Panther V-12 Madrigan for me while I lowered myself into the calf-leather seat.

"Nice car," I said.

"I shouldn't be driving it myself, I should've left it in the inventory." He circled around the front and climbed in behind the wheel. I think he was wearing Cary Grant's cologne. "If we could just push ten more of them off the line a month, we wouldn't be in the position we're in today."

"You can go ahead and release yourself from the guilt, Owen, and enjoy the car. A single Madrigan one way or the other isn't going to make the slightest difference. Neither will ten."

"I don't need you to remind me."

"I didn't think so."

"Do you want me to put the top up? It's probably going to get pretty cold once we're on the M-4."

"Absolutely not. It's perfect out." I tied my scarf snugly over my head.

"Aren't you worried about your hair?"

"Not in the slightest."

My reward was one of those sunrise smiles that set the world aglow. "Terrific," he said. Then he slipped the stick into first gear, and we glided away from the curb as though we were floating on air.

"This car is magnificent," I said, while we worked our way through traffic toward the M-4. "Are you happy with the way it handles?"

"Everything but snow—it's a disaster. Fortunately, it's not much of a problem around here, but in other markets, it's an issue. Even snow tires don't make a difference. It's ludicrous that people driving a hundred-thousand-dollar car have to put eighty-pound bags of sand in their trunks just to get out of the drive. But it doesn't seem to be fixable."

"Really." I could have told him that. I have a V-12 Madrigan convertible of my own in France. Dark green. I love my car so much, I think it's possibly a little sick.

He pushed it up to a hundred on the highway, making it too windy to talk, which was fine with me because I found myself being so drawn to Owen, so physically attracted, I'm not sure I could have spoken anyhow. I was filled with such an aching and a longing that I had to concentrate on restraining myself. Maybe it was the car. Maybe it was the remnants of my adrenaline glow from the night before, or from the dozens and dozens of stones worth millions and millions of dollars that lay in the dark of my safe, or from the sense of well-being I awoke with. I don't know, but whatever it was, the ride had become sensuous and arousing, and I found myself looking for flowering apple trees along the highway, even though it was wintertime, and thinking thoughts that gave me hot flashes. Maybe it was watching him handle the car. His hands were sure and strong, firm in their movements. His fingers gripped the steering wheel and gearshift with quiet assurance, and I pictured them moving across my body with that same confidence, the sure knowledge he knew exactly where to go and what to do. I felt them caressing my breasts and moving down my body, taking charge of every part of me. I felt his lips on me. I closed my eyes and leaned my head back and listened to the wind.

I became aware of my *Pasha* nestled close to my heart, its faceted edges grounding me, reminding me to control myself. I opened my eyes and began counting the roadside markers. By the time we exited for Henley-on-Thames, I was sufficiently frozen—my fires had smoldered to embers.

"We've got a few minutes," Owen said, as we approached the storybook town. "Let's grab a coffee."

"Great idea."

We ducked into an ancient little breakfast spot, with low ceilings and lace curtains along leaded windows. The room smelled homey, like slightly burned, buttered toast with honey.

"This meeting won't be long, but I need you there to keep the minutes—it could get complicated. I'm sorry to wreck your Saturday. I'm sure you have a number of pressing social engagements, you're so in demand." He made no effort to hide his sarcasm.

"Actually, I do have a lot going on"—I laughed—"and you cannot imagine how sorry I am if that offends you. We will be back by noon, won't we?"

"Absolutely." He dropped a sugar cube into his double espresso and slowly stirred. "Also, I wanted you to come with me today because I have a plan, an idea, that I put into place secretly several weeks ago, that I think could rescue Panther and Ballantine's. I'd like your input."

"What is it?"

"I'd rather just show it to you."

"I'll look forward to it," I replied, wondering what on earth he could possibly do without my knowledge. "You've aroused me. I mean, you've aroused my curiosity." Oh, God. I don't think he heard the slip, but I turned to look out the window just in case, just so I wouldn't have to make eye contact with him for a moment or two.

Whatever it is, I thought, it couldn't be much of a secret. After all, we're together most of the time, and the rest of the available time on his schedule I booked for him. Was it possible Owen was a man of secrets? He didn't seem the type, but then, I probably didn't seem like a woman of secrets, either, and I'll bet I've got more than he has.

"Like what?" he said.

My mind was a million miles away. "I'm sorry. 'Like what' what?"

"I was saying, like what kinds of social engagements do you have this afternoon?"

"Just this and that," I said vaguely. "Lunch and an opera matinee. Cocktails and dinner this evening. Just regular Saturday kinds of things. Why, what are you up to?"

"Same." He tossed off the coffee. "Let's go."

THIRTY

The Panther Automobile plant sat on seventy-four hundred acres behind a solid wall of greenery. The only indication there was anything at all behind the impenetrable screen of trees and foliage was a sign every fifty feet or so that said, "PRIVATE PROPERTY. CANINE PATROL. VIDEO SURVEILLANCE." The main gate materialized out of nowhere, and it was as well protected as the entrance to a top secret military installation. Four uniformed men, armed with machine guns, waited to greet us: two in the guardhouse and two by the gate holding on to German shepherds who strained to get off their leashes and rip our throats out.

"Have you been here before?" Owen asked me, as the guards approached, one on either side of the car.

"No."

"It's a whole different world. Just give him your driver's license."

"I don't have one."

"What?"

"I don't have a driver's license."

"What do you mean? You left it home?"

"No. I mean I don't have one. I don't drive."

Owen looked at me as though I'd been dropped onto his head from outer space. "You don't know how to drive?" He couldn't seem to grasp it.

I shook my head.

"You don't know how to drive?" he repeated.

"What on earth is your problem?" I muttered under my breath. It seemed to me that the guards were getting a little edgy. "It's not that big a deal."

"Well, you've got something with your picture on it, right?"

"Yes, my health card."

"Then use that."

"Fine." I handed my card out the window. "Sorry," I said to the guard. "It's not much of a picture."

Guy didn't crack a smile. Just handed it back.

"Are you going to want to use the track, Mr. Brace?"

"Is there anyone else on it?"

"No, sir. Not this morning."

"Then, yes. I'll take Miss Keswick on a quick tour."

"Very well. I'll let control know."

"Thanks."

We purred through the gates into the top secret world of the Panther and proceeded down a treeless boulevard toward a red stoplight that had barriers with flashing red lights running along the top, similar to those at a railroad track.

"As you can see," Owen explained, "it's all cleared out through this area so we can see if there's anyone on the track and they can see us, although they're not supposed to worry about if we're out here or not. They have the right of way."

We rolled to a stop. A whistle shrieked loudly enough to raise the dead, lights began to flash, and the barrier rose slowly. The stoplight turned green. Owen turned onto the track, which was as wide as the M-4, and pressed the accelerator. Within four seconds we were going sixty, within ten, a hundred and twenty. His concentration on the road and the car was absolute as we zoomed past various buildings, identified by small signs that passed in such a blur it was almost impossible to read them: PAINT SHOP, RESEARCH, WAREHOUSE, ASSEMBLY PLANT, FINISH PLANT, INTERIOR. Before long, he'd pushed the car to one hundred and sixty miles an hour but it felt like twenty-five—nothing rattled, nothing shimmied, nothing budged. The car was an animal. The sexy feelings returned. He pushed it faster, and took a split second to glance at me. I smiled and fought a shiver that seemed to have concentrated itself in the pit of my stomach.

I don't know how many miles we'd covered, the track ran through all sorts of terrain and elevations, but at some point, Owen took his foot off the accelerator and shifted down into fifth gear. The engine didn't scream, didn't whine, didn't overburden itself, it just powered down, and by the time we turned into the main administrative area, at a sedate city speed, it was humming like a pussycat.

"Well," he said. "What'd you think?"

"I think I'd like to do it again."

"You know, most of the girls I've brought out here and taken on the track start screaming for me to slow down once I get it over a hundred."

"Well, I'm a woman. That's the difference."

THIRTY-ONE

The headquarters building itself was basically brand-new, having been built one owner ago when the original, Tudor-style building burned to the ground. Its replacement was ultramodern—a two-story, black glass structure with an elegant air of mystery about it.

"I love this building," Owen said. "It represents the product perfectly. That tweedy, exclusive, men's club stuffiness isn't attached to the car anymore. Remember that ad campaign they used for fifty years—man leaning on the car smoking a pipe, leather patches on his elbows, hunting dog sitting next to him, a blonde in the background?"

"I do."

"That was part of the problem. Look at the difference." We stood at the end of the front walk, and Owen waved his arm across the expanse of the façade. "This building is about the car—money, power, speed, sex—not about who you know or where you went to school or what club you're in."

"Really," I said. "You mean the leather patches on the elbows of your tweed jacket, and the fact that I'm a blonde, make this picture all that different? All you need to add are the dog and the pipe. You're the guy."

"Okay. Point taken." He smiled at me. "At least I'm younger than he was."

"I don't think so."

He held the front door open for me. "Has anyone ever told you you have a serious attitude problem?"

"Just you."

Inside, we went up a staircase of green glass slabs that seemed to rise through the air unsupported by anything at all, and down the hall to the executive suite where Gil Garrett greeted us.

In a long-sleeved, cashmere polo shirt, loose-fitting gabardine slacks, and soft tassel loafers, Gil seemed perfectly cast as the president of the Panther Automobile Company. He was compact and graceful, catlike in his movements, as though he might have been a race-car driver himself, as a young man. Or a boxer. His blond hair was coarse and wiry, his nose had been broken a couple of times. There was nothing of the aristocrat about him—he looked like an affable, fit, formidable Mick.

"Morning, Kick. Thanks for making the trip, Owen." He shook his boss's hand. "I wanted to keep an eye on these tests."

Outside the windows of his corner office, a flat test track was busy with some sort of time trial involving three cars that appeared identical, but one of them was clearly faster. The whines of their engines were audible—not enough to interfere, just loud enough to remind visitors they were at the manufacturing plant of the world's most-sought-after, most highly valued, highest-performing, and highest-priced automobile.

Owen and Gil spread their papers out on the conference table while I took my own place at the far end and duly recorded the meeting. But my mind was elsewhere, trying to figure out exactly what the secret Owen alluded to earlier could be.

"Let's move on to the Caruso Project."

Gil's brows went up, and his eyes shot over to me and back to Owen.

"No problem," Owen said. "Kick has my total confidence. She knows what kind of situation we're facing, and the reality is, Gil, we can't make it work without her. We're stuck."

"You're sure? Because once this toothpaste's out of the tube, there's no putting it back."

"Positive. Let's get started—I don't want to spend the whole day out here, and I promised Kick I'd get her back to town by noon. Bring me up to date." He turned to me and tapped his finger on the table. "Kick, no notes."

I laid down my pen.

Gil didn't look completely sure, and he didn't look happy. Our eyes met, and I could tell he didn't like me and was struggling with whether or not to trust me.

"If you're wondering whether or not I can keep a secret, I assure you, I can."

"This is a whopper."

"Gil," Owen said, "get on with it. We've got to move forward and we've got no choice but to bring her in. You know how much you love this plant? How much you love these cars? Well, Kick loves Ballantine's that much, times ten. This is survival for all of us. We are literally up against the wall, and the firing squad is loading the guns."

"I know." Gil turned in my direction and leaned across the table toward me. His discomfort and aggression were obvious. "I want you to know, Kick, that once you see what we're doing . . . ," he began, but Owen interrupted him.

"Incidentally, I moved the date forward—it's in ninety days."

Gil's head jerked up. "You've got to be kidding." He frowned. "We can't possibly get everything done and meet that deadline."

"We'll have to go with whatever we've got by then, because, again, we've got no choice. Credit Suisse agreed to one more ninety-day extension, but then they're going to come in, and they mean it." Owen glanced at his watch. "I'm just going to take her out to the shed—it'll be easier to show her than tell her." Owen got to his feet and slipped into his jacket. "Come on, Kick."

THIRTY-TWO

"What is it?" I asked. "Project Caruso." I fastened my seat belt. The morning had clouded up, gotten cold, and I pulled my shawl close around my neck.

Owen smiled. "You aren't even going to believe it."

When V-12s leave the factory for public sale, they have their top speed limited to 165 miles per hour, but Owen's had no such governor. He was as revved as his engine, and at one point we were screaming down the track at almost 180. Shortly, we turned onto a narrow road that was marked with a sign that read, "KEEP OUT. PAINT TESTING FACILITY. DANGER."

Farther on was an empty guardhouse with a closed gate and another warning sign: "EXPLOSIVE FUMES. ALL VISITORS MUST HAVE PROTECTIVE GEAR. HIGHLY TOXIC COMBUSTIBLES IN USE. DANGER." The sign was painted in red and had a skull and crossbones to emphasize its point. Owen pushed a remote button on the sun visor, and the gate swung open. We entered a walled compound.

I knew something big was about to happen. Life was about to change. I bit the inside of my lip to keep from speaking, to keep from saying, Let's go back. Let's not go here. I want everything to remain the same. Leave your secret project a secret.

A gray, one-story, cement-block structure that looked as though it had been built to withstand a nuclear explosion hunkered at the end of the drive. Lights burned in the small square windows, and four or five various cars and trucks, nothing fancy, were parked in the lot.

Owen rolled to a stop in front of a steel sliding door and put the convertible top up before he turned off the engine.

"Don't you think we should put on masks or something?" I asked. He looked at me blankly.

"Exploding fumes and so forth?" I said. "Paint testing facility."

"Oh." He laughed. "That. No, that's just to keep everyone away. Come on, let's go. It's getting cold out here. I think it's going to rain." He rolled the heavy shed door open just enough to squeeze through and stood aside for me to pass, but our bodies brushed and our eyes met.

"Sorry," I said self-consciously as I entered a dusty, noisy maelstrom.

The room blazed with fluorescent lights suspended from the ceiling, so bright it was almost blinding. Wooden worktables ran down either side, and resting along the tops of the tables, leaning against the walls, were life-sized photographs of pieces of furniture. Blowups of Lady Melody Carstairs's pieces of furniture to be specific. Four craftsmen, their blue overalls caked white with dust from sanding, stopped working when we entered. Two of them pulled off headsets.

"Morning, gentlemen," Owen said.

"Morning, Mr. Brace," they answered in unison, their English heavily accented.

"Just a quick announcement. The timetable has been advanced. We need to be ready to go in eleven weeks—the auction is in twelve."

"Sir, we can't . . . ," the man closest to us spoke. He was French.

Owen held up his hand for him to be quiet. "I understand what we're expecting of you, and I'm aware that you won't be able to complete the full number of pieces. I want you to keep working as you have been—my criteria haven't changed, I still expect perfect, undetectable work. If we end up with fewer items, well, that's the way it goes. We cannot, repeat, cannot compromise quality for quantity— you know as well as I do what's at stake. You just needed to know that the deadline has changed. Any questions?"

The same man spoke, his tone perturbed. "Then I'll have to discuss the pieces. Somebody must prioritize them for us."

The other three nodded, their dark eyes grave.

Owen turned to me. "This is Miss Keswick, my senior executive assistant. She'll be out on Monday and meet with each of you."

Really. There was no way I was going to get involved with this scheme.

"More questions? No? Okay, thanks, gentlemen. We won't take any more of your time."

After a moment or two of Gallic harrumphing, they turned back to their projects. The pieces they were producing were picture-perfect. Working from photos of the front, back, top, bottom, and either side, their reproductions mirrored the authentic counterparts. In spite of my reluctance I was fascinated. I couldn't help myself. It was outrageous.

Owen stepped over to the fellow who'd spoken first and laid his hand on his shoulder. "Just keep working, Jean. I don't want to interrupt you, I just want to point a couple of things out to Miss Keswick. Look at this." He indicated one of the photographs that rested on the worktable. "Recognize it?"

"Yes, I do. It was in Lady Melody's library."

"Right. It's Louis XV, made by Adrien Delorme in 1766." The marble-topped, two-drawer chest was decorated with marquetry so intricate, I could almost smell the flowers—and flamboyant ormolu so well constructed, the gilded-brass laurel leaves, furbelows, shields, and scrolls were completely three-dimensional. "Jean, here, is one of the top cabinetmakers in the world," Owen explained. "As a matter of fact, each of these guys is. Three Frenchmen and one Italian. Each one of them is a master now, but they all started as apprentices to Jean."

Jean smiled up at me. "Mademoiselle," he said, and went back to work. He had drawn the design of the floral marquetry onto the smooth oak front of the chest and was using tweezers to select tiny slivers of wood, already cut into petal, stem, and leaf shapes, from three different trays, each with a different kind of wood: amaranth, tulipwood, pear, or maybe apple. I watched, fascinated, as he picked up a sliver, dabbed the back of it using a small paintbrush with a minute drop of what I assumed was authentic eighteenth-century glue. What would that be? Flour-and-water paste? I didn't want to interrupt to ask. And pressed it gently into place. The sides of the piece were finished except for the varnish and ormolu, and, to my eye, which—as I never seem to tire of saying—is better trained than most, they were indistinguishable from the original.

"It's beautiful, Jean," I said. "I could watch you work all day."

"*Merci*, mademoiselle." He kept his eyes on his task.

"Bertram has valued this piece at a million and a half. Come on. I want to show you the ormolu studio."

"Wait a minute. Do you mean Bertram knows about this?" I could not picture Ballantine's by-the-rules president and chief auctioneer approving of such a scheme, he was too up-and-up a gentleman. Besides, Bertram was single-handedly beginning to turn our ship, and I felt that Ballantine & Company, in general, and my personal 15 percent stake in it, in particular, were in good hands for the first time since Sir Cramner died.

"Absolutely not. And he's not going to, either."

"I wouldn't think he'd be too crazy about it."

"That's an understatement. He's such an old maid."

We passed a number of pieces in varying degrees of completion and out through a side door to a separate shed, where a man in a fire-proof suit, thick, quilted mittens, and a hooded mask stood in front of a smelter. He had just pulled the crucible from the fire and was pouring molten brass into an iron form of curved and swooping curlicues. We watched him through the window.

"As the pieces have arrived at the company warehouse from the estate, Wilhelm comes in and makes molds of the ormolu—ostensibly for any future restoration the piece may require—and then reproduces it perfectly. He's even devised a way to fire-gild the brass using mercury and gold leaf—same way they did it in the eighteenth century—without killing himself or anybody else. In those days, fire-gilding was a career with virtually no future. Come on, I want to show you the art studio."

Owen was transformed. He was animated, juvenile, half-baked. This was all a huge game to him. And that concerned me. It could lead him to make mistakes. I assumed he was planning to sell the originals at auction and then switch them in the delivery, that's how it's usually done, anyway. But he was about to play in a supersophisticated arena. He had no idea.

THIRTY-THREE

The scale of the venture was audacious. If it worked, it would be a miracle. If it didn't? Owen would be in a world of hurt for a long, long time because his customers were people of means. They'd screw him to the wall. Big-time. I'm talking hard jail time, something in which I have no interest. At least with my little enterprise, once the settings are melted, they're gone, and the stones are easily disposed of or hidden, and almost impossible to identify. Paintings and furniture were another matter.

We went from the ormolu studio back into the main building and through a room stacked with paintings, some of which looked pretty good.

"These are just a bunch of old pieces," Owen said authoritatively. "Eighteenth-, nineteenth-, twentieth-century filler stuff. You know, hotel art." He didn't exactly kick them, but his voice got across the message of his lack of regard for their artistic value. As though he could tell a Wyeth from a Warhol. "None very good. Our artists just scrape off the pictures and use the canvases for the replicas. Their frames are being retooled to match the originals."

He held a door for me to pass ahead. The art studio was warm and well lit, classical music played, and two middle-aged-looking artists, one man, one woman, sat at easels and worked on their forgeries. The man's face was lost behind a set of ultramagnification glasses, the sort worn by doctors to perform delicate surgeries, repairing nerves and so forth. His brush looked as though it had only a single bristle.

We then went to the frame shop, the varnishing shop, and the storeroom, where six completed pieces of furniture sat under padded quilts. And two paintings leaned against the walls—one of them the Gainesborough from Lady Melody's bedroom.

"Did you happen to see this when they brought it into Ballantine's? Would you believe someone had painted a mustache on it? I thought Bertram was going to have a stroke."

"I heard about it. Was there any serious damage?"

"Nah. The restorers got her all cleaned up. No problem."

"Owen, when did this start? How did you get it all set up?"

"Everything, including all the crew, was actually ready a couple of weeks before I went to meet with Lady Melody to ask her to consider giving us a chance to bid on the project." He gently redraped a Chippendale highboy. "I secretly took some snapshots that day, and we went to work that night. Then when our experts were out there assessing the goods for our bid, Bertram gave me photographs every afternoon, and I sent them to Gil."

"What if you hadn't gotten Lady Melody's estate?"

"If we hadn't gotten her estate, it would have been someone else's. We had so many proposals and solicitations out, it was just a matter of time and odds. It was a complete stroke of luck that she dropped dead. I mean, the business just fell into our lap—literally." He laughed. "Manna from heaven. Luck of the Irish, as my mama said. Come on, let's go."

"You know, Owen, and don't take this the wrong way, but when you stop to think about it, two bodies in one day to solve most of the problems in your life is pretty lucky—I mean it was propitious, wasn't it."

He stopped in his tracks and turned those hard eyes on me. "What exactly do you mean?"

"Nothing." I tried to laugh it off. "It was just something to say."

"Well knock it the hell off. It's unwarranted. And it's the kind of flip remark that causes trouble."

"Sorry."

"You should be." He walked out ahead of me, letting the door slam in my face.

By the time I got to the car, he was busy checking messages and ignored me. His anger sat there, filling up the tight cabin like a suffocating black cloud, and he drove too fast and too recklessly back to the main gate, doing everything he could to try to scare me.

I was upset that I'd made him upset. "I'm sorry," I said. "I was joking."

He didn't answer. We were back on the public road before he spoke. He checked his watch. "I've made you late for your lunch date, there's no way we can get back to the city by noon."

"It's all right." I lit a cigarette. "I don't think I could go through with a luncheon at the moment, I'm so . . . I don't know what. Astonished by your project, I guess. It's absolutely . . . great."

"You think so?"

"Yes, I do," I lied. I didn't think it was great. I thought it was insane. But I did admire his nerve.

His eyes met mine, and for the quickest second, I could see that I'd hurt him.

"Well," he said, "I'm sure you're going to say no, make up some excuse, but would you consider having lunch with me instead? I'm sure I won't be as scintillating as whoever you're planning to attend the opera with, what opera is that anyway?"

"*Otello*." First thing that came to my mind.

"Rossini or Verdi?"

"I haven't the faintest idea," I answered. "I was invited as a guest."

"They're both complete downers anyway. What a depressing way to spend your Saturday—sorry to make you miss it. Okay, it's up to you. I can get you back in time for the curtain, or, if you're hungry we'll stop on the way and grab a bite."

I considered his luncheon invitation. It was a quarter past twelve, and I was starting to get hungry. I had a lot of questions I'd like to ask him, and face it, my empty afternoon loomed like a black hole. I should have accepted Thomas Curtis's invitation after all. "Like where? I don't want to go to some kind of coffee shop and have a ham sandwich with chowchow piccalilli."

"Have you always been this high-maintenance? What are you? Some kind of goddamn princess?"

"Let's just go back to town."

"All right, all right, calm down. Let's see. Cliveden's not too far."

"Whatever."

"You could show a little more enthusiasm, Kick. Cliveden's not exactly Wimpy Burgers."

"Just put the top down," I said. "I don't feel like talking."

"In view of the fact that it's raining, I won't be putting the top down. But you don't have to say a word. In fact, I'd rather you didn't."

"Whatever."

"And stop saying 'whatever.' It's rude."

I checked my messages. One. Commander Curtis again calling to say he'd gotten Sunday off as well and would I like to go see the Rafael cartoons at the Victoria and Albert, have a late lunch at the museum, and hear their Sunday jazz concert. I'd call him from the ladies' room. I loved Sunday afternoons at the V & A and the lively jazz in their café. Plus, who could ever get enough of Raphael's colored chalk drawings for Pope Leo X's tapestries? Not I.

THIRTY-FOUR

Although, to my knowledge, Owen hadn't called for a reservation, it seemed slightly suspicious to see two of Cliveden's uniformed staff members waiting to greet us at the front door.

"Seems we're expected," I commented.

"This is what they do for everyone. When your car passes through the little laser at the far end of the drive, a bell goes off on the front desk, and everyone rushes out."

"I'll bet."

"I'm telling you the truth. What do you think? That I had this planned all along? Take you and show you a project that could land me in jail for the rest of my natural life, then bring you to Cliveden's and get you drunk and seduce you?" Owen's breath was fogging up the windows while the two staff members shivered outside waiting for our "discussion" to end. "Goddamn it, Kick. You are the most unfriendly, *suspicious,* independent goddamn woman I've ever met. First you cast some sort of weird aspersion about Lady Melody and Tina—I won Lady Melody's estate fair and square, and I won't have you implying anything to the contrary—and now you're bristling up because a couple of doormen are waiting by the goddamn door, which, just incidentally, in case you're interested, happens to be their job. Why can't you just lighten up for just a minute?"

"All right. All right," I said. "Calm down. It just seemed a little curious, that's all."

"Well, it's not. It's goddamn *lunch*. And if you shrug one more time, it'll be pow! Right in the kisser!" He smacked his fist into his palm and got me laughing hysterically.

This beautiful Buckinghamshire estate, Lady Astor's magnificent country home with its famous and infamous past—this was where John Profumo and Christine Keeler conduced the affair that toppled the British government—had been converted into an exclusive hotel several years ago, and its kitchen, under the hand of a three-star chef, was renowned.

A young man in a severe navy suit escorted us into the living room.

"Will you have an aperitif?"

"You bet," Owen answered. He was still pretty riled up. "We'd each like a Bloody Mary. Extra hot. Extra vodka. No ice."

"Excellent choice. Please make yourselves comfortable here by the fire, and I'll return with your drinks."

I excused myself to go to the ladies' room.

"Do me a favor," Owen said. "Come back with a better attitude. Put a goddamn smile on your face."

I looked in the powder room mirror. My cheeks were rosy, and my eyes sparkled. I looked like a kid. "Stop it, Kick," I said out loud. "Stop it."

THIRTY-FIVE

"Talk," I said, once Owen had approved the white burgundy I suggested he order, a 1989 Olivier Leflaive Corton-Charlemagne, and our glasses were poured. We were sitting by a window in the dining room, but, unfortunately, the famous grounds I'd read so much about were scarcely visible through thick fog.

"I came up with the plan years ago, but the timing wasn't right until recently, for obvious reasons. For some time now, I've collected furniture and paintings at auction, and I'm not an expert on either, but the point is: neither are most of the people who are doing the buying. I don't mean they're ignorant, in fact they're generally pretty savvy, but when it gets down to the extra fine points of confirming what's authentic and what's not, most of them don't have the expertise. I'd never try to trick a dealer, or a museum expert, but face it, if you bought that Louis Quinze chest—and what you examined at the auction itself was the real thing—and if Jean's reproduction were delivered to your house, would you be able to tell the difference?"

"No, actually, based on what I saw, I don't think I could."

"And you're in the business."

I resisted saying anything about my "eye," and how fine it was, because in this case evidently it wasn't. "So what you plan is, depending on who buys a piece, whether it's furniture or a painting, you'll swap it during delivery, then sell the original privately?"

"You learn fast."

"Well, I'm sorry to break this to you, Owen, but it's not exactly an original plan—our business has always been vulnerable to fraud. But I'm pretty sure the scale you're contemplating is something new." The two Bloody Marys had warmed and relaxed me. The soft cashmere of my sweater caressed my skin. I toyed with my pearls. Owen put his hand on mine, and I could feel myself responding, enjoying his touch.

The waiter and his aide arrived with a gold-rimmed tureen big enough to hold soup for thirty, and we suspended our conversation while he ladled out bowls of steaming lobster bisque, adding a dollop of sherry.

When they were gone, Owen lifted his glass. Our eyes met. "*Bon appetit*," he said. "Here's to Project Caruso."

The wine tasted like ambrosia.

"Owen, I know you think this is going to generate a huge amount of cash, and it might, but has it occurred to you that you need a financial fix that is *not* high-risk and labor-intensive? You need something conservative that generates a steady, dependable cash flow. What will you do if you get caught?"

"First, I'm not going to get caught." He put down his glass and picked up his spoon. "Do you have any idea how much of a priority this sort of scam is for Scotland Yard? Zero. Plus, what I need is *cash*. Now. Plus, we can always say our experts' assessments were wrong. We don't have any liability. Caveat emptor."

"You do have a reputation to protect," I observed, and took a small sip of soup, but my appetite had vanished. Being in this beautiful spot with this dangerous man had filled me with unfamiliar sensations. Pure animal attraction. All I could think about was going to bed with him.

"Don't worry about it. It's not going to happen."

"I hope for your sake, it doesn't. But I think you're crazy."

"I want to change the subject."

"Go ahead," I said. "You're buying."

"You look particularly beautiful today. I'm glad you agreed to have lunch."

"Owen, I'm not one of your models. You don't need to use your lines on me. I'm happy to be here. Let's leave it at that."

"Why can't I just give you a simple compliment? Why do you turn everything into a federal case? It's not a line. You do look beautiful."

"Thank you." The fact is, his comments flooded me with happiness. However attracted I might have been to Owen in the car that morning had multiplied itself times a thousand. The car was a turn-on, but nothing compared to grand larceny and fraud! It was just unbelievably sexy. Oh my, I thought, the things we could share. Of course, I never would, but the idea of it made the butterflies in my stomach churn up a storm.

"How are you going to work the money?"

We'd finished the soup and white wine, and started on grilled veal chops with perfectly prepared carrots, broccoli, gratinéed potatoes, and a perfectly selected burgundy—a 1989 Bouchard Beaune Grèves Vigne de l'Enfant Jésus—one of the most hard-to-find, sensual, beguiling wines on the planet, which could not have complemented the food more perfectly. I spotted it immediately on the wine list and told Owen to order it. The sommelier almost fainted with joy at Mr. Brace's connoisseurship. And me? I was feeling perfectly relaxed.

"I set up a dummy corporation that will become a major investor in Panther. That's what's hemorrhaging the most at the moment."

"Amazing." I didn't seem to be able to take my eyes off Owen's lips. He seemed to be having the same struggle with mine.

It started to snow.

We had orange marmalade bread pudding for dessert. And cognac. We were both warm and comfortable, satiated. Owen reached over and put his hand on my cheek and stroked it along my jaw, and the touch ran through me like an electrical current. I held his fingers to my lips and kissed them. I touched them with my tongue.

"My car won't go in the snow," he said.

"I know." I kissed his fingers again.

"Do you want to?" he asked.

"Yes," I answered.

Okay. I guess there's something wrong with me. I don't know. I suppose I could blame it on the Bloody Marys. The bottle of Corton-Charlemagne. The bottle of Beaune. The cognac. The fact that it started snowing during lunch and we all know the Panther Madrigan couldn't make it out of the parking lot, much less down the drive and back to London. For that matter, with all the drinking we'd done, even if it were a summer's day I don't think Owen would have been capable of making the drive.

I could blame it on the laughter. Or the scheme. Or the passion that had been mounting all day. What difference does it make?

"Excuse me for a minute," he said, and left me at the table.

I knew I was about to do something like I'd never done before, with a man I had no business doing it with. So what. I was a grown woman. I felt happy and excited. Everything would be all right.

Minutes later, Owen returned. "Come with me." He put his hand on the small of my back and guided me out of the dining room. It was a familiar, intimate gesture, and it made me feel special, close to him. We went up the stairs and Owen put the key into the doors at the top of the landing. LADY ASTOR SUITE, a small plaque read. The room was spectacular. A fire blazed in the fireplace, and outside the wind whipped the snow into a frenzy. He locked the door and very slowly turned me around to face him and kissed me. His lips were warm and sweet, almost tentative, and then he kissed me more hungrily. I felt him hard against me and his tongue on mine.

"Oh, my God," he whispered, pressing his lips to my neck. "You are so magnificent."

He kissed me again. His strong fingers stroked me gently through the cashmere, just the way I'd imagined. My knees weakened. My breath ran out.

From that first touch, Owen brought me to a new world. I can safely say I'd never been made love to before.

I melted like platinum.

THIRTY-SIX

The snowstorm wasn't a blizzard. In fact, it had stopped and was melted, for all intents and purposes, by six o'clock that evening. But it was dark and might have been icy, and so we stayed all day Sunday, too. We stayed until five o'clock Monday morning, just to be safe.

"See you at the office," Owen said, when he dropped me off at home. His mind was back at work, and mine, I'm sorry to say, was filled with complications. And exhaustion. Plus, I had a huge, red, bruiselike sore on my neck. I had a hickey.

"I can't believe you did this," I said. I was angry and embarrassed, and embarrassingly thrilled. "I haven't had this happen since tenth grade."

"Yeah. Well, there it is. It's like a sexual badge of honor."

Just what I needed.

I took the morning papers in and, while I waited for the coffee to brew, searched for news of the theft. There it was, a tiny article in the city news section:

THEFT IN MAYFAIR. Mrs. Cavanaugh Fullerton, daughter of Lord Ishmael Winthrop, reported that Renoir's priceless painting, *Polonaise Blanche*, as well as some of her jewels, have been stolen. The theft was apparently suffered during a break-in at her Stanhope Gate home Friday night while she attended her father's ninetieth birthday gala. Further extent of the theft has not been revealed nor has any information been made available on how the thief gained entry. Police would not confirm or deny whether it was the work of the Shamrock Burglar, who has taken credit for a number of Mayfair jewelry burglaries in the last year but is not known to steal works of art.

WHAT? I could not believe my eyes. Had the Samaritan taken back his card and kept the painting and let me take the blame? Where was the Samaritan-ness in that? I guess he was sore, literally and figuratively, that I'd whacked him on the head, and this was his way to get even. What a mess. That was definitely the end of Mayfair for a while—I'd have to move down the park to Kensington. Oops. I just remembered, I'm not doing this anymore. Old habits are hard to break.

I left a message for Commander Curtis apologizing for not returning his call earlier. "I was away for the weekend," I said. It was the truth. The other part of the truth was that, until I checked my messages, I'd completely forgotten he'd called.

Later, as I sat on the bus on my way to work—an animal-print chiffon scarf wrapped high around my neck to conceal the hickey—eating my warm cruller, and watching the city creep past, I reflected on what had happened to me over the last two days. I was filled with self-recrimination. What a terrible mistake I'd made falling into Owen's trap and bed. It was the stupidest thing I'd ever done in my life, not just because it put me on the same level as all the other silly girls who panted after him, but because I'd had such a good time, and now I was sorry. More than anything, I felt ashamed. And embarrassed. And I was getting angry about the hickey. You can make up all the lies, stories, and explanations about something like that you want, and you can't fool anyone. If I'd had any idea what he was doing, sucking on my neck like that, I would have stopped him. And by the time I figured it out, it was too late. At the time, I'd laughed and laughed, like a love-struck teenager. What a fool I am. A hickey is a hickey and there's only one way to get them and everyone knows what that is. And FYI: Miss Kathleen Day Keswick of Ballantine & Company Auctioneers does not get hickeys. Oh, hell.

I adjusted the scarf higher.

Also, while I'm not a total sophisticate about men, I do know a few things about them and I knew as well as I knew my own name that, in spite of his declarations of affection for me: *Men will say anything to get into your pants.* Okay, so he's had his little conquest, and now he's over it, no doubt fed up at his lack of self-control, his inability to keep it zipped, and trying to figure out a way to extricate himself and not jeopardize his business, because he knew as well as I did, I now knew as much about his business as he did.

I got myself so stirred up, for a second, I thought my brain was going to blow a gasket—that I'd keel over of an aneurysm right there on the bus.

"Oh, for heaven's sake, Kick, get ahold of yourself," I said out loud making my busmates lift their heads from their papers and look at me. "Sorry," I mumbled, and returned to my cruller and window. But the fact of the matter was, in a forty-eight-hour whirlwind of an orgy, our business relationship, which had been so ideal, was now ruined by a few expeditious (and exhilarating—oh, my God, just the thought of him made me tingle) collisions. Our world had flipped: We'd gone from friendly friends, boss and secretary, not only to being lovers, but also partners in a major confidence scheme.

We'd gone from sailing along the surface to twenty thousand leagues beneath the sea.

I pulled my little book out of my purse and made a note to pick up some boxes and start shipping a few things to France. The idea seemed to calm me down.

THIRTY-SEVEN

Owen was on the phone, behind closed doors. I stuck my head in and he gave me a big smile and blew me a kiss. I gave him a tight smile in return. Nope. This will not continue. Period. The end. Was I going to let a little attention make me lose years, decades, a *lifetime* of equilibrium? No! Then it dawned on me that my problem was I needed some sleep. I was a completely exhausted wreck.

My interoffice phone rang. "Miss Keswick speaking."

"Miss Keswick," the guard said. "There's a gentleman here asking for Sir Cramner. And he said if Sir Cramner wasn't here, he'd like to see you."

"What's his name?"

"He prefers not to say."

It's not especially unusual that a client prefers to keep his identity to himself. After all, Privacy and Trust, with a capital "P" and capital "T," are cornerstones of our business. "Ask Alcott to bring him to the first-floor conference room."

"Right."

Poor old soul, I thought as I touched up my makeup, added concealer over the stupid hickey, and smoothed my hair, happy to see that even though I was dead tired, I didn't look it. I looked like a damn rose. I started to giggle. I was turning into a complete idiot.

Poor old soul, I started again. Although Sir Cramner died over three years ago, every now and then one of his few surviving, old regimental buddies shows up, having forgotten.

Who I found in the conference room was not an ancient regimental relic but a well-dressed man in his thirties. Black hair and blue eyes, a bladelike nose in a taut face. He stood up when I entered, and we shook hands. His grip was firm.

"Miss Keswick?" His accent was unidentifiable—maybe a little Eton mixed with something mid-Atlantic. "My name's Dimitri Rush."

"Good morning, Mr. Rush. Please have a seat. Tell me, how can Ballantine & Company be of service to you?"

"Is Sir Cramner available?"

"I'm sorry, he's been gone for quite a while now."

"You mean gone as in . . ."

"Dead."

"Oh, I'm sorry. I was given his name as well as yours. Well, that's neither here nor there, is it?" He smiled briefly. His lips were well-defined, and his teeth were white and straight. He had a winning, well-exercised air about him.

"How can I help you, Mr. Rush?"

"I'm here about a matter of the utmost secrecy, and I've been given to understand that I can trust you."

"Of course you can. As long as you aren't bringing us stolen goods or asking us to do anything illegal." I am such a hypocrite, sometimes I amaze myself.

"Most assuredly not. It's family property. But if news of our conversation were to reach the public before we've come to terms, it could cause an international incident."

"Mr. Rush, Ballantine & Company has not been in business for almost 250 years by betraying confidences." Oh, God, may lightning strike me dead. "Whatever you divulge will stay here within these walls. You have my guarantee."

"That's what I needed to hear. Do you mind if I smoke?"

"Please." I slid an ashtray across the table. He fiddled around with his lighter, sipped his coffee. I checked my watch. "Mr. Rush?" I smiled at him with what I hoped looked like encouragement and not impatience. "I'm ready when you are."

Based on my experience, I was pretty sure all this fiddling around would turn out to be over another set of hunting prints. He looked the type. Here to sell great-great-great-grandfather's etchings— maybe there'd even turn out to be a small Rembrandt pencil sketch or a Holbein miniature among the lot—he was dying of guilt. "But," he would tell me any minute, "it simply *has* to be done, they have to be sold, because the manor house needs a new roof." Heaven forbid he, or any member of his elbow-patched, broken-down family, should actually get a job.

He gave another quick, slightly apologetic, smile. "I'm sorry, this is such a momentous occasion for me and my family. The responsibility is somewhat awesome."

"I understand, sir. But if you don't tell me what it is, we can't help you." We'd been at this for about five minutes. I stifled a yawn.

"Tell me, Miss Keswick, did Sir Cramner ever mention to you anything about the missing Romanov Treasury? The jewels that disappeared during the Russian Revolution?"

Well, that got my attention quicker than a cold shower. The mist in my head evaporated like fog. I sat straight up and shivered. Goose bumps covered my arms. "Yes, as a matter of fact, he did. A number of times."

"Good. Good. What did he tell you?"

"He said one day we'd hear from someone about selling them. Are you saying you're that someone?"

Mr. Rush nodded. His expression was grave. "Yes. He met with my great-great-grandmother, Dowager Empress Marie Feodorovna, and told her to talk to no one but himself, and later, long after she was gone—he'd stayed in contact with my grandfather and then my father—he added your name to his. So"—he examined his hands— "the time has come to sell them. The proceeds will enable us to reclaim our properties."

I now studied him very closely. This was what Sir Cramner had insisted would happen one day, and all of a sudden, here it was. Right out of the blue. We never know, do we, when life will change.

Just bang, whole different picture of the world. In the blink of an eye, our perspective is shifted forever.

This could be the golden parachute Ballantine's so desperately needed—Sir Cramner's final gift to the firm he loved so much. My mind spun from one end of the spectrum: From a bonanza of spectacular publicity—Bertram would be positively orgasmic on the podium, gaveling us to higher and higher records. The publicity would be unstoppable. To the other: We would be blamed for launching World War III—Bertram would resign, and the government would close us down and sue us for ending the world.

"Forgive me, Mr. Rush, to say this is a momentous occasion is extraordinary understatement. It's mind-boggling." I knew I needed to say something, ask some sort of intelligent question. "When you say 'reclaim our properties,' what exactly does that mean? Reestablish the monarchy?"

He shook his head vehemently. "No. No. We'd never make such a presumptuous, or ridiculous, claim. In spite of what some loyalists may proclaim over the Internet—and believe me, they're everywhere—restoration of the monarchy in Russia is completely unfeasible, if not impossible. It's not even desirable, unless, of course, the people were to clamor for it, which they're not. Unfortunately." That self-deprecating smile again. "No, what I'm talking about is that, during the revolution, all of my family's possessions, our estates, furnishings, everything, except those small items they could carry out with them—if they were lucky enough to escape—were appropriated by the state."

I opened my mouth to speak, but Dimitri Rush held up his hand.

"If I may," he said. "Let's face the truth: Many of those palaces, properties, jewels, and furnishings are, in fact, rightfully the possessions of the Russian people. And should remain so. They're national treasures. But many others aren't. Some were gifts to family members; others were bought legitimately and legally. It's those properties we want to buy back, because they're rightfully ours. We have deeds and bills of sale to prove it."

"What about the jewelry? What is the condition of the provenances?"

"Unimpeachable. These are family, not state, pieces, and each one is fully documented."

Well, first of all, when a family is the monarchy of a country, there is a not-so-fine line between what's "family" and what's "state." If you were a regular citizen, especially in Imperial, pre-Revolutionary Russia, nobody went around giving you fabulous gems or estates. And when it came to the money? Well, that was another big part of the problem in Russia: The monarchy was keeping all the money—they might have bills of sale for certain goods or properties, but they'd bought them at fire sale prices because the people who'd owned them didn't have any choice but to sell. If they wanted to thrive, survive, or live. Maybe if the Romanovs had reinvested a little of that cash in the economy, they'd still be in power.

Plus, the chances of having verifiable provenances of a collection that has been through what this one has would be slim, at best. Although—and I had to remind myself that "althoughs" are what make exceptional things happen—the personal jewelry that the Dowager Empress had brought with her to England when she fled, and sold to today's royal family in order to pay for her upkeep, was fully documented. Some of the pieces could be traced back to the 1400s. So it was possible this collection was in the same condition.

"I'm sorry to sound skeptical, Mr. Rush, but as we've all seen over the last years, keeping the provenance intact on something as big and singular as a painting that went through World War II has proved almost impossible in many cases. So to have an entire collection of jewelry that survived not only the Russian Revolution *and* World War II, securely documented, seems unlikely."

"I know. But it's true." Mr. Rush wasn't defensive. He was relaxed and confident.

"Where is the collection now? When can we see it?"

"I have it with me. It's in the back of my car."

"In the back of your car," I repeated. "I see." It occurred to me Mr.

Rush was a crackpot who'd somehow stumbled on Sir Cramner's fantastic claim.

He sensed what I was thinking. "Hidden in plain sight, Miss Keswick. It's always the best way. It's what's kept them safe all these years."

"Where is your car?"

"At the front door."

"Okay. I'm going to call the loading dock—I think it'd be a good idea to move the car inside before we unload it."

Mr. Rush shook his head. "Not necessary. No one knows what's in there. Besides, I've got guards—believe me, nobody can get past them."

This was a tricky game. If he were legit, then this was the first of what would become many, many negotiations, large and small. If I were to dig in now, he could very easily get in his car and drive a block or two to Christie's, or across the way to Sotheby's, and they'd welcome him with open arms.

"Believe me, miss, my family has been responsible for the safe-keeping of this treasury for more than eighty years. I'm certain I can get it across the sidewalk and through your front door."

"All right, I'll notify security. Please tell me you won't mind if I do that."

"By all means. We'll need a couple of strong backs and dollies as well."

THIRTY-EIGHT

A mud-splattered, slightly dented, aged, white Range Rover—the perfect car for a country gentleman living on fumes—was parked at the bottom of the steps under the watchful eye of our elegant doorman, Winston. He'd come to us from Claridge's, seduced by one of Bertram's irresistible offers, and now classed up our establishment in his black-and-gold livery. Watching him greet the early-bird arrivals for the morning's auctions, it seemed he knew everyone in the world by name. Winston was a London institution. I doubted Owen knew how lucky we were to have him.

Two Airedales sat patiently looking out the smudged, Range Rover windows—one in the driver's seat, one directly behind. I'm not a dog expert by any means, but these looked to me to be the perfect standards for the breed, with large intelligent eyes, alert expressions, cocked ears, and dark black saddles with rich tan legs and faces. They were an ideal choice for guardians—the fearlessness and brute strength of the breed was legendary. The minute they saw their owner, they stood up and wagged their tails.

Dimitri Rush opened the rear cargo door, snapped on the dogs' leads, and let them leap out, where they automatically took up their duty stations next to him. Then he leaned into the cargo area and pushed aside a jumble of athletic, hunting, and fishing equipment and tossed back a black tarp, revealing six black metal, padlocked, tackle boxes—each about three feet long, a foot and a half wide, and a foot tall. I don't know how much each case weighed, but it required two of our burly furniture movers to lift them from the bed of the wagon and muscle them onto the dollies. Armed guards stood by as the cases were stacked.

That done, Mr. Rush and the dogs, who I noticed had not taken their eyes off the cases, followed closely as the carts were rolled down a service ramp into what was known as Cellar A (Ballantine's had four basement levels). Once we were all in, a three-inch-thick, solid steel door clanged shut and was bolted behind us.

Life in an auction house is dynamic, the backstage activity is non-stop, and Cellar A was the center of the action. We proceeded through an alley of storage lockers with open-slatted walls, their contents visible inside. Moving men swarmed on and off ancient service elevators while supervisors in headsets called out directions for what went into which bin. Today was Monday, and goods were being organized for Wednesday's auctions. The names of the consignees, time of auction, assigned room, and auctioneer, were displayed at the door to each bin. As soon as today's sales were over and the goods moved out, these items would be moved up to the showrooms tonight for tomorrow's exhibitions.

No one paid much attention to our silent parade moving through the maze and maelstrom and onto an empty elevator. We ascended to the mezzanine and went directly to a windowless conference room accessible only by passing behind my desk. The fireproof room, itself a safe of sorts, was reserved for review of highly sensitive or fragile goods, such as documents, illuminated manuscripts, or ancient books; or small items, such as fine jewelry, coins, or stamps. Items that were easily pocketed.

The movers gently hefted the cases onto the baize-covered table, and left.

The guards closed the door and took up their watch, and I locked the door from the inside and pushed the rheostats of the track lights and the air-conditioning thermostat up to high. The lights would force the temperature up in the close little chamber, and it would quickly become unbearably hot. But, the intense lighting was essential. Close examination of the goods would quickly show us what we had in terms of the gems—the real thing or a pig in a poke.

The atmosphere was charged with anticipation. I needed to go get Owen, but I also felt Mr. Rush needed some time to gather himself. I'd recognized in our brief meeting that he was a deliberate, thoughtful man, so I watched quietly from the door while he and the dogs slowly circled the table, his hand sliding familiarly across the boxes. He seemed almost to embrace them. His face was pale. He was about to change history by opening these boxes, to step into the spotlight, and assume a perilous mantle. So aware that I was a witness to the occasion—the last anonymous moment of this man's life—I remained silent, respectful. His posture was ramrod straight, his shoulders square. There was no fear or trepidation there, only duty.

Shortly, I said, "If you're ready, I'm going to get Mr. Brace."

"Mr. Brace?"

"Chairman of the board of Ballantine's."

"Ah. Yes. I suppose we have to tell someone sooner or later." His lips tilted.

"It's going to be all right," I said, knowing I didn't have the slightest idea what I meant by that, and while he didn't look to me as though he could use an encouraging word or two, I knew it wouldn't hurt. "I'll be back in a second."

Bertram's office was empty, and Owen's door was closed. I rapped on it and walked in. He was on the phone. His feet, in their thin-soled, glossy black, banker's shoes, were propped on the edge of the Edwardian desk. He was leaning back in his chair, a hand covering his eyes as though he were trying to concentrate on every word and it was taking every ounce of his energy. We were both suffering from sleep deprivation and running on sheer will, but I now had the advantage of adrenaline.

Bertram sat across from him, his laptop on the edge of Owen's desk. He was studying a spreadsheet.

"I'm sorry to interrupt," I said, "but something urgent has come up."

Owen lifted his hand and frowned.

"Seriously. This is important." I removed his jacket from the coat rack and held it open for him to slip on.

"Okay, Gil." He sat up and swung his feet to the floor. "I've got to go. Keep me posted." He hung up the phone. "What?"

"You both need to come into the small conference room." I could scarcely contain myself. "You aren't even going to believe it."

"What?"

"Do you remember that night when you came to my apartment, the night of Tina's press conference, and you were thumbing through a book about Russian crown jewels and I told you the story about Sir Cramner? That he said one day someone would show up at Ballantine's with an even bigger collection of Imperial jewels?" I smoothed the jacket along the top of his shoulders.

"Vaguely."

"Well, he just showed up."

"Who just showed up?" Bertram asked.

"The Czar of Russia."

They both returned to what they'd been doing.

"Listen to me. Did I steer you wrong about Lady Melody? No. I gave you good advice, and I'm telling you right now that there's a man in the vault room with a half dozen cases he claims are full of Romanov jewelry that belonged to his great-great-grandmother the Dowager Empress. Now, you both can just stay in here like a couple of nincompoops, or you can come in and meet him and see what he's got."

"Quite right," Bertram said, and got to his feet and straightened his tie. "No harm, no foul. Heaven forbid I should ever be accused of being a nincompoop."

"Whatever."

The dogs went on full alert when the three of us entered, growling deep in their throats, and waiting for instructions.

Once I'd made the introductions and Mr. Rush repeated the circumstances, I realized how completely preposterous it sounded. Owen kept looking back and forth between us, as though we were speaking Swahili.

Bertram just nodded his gray head, like a psychiatrist pretending to listen but trying to remember when his tee time was.

"Sir, will you excuse us a moment?" Owen took my elbow and guided me out of the room and into his office. "Is this some kind of joke?"

"No." I couldn't help but laugh. I was as bemused as he was. "It's just what I said. I mean, I don't know if he's telling the truth, but I told you what Sir Cramner said would happen, and you've heard what Mr. Rush has to say. For all I know, the boxes could be full of sandwiches, but on the chance he's the real thing, you need to be there."

"Who else knew about this besides you and Sir Cramner?"

"I haven't got the slightest idea. But I'm pretty sure no one else in the firm knew about it. No one that I know of."

Owen jammed his hands in his pockets and shook his head. "I don't know what the hell's happening, but I feel like I jumped off a cliff forty-eight hours ago and terra firma is nowhere in sight. You have completely turned my world upside down. Every time I get near you, something happens."

"Is that a bad thing?"

"Did I say I didn't like it? All right. Let's go back and see what he's got."

When Mr. Rush unlocked the boxes and opened them up, and as those halogen lights hit that jewelry, it was blinding. The contents were beyond imagination. Other than the English crown jewels, this was, without question, the most fabulous collection ever assembled.

For once, neither Owen nor Bertram had anything to say.

THIRTY-NINE

We trailed Mr. Rush along the row of armored cases. They were lined with rich red velvet that was in perfect condition. The first held tiaras, including one that looked identical to the tiara that had been the English royal family's favorite for most of the twentieth century, known as the Grand Duchess Vladimir of Russia's Tiara.

"Is that what I think it is?" I asked.

"You recognize it?" Mr. Rush's face brightened. "The one you're familiar with is Grand Duchess Vladmir's, of course. This"—Mr. Rush lifted the tiara out of the case and held it up—"is the original. The Dowager Empress had it made in the 1870s—it became one of her favorites. It's quite astonishing, isn't it?" The fifteen interlaced diamond circles blazed in the strong light, as though they were on fire. Inside each circle was a robin's egg–sized cabochon Kashmir sapphire—they hung suspended like giant, royal blue teardrops, quivering slightly, ready to fall. "Do you know the story?"

"No. I didn't even know this piece existed. Do you mind telling us about it?"

Flattered, he continued. "The Dowager Empress was very attached to her niece, Miechen—Grand Duchess Vladimir—who was considered the leading hostess in St. Petersburg."

I knew well about Miechen. A bright, jolly, politically astute, twenty-year-old German princess who married the forty-year-old Grand Duke Vladimir, Russia's richest and most influential aristocrat. Little Miechen was a very savvy, brainy gal. She went right to work building her own power structure, and within no time at all, their home, the spectacular Vladimir Palace—today it houses part of the Hermitage Museum—on the banks of the Neva, became the alternative court. Miechen was able to pull this off for a couple of reasons: not only because of the power of her personality and financial wherewithal, but also because vague, vapid, overwrought, and not-terribly-bright Empress Alexandra was so totally wrapped up in her family and under the spell of her "counselor," the rascal Rasputin, she had virtually no interest in anything that had to do with society or the official court—to the obvious detriment of the family, the monarchy, and all of the history of Russia, to put it mildly.

"Anyone who wanted to accomplish anything," Mr. Rush explained, "whether in the court, the military, or the government, knew that Miechen and her husband were the center of Imperial power, not the throne."

It's difficult to describe my feeling at seeing this piece face-to-face. It was so dazzling, it almost seemed fake, like a crown in a movie. "May I?" I asked, and held out my hands.

He placed the tiara in them. I held it up to the light and watched the reflections move through the thousands of facets. "Magnificent."

"It's like looking into the center of a lightning storm, isn't it?"

I nodded and handed it back.

"As I was saying," Mr. Rush continued his history, "the Dowager Empress adored Miechen. They had a great deal in common, including a passion for jewelry. Even though the Czarina was her daughter-in-law, the Dowager had no patience with her, thought she was a fool, and more than that, blamed her for the Czar's weaknesses, for his refusal to accept reality and adapt to it. But we won't go into that today. Too long a story."

Owen gave him a tight grin. I know he was thinking, thank God, but it didn't have any effect on our guest.

Mr. Rush sat on the edge of the table. "Family legend has it that the Dowager Empress insisted the Czarina hold a state dinner for some visiting dignitaries and include Messrs. Lenin and Trotsky.

Alexandra refused outright. So, she convinced Miechen to do it. We all know now what a naïve, misguided, well-intended gesture that was: letting the revolutionaries see firsthand the sumptuousness of a state dinner while peasants were literally starving and freezing to death virtually at the palace gates—the occasion only gave the rabble-rousers more ammunition."

"Quite so," interjected Bertram, sympathetically. "Very unfortunate."

"Quite," agreed Mr. Rush. "At any rate, out of gratitude for Miechen's making the effort, the Dowager Empress had a copy of her favorite tiara made for her, but she had oriental pearls suspended in the circles instead of sapphires. As you can imagine, a gift of this importance did nothing to improve family relations."

"I'll bet." I was enthralled. Owen was trying to look polite. He had no choice—it looked like the crown prince, or archduke, or whatever this fellow's official title was, was on a roll. We needed the business. He sat down and lit a cigarette.

"Forgive me, Mr. Rush," Bertram said. "But I must excuse myself. I have a sale starting in half an hour, and I need to be on hand. But on behalf of Ballantine & Company, let me tell you how honored we are to have you here in our house. Here's my direct line"—he handed him a card—"if you have any questions, or need any assistance of any sort, please call me straightaway. I'll see you again shortly." They shook hands warmly, and Bertram exited, leaving a look of envy of Owen's face.

"Then when the trouble started in 1917 . . ." Mr. Rush also took a seat and helped himself to fresh coffee.

My God, I thought, are we going to go through the whole Revolution? We'll be here for the rest of our lives.

". . . Miechen and her household moved to Kislovodsk, and in 1919 escaped to Switzerland. She'd taken a case of jewels with her, but the bulk of her collection was in a safe sealed up behind a plaster wall in the Vladimir Palace. Do you know the story?"

"Well . . . ," I began. I knew the story like I knew the back of my hand, and it was perfectly fascinating, but this man didn't know when to stop. He obviously lived to tell these stories to people who didn't know them, and the fact was, it was in our best business interests to draw him as close to us as possible, because if we didn't, our competition would—they'd sit for a week without a break if they had to, listening to him go on. And on. And on. If it meant they were going to get this business. Well, so would we. But good grief, give it a rest. Cut to the chase.

Owen and I sat on the edges of our seats, enraptured. I don't know what Owen was thinking, but I know what I was thinking, and it didn't have to do with Grand Duchess Vladimir.

"It's such an amusing tale." Mr. Rush took a bite of a sticky bun. "Oh my, these are delicious." He pulled a couple of dog biscuits out of his pocket, dabbed a little of the brown sugar syrup on them, and handed them to the terriers. "A young Englishman named Stopford who was attached to the English Embassy, probably what we call today a cultural attaché, no doubt an espionage specialist, was a protégé of Miechen's—a polite way of saying he hung around her salon and gathered information—and stayed in touch with her after her escape. Once Miechen and her entourage were safely abroad, Stopford and one of her loyal retainers sneaked into the palace one night—by then of course the place had been completely ransacked, 'trashed' to use today's vernacular, so one or two more scavengers didn't draw any attention—and rescued the jewels, which he wrapped in newspapers and stuffed into two Gladstone bags, except for the tiara. This Stopford was a very clever fellow. He disguised himself as an old woman and hid the tiara in the lining of his bonnet, stuffed the pearls into cherries that were part of the hat's decoration, and escaped to the West. Ingenious, isn't it?"

"Amazing," Owen said.

"He returned the jewels to the Grand Duchess. She died in 1920, somewhere in France, I can't quite remember where, and two years later, her daughter, who was by then Princess Nicholas of Greece, offered the tiara to Queen Mary, who bought it for practically nothing. But the princess had no choice but to accept. She was desperate for money." There was clearly some lingering bitterness and resentment there between the Russian and English royal cousins. "Since then, Miechen's tiara—the copy of this"—Mr. Rush stood up and laid it reverently in the case—"has become the British State Tiara for major occasions. They really took the most terrible advantage of my family." His eyes flashed at us with what could have been either humor or the start of another blood vendetta. "That's water under the bridge. There are many extraordinary pieces in this collection, but to me, this tiara is the undisputed centerpiece. All the pieces have as much, sometimes more, history."

"I wish we could hear about every single one of them right now," Owen said. "But I'm afraid if we do, we'll have to have cots brought in."

"Good point." Mr. Rush laughed. He and Owen looked as though they could be father and son.

"Let's see what else you've got."

The rest of the tiaras were antiquated and fussy, encrusted with jewels and heavy. Constructed of white gold and yellow gold, long before lightweight platinum came into use, each weighed between three and six pounds. Some had stones so big that if you dropped one on your head it could give you a brain concussion. Another case had necklaces—stomachers so detailed they looked like lace; and hundreds of pearls—one strand of ten-millimeter pearls was six feet long. There was a sapphire-and-diamond *devant de corsage*—a necklacelike affair that is draped across the corsage of an evening gown from side to side—that was so sensational, I would put it in the same category with my Queen's Pet bracelet and the Dowager Empress's tiara. Another case was strictly medals and royal orders, some jeweled, some enameled, some both, all with matching ribbons. One had brooches, many set with elaborate gems. And finally bracelets, earclips, and loose stones. They were all, as one would expect them to be, very, very Russian in style: ornate and complicated.

"What's this?" Owen said when we reached the sixth case, which remained closed.

"Documents."

The survey had taken more than two hours. We sat down. The conference room was silent. Owen snapped open a can of Diet Coke, leaned back in his chair, and studied Mr. Rush. "I'm not an expert, sir, but either this is going to set the world on its ear or it's a hoax of monumental proportions."

"This is no hoax."

"I want to go very slowly. I first want every piece authenticated, and then I want to talk to David, David de Menuil is our attorney"— Owen explained to Mr. Rush—"who can guide us through what obviously is going to be a political minefield."

Mr. Rush nodded. "I think we have no idea how complicated this could become."

"Well, we know that both governments—Russian and British— will be involved, not to mention every nutcase on the planet who probably thinks he has a legitimate claim to this stuff. And we can be sure the Queen and her family will want to put in their two cents' worth. Are your attorneys aware of this?"

"Naturally."

"Good, because this is the sort of situation that will either end up a big plus, or turn into the shitstorm of the century."

FORTY

There're a couple of old sayings about public relations: If you're in business, there's no such thing as bad publicity, because with the right spin, any negative can be turned into a positive. And: Say whatever you want to about me, just spell my name right. So while Owen was talking international public relations nightmare, I knew he was thinking, no matter what happened, this was going to be a win-win situation. "We're going to take this nice and easy."

"I agree completely, Mr. Brace."

"Kick, I want company security beefed up and guards on this jewelry twenty-four hours a day. Who else knows what we've got in here?"

"Only the four of us, so far," I answered. "As far as I know."

Owen looked to Mr. Rush. "My immediate family and counselors, of course," he answered. "This wasn't my decision alone."

"I understand," Owen said. "I'm not worried about your family spilling the beans. Are you sure there's no one else?"

"Well, naturally, there are those who suspect the existence of the collection. There are always rumors that this faction or that have us under surveillance, and we receive occasional threats, but we don't give them much credibility."

"'This faction or that,'" Owen repeated. "As in the Russian government? The KGB, or whatever it goes by now, for instance?"

Mr. Rush shrugged. "Yes. Or diehard extremists. You know, the usual fringe elements—Communist-Leninist-Marxist loyalists, monarchist fanatics, so forth."

Owen looked at me, and I knew he was thinking, Here I am looking down a ninety-day gun barrel to save the company, about to launch my big furniture scheme, and now what do we have on our doorstep? Fringe elements. "All right. We'll take it as it goes. Kick, would you ask Mr. Gardner to join us?"

"Yes, sir."

Andrew Gardner was our director of jewelry. A plain, esthetic little man in his midforties, he was a consummate professional, trained from birth—as are all expert jewelers—never to have any facial expression, any reaction at all, to anything. I think you could have said, "Andrew, your wife and children have been kidnapped, and if you don't have the ransom by three o'clock, they'll be set on fire," and he would say, "Fine." And then he would take care of it, but he wouldn't blink. He ran Ballantine's three-man jewelry division the way a butcher would run his walk-in. The whole department was like a giant freezer.

He really knew his stuff, and coming from me, that's a big compliment.

"Very impressive, Mr. Rush," Andrew said as he walked the length of the table, then circled back around, examining various pieces as he went, his loupe screwed into his right eye. While Owen was giving the Airedales a wide berth, Andrew seemed unperturbed by their presence, and they by his. He picked up a necklace with shilling-sized rubies, each one encircled with two-carat diamonds. "Very nice." He laid it back carefully in its velvet-lined box. The tiara scarcely got a nod. "Shall we be seated? And you can tell me a little about this collection. How did you come into possession of it?" His tone was flat and his manner flatter. He sounded like a pompous ass, and that was my fault. I hadn't had a chance to brief him. Owen shot me a look.

"With pleasure. I am Archduke Dimitri, great-grandnephew of Czar Nicholas II, and the spokesman for the Imperial family. When my great-great-grandmother, Dowager Empress Marie Feodorovna, fled to the Crimea in 1917, Czar Nicholas asked her to take the bulk of the family jewels with her for safekeeping."

"It's always been my understanding that she and her son were estranged. I find it curious that he would ask her to do such a thing."

"Well, that's how it is with publicity," Mr. Rush said generously. "Sometimes the wrong story gets out, and there's no correcting it. In fact, she and the Czar were always very close. It was the Czarina from whom she was estranged. Believe me, sir, I have full and authentic provenance and proof of ownership for each one of these stones and pieces."

"You are no doubt aware that many items in the British Royal Family's crown jewels are Russian? Sold to the crown by who you claim was your great-great-grandmother." His tone was haughty. "You're asking us not only to believe there was more jewelry than what we know she brought? Which was substantial. But also that you are the Romanov heir-presumptive to the monarchy?"

"Uh, Andrew . . . ," I started, but Dimitri Rush stood up. The dogs went on full alert and boy, oh boy, if there'd been any doubt that this man was a direct descendant of an Imperial family, it was dispelled by his bearing. I've never seen a back so straight or shoulders so square, or a neck so arched, or heard a tone so dismissive.

"Forgive me, Miss Keswick. Mr. Brace. I've been laboring under a delusion. I'd been led to believe that I could count on your assistance."

"Whoa! Hold it." Owen held up his hands. "You can count on our assistance. You have my word."

"Mr. Rush," I explained as quickly as I could, "Mr. Gardner hasn't had the benefit of knowing about Ballantine & Company's long-standing arrangement with your family, so he's understandably skeptical." I turned to face Andrew. "This is a day long anticipated at the company, Andrew. I've been expecting this collection for over thirty years, and the company's been expecting it for eighty. Believe me, it's legitimate." I turned back to our guest. "Mr. Rush, we are so honored to have you here, and, believe me, the promises made to your great-great-grandmother, *the Dowager Empress . . .*" I shot a look at Andrew and thought, if you say one more word, you son of a bitch, I'll kill you, ". . . by Sir Cramner are in force. Please, let's proceed."

Bright spots had bloomed in Mr. Rush's cheeks. He was unassuaged. He was ready to walk. And Owen was ready to hyperventilate.

"Why didn't you tell me in the first place?" Andrew said to me, his eyes as bloodless and flat as a snake's, his tone accusatory.

"There wasn't time."

"I'm very embarrassed." He crossed the room and offered his hand to Mr. Rush. "I hope you understand. I had no idea. We frequently have individuals come to us with stolen goods and outlandish stories of lost provenances. It's my responsibility to assure Ballantine & Company, and therefore our customers, of provenance, authenticity, and rightful ownership, and sometimes it's left to me to bring a dose of reality. I hope you understand. Please accept my most sincere apology."

Thunderclouds still darkened Mr. Rush's expression. He looked at Owen and then me. Our eyes locked.

"Please, Mr. Rush," I said. "You have my word. Which is that of Sir Cramner."

He reluctantly extended his hand to Andrew. "I accept."

They shook, and after another couple of tense moments, the tension began to leach out of the room like a wave getting sucked back into the sea. I took a deep breath.

"So," Andrew said—I couldn't believe it, his neck was actually a little pink, he did have blood!—"tell me, sir, if we may proceed, do you have the documentation with you?"

"I do." Mr. Rush unlocked the sixth case and removed a rectangular storage bag, the zippered, plastic kind blankets are stored in. It was packed with red leather portfolios and document boxes embossed in gold with the Romanov's magnificent double-eagle coat of arms. Each portfolio held sheets and sheets of paper, some with large wax seals and ribbons. Others plain and flat. Some were rolled and tied with ribbons. On top was a file folder of typed sheets, which he offered to me. He looked straight at me, and I knew he was thinking: "I trust you to live up to your promises. I am putting the entire future of the Romanov family in your hands." Great.

"This makes it easier to find your way through these old documents. As you will see, some are in Cyrillic hand and others in Roman, others in Arabic. There are a number of languages as well— Russian, German, Persian, English, French, Hindi, Mongolian."

I passed the file to Andrew. I know I should have been thinking about what a big deal this was, but the truth is, at the moment, all I could think about was how much I wanted to tear Owen's clothes off.

FORTY-ONE

Well, of course, I couldn't rip his clothes off any more than I could steal the Russian crown jewels, but I looked at him and swallowed. I felt warm, and excited. The Pasha burned over my heart like a hot coal. I couldn't decide which I wanted more, the jewelry or Owen.

"I'll have some safes brought up, then we'll begin the inventory," Andrew was explaining to Mr. Rush. "It's going to take us several weeks to authenticate and catalog this lot, but using your list, you and I should be able to complete an inventory in a matter of two or three hours. Then we'll give you a receipt and store the goods in our central jewelry safe."

Owen got to his feet and offered his hand to Mr. Rush. The two men shook. "You'll let me or Miss Keswick know if there's anything I can do for you. My office is just across the reception room."

They'd begun the painstaking inventory process before he was out the door. Andrew read an item off the list, Mr. Rush held the corresponding piece up for view. It was checked off and laid aside. After watching them for a while, I excused myself. I don't think they even noticed.

Downstairs, a few stragglers arrived for today's sale of Antiquities, which Bertram had gaveled into action fifteen minutes ago—it was a testament to his personal celebrity and irresistible personality that he could get such a fine turnout for such an arcane field as today's: fourth-, fifth-, and sixth-century B.C. Greek urns, vases, and so forth. But he was putting his mark on Ballantine's, people were starting to pay attention. Today's latecomers clutched their catalogues, whispering back and forth to one another as they slipped into the saleroom.

I took a deep breath and poured myself a glass of water. I needed to settle down, cool off. Not to be vulgar, but the fact is, I was as hot as a firecracker. Hopefully, a little cold water would get rid of my fever. I took a long drink and held the chilly glass on my neck. My hickey throbbed, and I had a feeling it was flashing through my scarf like a neon light.

The intercom rang. I picked it up and heard Owen's voice. "Kick," he said, all business. "Would you come in here, please. And bring your book."

"Right."

"Oh, and one other thing."

"Yes?"

"Don't wear your panties."

I slammed the phone down as though it were radioactive. An uncontrollable, adolescent feeling of hysteria bubbled up in me. But, heaven help me: I did what he said!

The second I stepped into his office, Owen closed and locked the door and grabbed me, and we were instantly on the new sofa that had replaced the one where Tina expired. It wasn't really a "new" sofa, it was a salmon-colored, damask silk, Regency affair with big, soft, down cushions and some very comfortable fringed side pillows—I knew when I selected it, sooner or later, someone, some girl, would benefit from its comfort. I never dreamed it would be me. Of course, at the moment, we could have been on a cement floor for all the difference it made. We were breathless and insatiable. I don't think even dousing us with a cold fire hose could have gotten us apart.

"I can't control myself around you," Owen said when things had calmed down a little. "You are the most luscious, exquisite woman I've ever known."

"It's the jewelry, Owen."

"No, I mean it."

"I think that's going a little far," I answered. "But you're nice to say so. You aren't bad yourself."

"All I can think about is how much I want you. All of you."

"Well, I'll tell you what, you can think about whatever you want, but you'd better let me up because I have to go back to work."

"I'm the boss, and I'm telling you, you don't have to leave quite yet."

It always made me laugh when he said he was the boss.

Just when things were getting interesting again, there was the sound of a huge explosion. It was as though a bomb had gone off.

Owen was instantly on his feet. "What in the hell was that?"

"You've made the earth move."

FORTY-TWO

The conference room door flew open and Dimitri Rush charged out, his face registering the shock we all felt. "Get back in there," Owen yelled as he ran for the stairs. "Bolt the door. Don't let anybody in." There was pandemonium throughout the house.

Downstairs, the front door hung from its hinges, and the front windows were gone—blown out. Impenetrable smoke, falling plaster, and floating bits of debris thickened the air. I could see people screaming, but I couldn't hear them—everything seemed to be happening in slow motion, with the sound track at the wrong speed.

What in the hell had happened? Obviously a bomb had gone off. But where. And why? Why us?

Owen descended the steps two steps at a time, and I followed. The main floor was in chaos. Our security guards, many of whom were off-duty policemen, called for calm at the tops of their voices, but they were completely overwhelmed. I could hear Bertram calling from the podium at the far end of the saleroom, "Please, please, people. Nobody panic. Try to stay calm." To little avail. I'd never seen panic—it was unstoppable, a virtually unstoppable force with a life of its own. A number of people, patrons and employees, were completely out of control, screaming at the tops of their lungs and willing to trample one another as they tried to cram themselves through the bottleneck of what remained of the front door. Their desperation to get outside for fear the building was in danger of collapse was as palpable as the dust-and-debris-filled air. They pushed and shoved and stumbled down the steps, into the rain, and into the busy square, where all that remained of Mr. Rush's Range Rover was a smoldering black smudge. Our wrought-iron fence twisted off its posts like licorice. The front gate was gone and large chunks were missing from the granite steps. The cars on either side of Mr. Rush's—a Mercedes sedan and a Rolls Silver Cloud—were on fire. People struggled to pull their unconscious drivers to safety while others scrambled for their lives around them, before those cars, too, exploded.

Inside, many stood frozen in place in the midst of the panic, deep in shock. Roger, our senior guard, lay motionless in a corner, evidently thrown there by the blast. Then it began to register that throughout the front of the house, wherever there'd been windows, people were injured, slashed by broken glass, some horribly. Some were on the floor, others stood clutching themselves. Blood seemed to be everywhere.

As quickly as the panic started, it was replaced by an eerie calm. Cooler heads began to prevail. There was no fire inside. The explosion had come from the outside in, not inside, and the most pressing danger was the burning cars.

"Get back from the windows," the security team called out instructions. "Move back into the house." The individuals who'd maintained their composure and self-control rushed to assist the injured, carrying them back behind the stairs to the kitchen and meeting rooms, pressing jackets, scarves, handkerchiefs, whatever they could get their hands on, against the wounds to try to staunch the flow until the paramedics came.

It was miraculous how quickly help seemed to arrive. The fire department put out the two car fires immediately, eliminating the most urgent threat. Police and emergency support personnel flooded in and took over, bringing order and assurance.

Outside, emergency response personnel started to round up the terrified victims. Blankets materialized, and cups of tea, dozens of umbrellas and cell phones for those who didn't have them, and Red Cross volunteers to help make the calls. I don't know how long it took for all this to happen, but it seemed as though help appeared out of nowhere, and suddenly, and blessedly, it was everywhere.

The rain slowed to a heavy mist, making it easier for the police and firefighters to complete an orderly evacuation of the building and for the paramedics to evaluate, triage, and transport the injured. One of the first to be taken to the hospital was Bertram who, in spite of his insistence he was fine and should be left till last, had sustained multiple, deep, cuts on his face and hands, had a serious gash in his head, and what I overheard somebody say was a collapsed lung. It was a miracle his eyes had been spared.

"Will you kindly tell them I'm fine," he complained breathlessly to Owen, who jogged alongside his stretcher as they dashed to the ambulance. "Tell them to take the people who need it." He had no idea how badly injured he was.

"You've got to go now—you need to get back here as soon as possible." Owen said it as an order. "The quicker you get checked out, the quicker we can assess what's happened."

"Righto," Bertram whispered as they slammed the ambulance door shut and took off, sirens screaming full blast.

The devastated look on Owen's face as they carried off his complaining president said everything. The losses—human and material—were mind-boggling.

We watched stretchers with the most seriously injured victims whisked away: Winston, our doorman; Roger, our senior guard; a passerby, two customers; and the chauffeurs of the now-burned-out carcasses of the luxury sedans. What we read in the papers about happening to others had happened to us. We'd been attacked. Bombed. Terrorized. It was surreal. There was no safe place on the planet.

Many of our customers were old enough to remember when London was bombed in World War II, and not surprisingly, they seemed the least affected by what had just happened. They knew exactly what to do, and how to behave, and began to rally the younger patrons in the crowd, who were in shock and verged on tears.

"Let me see here," I overheard a distinguished older woman say to a spoiled-looking girl who looked to be in her thirties and close to blubbering, "Do you have both your legs?"

"Yes." Her lips quivered.

"Do you have both your arms?"

"Yes."

"Can you see?"

"Yes."

"Are you injured anywhere at all?"

"No."

"Well, then, I suggest you get yourself under control, stop whimpering, grow up, and make yourself useful." It worked better than a slap in the face or a splash of cold water.

The library at the opposite end of the square opened its doors and welcomed the survivors in out of the cold, where they were questioned by Scotland Yard detectives (under the command of our friend Thomas Curtis), calmed and soothed by aid workers, then taken home.

Owen, Dimitri Rush and his dogs, Andrew Gardner, and I stood shivering under a tree in the square across the street. A police command post with sandbag walls was being erected between us and the building. We were in shock. All we could do was stare at the building and think how this was simply not happening.

"Sir," Curtis said to Owen, who seemed not to hear. "Mr. Brace," he said more firmly until Owen's eyes focused on his face. "I'm going to have to ask all of you to go to the library down the street."

"Are you out of your fucking mind?" Owen said.

The distinguished commander looked disappointed. "Sir, please . . ."

"Listen. The value of the goods in this building is similar to the British Museum, and I'm personally liable for them."

Curtis opened his mouth to speak but Owen kept after him.

"I'm not moving, and if you want me to get the prime minister on the phone, or the lord mayor, or the head of Scotland Yard, or the Queen of England, to tell you to let us stay here, I'm happy to do it. But we're not budging."

"The building is in danger of collapse."

"That's bullshit, and you know it. Listen, Commander, I'll sign whatever you want, I'll indemnify whoever you want, but I cannot and will not take my eyes off that building until I am one hundred percent confident it, and all the goods inside of it, are secure. It would be like leaving the Waterloo Barracks and the National Portrait Gallery unsecured with their faces blown off and me liable for all their contents."

The two men studied each other.

"Please," Owen finally said.

So, Owen, Dimitri, Andrew, and I stayed behind the police command post. Since there'd been no time to grab our coats, we huddled beneath gray army blankets draped around our shoulders. There was no way any of us was going to take our eyes off the building with Mr. Rush's jewelry sitting in the conference room, unsecured and uninventoried: None of our multiple insurance policies would cover it. If any of it were stolen, we'd be completely liable. Owen's face was a mask, so I couldn't tell his exact thoughts, but if they were anything like mine, then they ran along the lines of tallying up precisely what the insurance would and would not cover, and estimating the inevitable tidal wave of lawsuits, some of which were unquestionably being filed at that exact moment over the emergency cell phones provided by the Red Cross volunteers.

Media trucks lined up on three sides of the square behind the perimeter of police ropes. I watched them as though they—or we— were in the Twilight Zone. I saw them interviewing people. I noticed big cameras pointed in our direction. I watched policemen holding up their arms to keep the reporters away. And I thought, so this is how it works when something like this happens. It didn't seem real or as though it had anything at all to do with us. We were observers from a different dimension.

FORTY-THREE

Commander Curtis finally got around to focusing his attention on Dimitri Rush, whose dogs lay curled up on either side of him. There was a slight frown on the commander's face, the expression of a confirmed skeptic. "Mr. Rush," he paused and ran his hand over his forehead, gathering his thoughts, "why would somebody want to blow up your car?"

"Any number of factions," Mr. Rush answered.

"Factions?"

"Monarchists. Communists. Extremists. Even the government."

"The government?"

"The Russian government."

Thomas shook his head. "Lord have mercy." He turned back toward the blind-eyed building.

Bomb squad experts, accompanied by specially trained, bomb-sniffing German shepherds—men and dogs alike, covered in heavy protective gear—were combing the building for what Thomas said were "secondary devices."

" 'Secondary devices?' " I asked.

"Bombers are particularly cruel," he explained. He kept his attention on the comings and goings of his assistant, who shuttled back and forth between the command post and various staging points. "Sometimes they let a bomb go off, and then time the next one to go off right where people will be trying to get away and rescue workers are trying to get in."

I felt a chill run through my entire body.

"It's sick business."

The dog teams exited the building. Signals were given. No other devices had been found. Thank God.

"Okay," I said, "let's go get this collection secured before we all have a heart attack."

The commander shook his head. "I'm sorry, Miss Keswick, but until we get a green light from the structural engineers, the building remains off-limits."

I opened my mouth to speak, but he continued, talking to us as though we were thickheaded. I wanted to hit him. And then Owen walked up and from the expression on his face and the way his hands were balled into fists, I was pretty sure he was about to. I stepped between them.

"I'm sorry, Commander," I said. "I don't mean to be disrespectful, but that won't do. You don't understand the vastness of what we're dealing with. Mr. Rush's collection alone is worth possibly five hundred million pounds, and it's just lying there on a conference table. And obviously, somebody has gone to a great deal of effort to try to get it. It's got to be put in the jewelry vault."

"Five hundred million?" His bright blue eyes stared hard into mine.

"For starters. Much of it's priceless."

"Where is the vault, Miss Keswick?"

"In the fourth cellar," Andrew answered. He was shivering, and his glasses were foggy. I don't think he was accustomed to being out-doors. "It was built to withstand a nuclear attack. The jewelry's unguarded at the moment, sir. I'm sure you don't want that respon-sibility on your shoulders in addition to everything else."

I felt sorry for Commander Thomas Curtis. I don't mean he was a weak man, far from it. I just think he didn't like his job very much. I think he agreed with the logic of our argument in spite of the fact it went against all department policies. I also think he was burned-out and didn't have the wherewithal or the desire to fight back.

"Wait here." He pulled the collar of his raincoat up around his neck and limped over and had what looked like a heated discussion with the head of the bomb bureau. The conversation concluded with a lot of nodding. He returned. "Follow me," he said. "Be extremely careful where you step. The structure is now officially a crime scene, and we don't want you rearranging any evidence."

Owen rolled his eyes at me. "Mr. Important."

"Shut up, Owen," I said. "This guy's sticking his neck out for you."

It took additional convincing of the structural engineers that we should be allowed to use one of the service elevators to transport the cases and safes; the fact was, the elevator we wanted to use was in the back of the building, far from the scene of the blast, and they conceded that the chances of its having been damaged were slim.

We were a shell-shocked group, numbly accompanying police officers and our in-house guards as they ferried the safes down to the safety of the cellar and the jewel vault, where the inventory would be recommenced and completed. Owen was on the phone most of the time with David, and I was on the phone with the hospital, checking on Bertram and the other injuries.

"He's still in surgery," I glumly reported. It was late afternoon. It seemed as though he'd been in surgery for hours.

It took an inordinate amount of time to get the cases moved, not only because they had to be repacked, but also because so many of us were involved in their transportation and we were all feeling territorial: Nobody wanted to let any of the goods out of his or her sight for a second.

Finally, they sat on padded worktables around the edge of the jewelry vault and Dimitri and Andrew were ready to proceed. They placed the first case on the velvet-covered center table and unlatched it.

I leaned against the wall and closed my eyes. I felt like crying. I wanted to go home and put my head under my pillow.

"Kick," Owen said, "it's starting to hit the fan, and I've got to get to the hotel and meet with David—he's hired a public relations/damage-control specialist who insists we get on the air with the company perspective as soon as possible. Will you stay till they're done and just double-check that everything's squared away? Locked up the way it should be."

I nodded. I would have stayed anyway. My home had been attacked, my life. I couldn't leave her bruised and bleeding until I was sure I'd done all I could to help.

In reality, there wasn't much for me to do but hang around and wait for them to finish. I couldn't very well go upstairs and help hammer plywood over the windows. After about an hour, Thomas Curtis appeared.

He handed me a cup of steaming black coffee and held his lighter for my cigarette. "There are some sandwiches and cakes out in the hall from the Red Cross."

I followed him into the wide, dark corridor. The furnace had been turned off in case of a gas leak, and it was starting to get cold.

I was suddenly so tired, so permeated by sadness and grief, I thought I'd collapse.

"Why don't we sit down?" Thomas suggested. "I think I saw some folding chairs in that storeroom."

He retrieved the chairs and set them up on either side of the scratched, Danish-Modern-looking side table (probably unbought or unclaimed from a sale) which held the tray of sandwiches. "More coffee?"

"What I'd like is a drink." I smiled and took a deep breath.

"A whiskey would hit the spot right now. Unfortunately, it's not in my cards, but it shouldn't be much longer before you can go."

"I'm sorry Mr. Brace was rude to you. There's just so much at stake."

Curtis nodded. "I'm used to it. His reaction was very common—threatening to call the higher-ups. Textbook. The fact is, the lord mayor and head of Scotland Yard are out of the country—at a conference in Oslo, so he wouldn't have had much luck getting them on the phone. He might have been able to get through to the prime minister, but the prime minister would have reasserted my authority. It was my decision to permit the four of you to remain—I knew there wasn't any harm in letting you stay close by. Made it easier for us to get quick answers. Believe me, I've had much tougher adversaries than Mr. Brace."

I wasn't so sure of that—Owen could be more diabolical than Professor Moriarty—but I didn't say so. "I'm sorry I couldn't go to the V and A with you yesterday, Thomas—I love the Rafael cartoons and their Sunday brunch. Was it terrific?"

"Very."

"I was away for the weekend."

"So I see." He smiled broadly. He was looking straight at my neck. "Lucky fellow."

"Oh, my God." My hand flew up to my neck, scene of the incriminating hickey—my scarf was gone. "Oh, God."

We both started laughing, and within seconds had tears running down our cheeks. I know my face was bright red. I don't think I'd ever laughed so hard in my life. It was so ludicrous, so naughty, so ridiculous. And what made it even funnier was that we both knew it. Things like hickeys simply did not happen to people our age, whatever that was.

"I swear to God this has never happened to me before," I told him, although I don't know why; it wasn't any of his business. "I'm just absolutely horrified by it."

"Don't be embarrassed on my account. Believe me, whatever you were doing was possibly as much fun, maybe even more, than the museum. Although I wouldn't bet on it. I haven't seen a raspberry like that since I was at Oxford."

"*Raspberry*? Oh, my God. How unbelievably cheap."

We both went hysterical again.

When Mr. Rush and Andrew emerged from the safe, we were still trying to compose ourselves. Then, as bad luck would have it, just as we got outside, the lord mayor of London and the head of Scotland Yard drove up, right off the plane from Norway. That wiped the smile off Commander Thomas Curtis's face. His jaw set. His troubles were just beginning.

FORTY-FOUR

Once the initial shock subsided, the sheer magnitude of the event, its repercussions and ripple effects, set in.

The bombing had quickly been claimed by two separate groups, each proclaiming itself as the true monarchy. But the sad fact was, within hours of the attack, a number of other arrests were made, including a gang of common, bumbling criminals who had followed Dimitri around for a few months looking for the right opportunity and almost blown themselves up in the process. They knew somebody, who knew somebody, who knew somebody who worked for Dimitri's family. Two of the suspects were the drivers of the Mercedes and the Rolls, and they were arrested in their hospital beds once they regained consciousness.

"That's the problem most criminals suffer from," Thomas explained. "They aren't very intelligent. They don't have the horsepower to think things through."

We were grateful for the arrests, but wished they'd find someone with a more authentic agenda. It didn't seem fair or right that a burglary gone awry by common and inexperienced thieves had caused such destruction and suffering.

Mr. Rush and his family went into seclusion and were provided a round-the-clock, maximum-security detail.

————

Everything was on hold. Everything. Except Owen's and my growing infatuation with each other which "the Troubles," as Bertram had taken to calling them from his hospital bed, had thrust into high-gear. I experienced each day with a sort of mindlessness, doing my business but really only wondering when I could touch Owen and he would touch me. It was stupid and immature and irresponsible, and I knew it. But I justified it with the fact that I could have been one of those injured in the blast—I could have been killed. What a gratuitous, selfish excuse. I should have been ashamed, and deep down, I was. But for the moment, all I cared about was my physical pleasure. Life was short. I didn't stop to look at our relationship or wonder where it might be headed, although deep down I probably knew the answer to that, too. If I had any thoughts about the long term, I kept them to myself. Everything was about now.

Our poor building was condemned until the police completed their investigation and the engineers could determine the extent of the structural damage, which they did in record time. Except for the front of the house, the building had been constructed so solidly two hundred years ago—dirt from the excavation had been used to fill the walls—it was generally sound. Reconstruction commenced and proceeded, at a snail's pace.

Every day I walked over to survey the progress, or lack of it, and it broke my heart. Our beautiful home with its windows and front door boarded up and police tape looped along the temporary, plastic mesh fencing like bunting. A police guard in full military combat/riot gear patrolled, front and rear, night and day. I was glad Sir Cramner wasn't here to see it. To see what the reality of his "fantasy" had wrought. It would break his heart, too.

Even though certain key employees were permitted access to the St. James's Square headquarters, the public was not. So, we on the executive staff, who dealt with the public on a regular basis, were obliged to set up interim operations as best we could. The executive offices were temporarily relocated to a ghastly, white-elephant office building at the corner of St. James and St. James's Place. But when filled with unclaimed furniture and paintings from our warehouse, our quarters had a comfortable, eclectic look, a little Biedermaier here, a little Chippendale there.

Bertram was released from the hospital. He had a long way to go before he'd be completely healed—he still couldn't get his full breath—but his sense of humor hadn't suffered. He began to fancy that the stitched-up cuts on his face made him even more dashing. "Quite Bondian, I think. Don't you?"

He spent every day on the phone reassuring clients and potential clients that the losses weren't as catastrophic as they seemed at first glance. Far from it, in fact. To be sure, the items that were in the process of being auctioned at the time of the explosion were complete losses, as were the displays in the Square-side exhibition rooms. But all the other goods stored in back and underground had escaped unscathed. So, it could have been much, much worse.

On the plus side, the bomb solved a few problems. Ballantine's carried a huge amount of expensive insurance, which began to pay damages right off the bat and put our cash flow in a steadier, more dependable and much healthier position than if we were engaged in business as usual. Also, in a special emergency board meeting, Credit Suisse agreed to a further ninety-day extension of the notes. If they foreclosed on us now, their loans would be complete write-offs. It gave us almost six months.

The Romanov collection itself, slept safely in the cellar vault, protected round-the-clock by heavily armed, private guards. Under their watchful eye, Andrew and his team began the meticulous process of cataloging and authenticating the pieces.

The collection was the superstar of a glamorous international incident, and because we were its caretakers, we had ringside seats. It was a public relations gold mine. Not the one we'd envisioned, but every time the incident was mentioned, we were, as well. Every time a story appeared about any auction or any auction house, or any kind of jewelry collection, or practically anything Russian, Ballantine & Company got some ink. When it came time to reopen and begin the business of auctioning, we wouldn't be able to keep the crowds away.

I'm ashamed to say it, but it crossed my mind that Owen and Dimitri Rush engineered the catastrophe for the publicity.

FORTY-FIVE

Scotland Yard and Her Majesty's Home Office had claimants of the jewels coming out of the woodwork and weren't taking any chances on another robbery attempt. The Ballantine & Company employees who were lucky enough to go back to work in their regular offices and workrooms passed through a harrowing phalanx of security. They were required to carry not only their company identifications, but special police-issued ones as well. Security personnel were rotated daily so none of the employees got to know any of the guards and vice versa.

We all had to get these special IDs. The background checks and security clearances were intense. When it was my turn, I took special care with my hair and makeup. I knew I was going to be videotaped, so everything I put on—my best three-strand pearl necklace, day-time pearl-and-amethyst brooch and earrings, and a sedate espresso brown Rena Lange suit—was designed to reflect, soften, and flatter. Oh yes, quite a lot of lip gloss, too. So I was feeling quite sharp when I stepped boldly into the interrogation room at Scotland Yard—well, I'm being dramatic, of course. It wasn't an "interrogation" room like we see on television, where people get slammed up against the wall and bullied and burst into tears. It was actually a regular conference room, equipped with a video camera on a tripod at the end of the table, a tape recorder, and Commander Curtis, done up today in a nice-looking navy blue suit with a clean shirt and tie. His hair was combed.

"Commander," I said.

"Miss Keswick," he greeted me formally, as though we'd never met, except his eyes darted to my neck, where makeup concealed the small shadowy remnants of my hickey. He invited me to be seated and explained the interrogation procedures, which were basic and brief. After a few warm-up questions, he headed to the heart of the matter.

"You have a sealed juvenile record in Tulsa, Oklahoma, Miss Keswick. You're not required to reveal whatever your infraction was, but I wonder if you'd care to comment?"

I knew that someday, some way, this would come to light, and I was always ready. I paused to collect myself. "That was so long ago." I smiled, as though warmed by a fond memory, just as I'd practiced a million times in front of my mirror. "I'd almost forgotten about it, but the fact is, a number of us were arrested for malicious mischief, Commander."

"*You* were arrested for malicious mischief?"

"It was the sixties—all the students in America were doing something to be bad."

"What sort of mischief?"

"I don't know if you've ever been to Oklahoma, but it's not exactly a hotbed of dissention. Or activity."

"Never had the pleasure."

"You haven't missed much, unless you like oil wells and cows. Anyhow, we draped toilet paper over the trees and the teachers' cars and tossed paint on the school building and marched around with signs."

"And for that, you were arrested?" He was having trouble keeping a straight face.

"Everyone was getting arrested in those days."

"And you were protesting what?" Thomas set out on another tack.

I cleared my throat. "We were protesting just about everything, but I can't remember what all our signs said. It was all kinds of things—not so much the war, we weren't big antiwar people in Oklahoma—mostly we were against curfews and in favor of love, peace, free sex, you know, things teenagers care about."

He laughed. "You're the last person I'd envision doing something like that."

"Well, I did."

"What did your sign say?"

" 'More Pay for Cops.' " I smiled.

Thomas put his hand across his mouth and sat very still. When he looked at me, his eyes twinkled. "More pay for cops."

"That's Oklahoma for you. It's a real law-and-order state."

"Excuse me." He left the room, returning shortly with fresh coffee and a new pack of cigarettes, and began again, very sober this time, and we got through it.

"I'd like to ask you a favor, Commander," I said. The camera was still rolling. "No one knows about this indiscretion in my past. I'd appreciate your keeping it a confidence."

"You have our word, Miss Keswick. Unless it turns out, of course, you were involved somehow in the bombing."

"I can assure you, I was not."

We stood and I gathered my purse.

"One last question, Miss Keswick," he said offhandedly. "What do you know about Gil Garrett?"

"Excuse me?"

"Mr. Garrett, the president of Panther."

"Oh, I know who he is . . ." I was perplexed. ". . . but I really don't know anything at all about him. Why?"

Thomas shook his head. "Just curious. He seems an unsavory type, his background is obfuscated."

" 'Obfuscated'? What do you mean?"

"As far as we can tell, he's only been Gil Garrett for twenty-or-so years, since he went to work for Mr. Brace in the eighties. He materialized out of nowhere. Well, we'll get to the bottom of it—probably nothing. Thanks for coming in." Thomas switched off the video camera.

"That was the most unprofessional interview I've ever done." He walked me through the maze of offices. "I imagine dinner is still out of the question."

"Pretty much," I said. "I'm still sort of taken."

"You are a world of wonder to me, Kick. A bundle of contradictions. On the one hand you're self-possessed, composed, sophisticated— you're establishment, upper-crust. Yet, you've been arrested for mischief as a teenager, and you've gotten a recent hickey on your neck."

"Can we just forget the hickey?"

"One of these days, I intend to get to know you better. I have a feeling you're probably lots of fun."

"Well, of course I'm fun. That's why I'm taken, isn't it?"

"I'm not going anywhere, and even though I don't know you well, I know you well enough to be confident you'll get tired of Mr. Brace and his ways before long."

"Really."

Thomas nodded. "Really. You need a grown-up man, not a peacock."

"Well, he is that."

"Tell me, do you ever miss Oklahoma? I mean, it couldn't be more different from here."

I shook my head.

"Do you still have family there?"

"No. Everybody's gone now."

"I'm sorry. My family's all gone, too. It's strange, isn't it?"

"Yes, I suppose it is. I haven't really given it much thought."

"You're lucky." He held the taxi door for me. "I think about it all the time. Incidentally, did the cops in Oklahoma City get more pay?"

"It was Tulsa, and I haven't got the slightest idea. But I know they deserved it."

In the taxi on the way back to the office, I was almost light-headed with a rush of emotions. I'd talked about my past for the first time. Ever. I mean, none of what I'd said was the truth, except that I had been involved in a small protest march in high school, that was true. Were my mother and father alive? I had no clue and no interest. My child? Oh my, what a complicated, haunting issue that had become for my soul. But that's not the point. The point I'm trying to get across is that it'd given me a strangely liberating feeling to discuss, in a perfectly relaxed way, the fact that I was from Oklahoma and had a juvenile record. To tell a story from my high school years. To mention that I'd even been to high school at all, or had a life before Ballantine & Company.

No one had ever asked to hear anything about me, expressed even the slightest interest in my past. Sir Cramner seemed to know that it was a closed and painful subject. And Owen—who wasn't ever interested in anyone but himself—had never asked again about my past beyond that first evening we had sandwiches in my kitchen, which was fine with me. Our connection was adult, physical, and contemporary. We were of the moment. Our lives might as well have begun the day we met for all we knew about each other, or cared to know.

So now, to have even this minimal discussion with Thomas had been a very peculiar experience. I liked it and I didn't. Someone—Commander Thomas Curtis of Scotland Yard of all places—knew something about me that no one else knew, something big, something true. The fact that he thought I was a reformed juvenile delinquent didn't seem to make any difference to him. He still wanted to take me to dinner. Wasn't that nice? Okay, so if he really knew the truth, that I'd never reformed, that I was still delinquent, the Shamrock Burglar, in fact, he probably would have felt very differently. He would have arrested me, no matter how charming he thought I was.

One of these days I'd need to straighten up this messy life of mine. It was getting to be burdensome.

I also ruminated on his remarks about Gil and his "unsavory, obfuscated" background—no news to me. I could have mentioned that, for starters, he and Owen were planning a scam that would make the Sotheby's/Christie's price-fixing scandal of a few years ago look like a business school assignment. That they lived on the edge of their financial seats, much more in the dark than the light. It was obviously out of the question for me to make any such observations, but Thomas's comments did give me something to think about for a few minutes besides Owen. And sex.

FORTY-SIX

The Carstairs auction had been postponed for ninety more days, giving Owen and Gil's crew of forgers and workmen much-needed time to make progress. I didn't want to have anything to do with that project and told Owen so.

"It's exciting," I said, "but it makes me really, really, uncomfortable to have such an active and visible role. I mean, the fact is, Owen, if this thing were to get blown open, I don't want to be the one going to jail because I was the one out there giving them orders."

This was the truth. My own little operation was just that: mine, and I had it controlled down to the smallest detail. And speaking of small, if I felt I was about to be apprehended with a load of goods, they could vanish in the twinkling of an eye, off a bridge, down a sewer, into someone else's purse, someone unsuspecting, into an Underground wastebin. I could stand my ground without physically running from the law and making myself suspect. But these men were involved with physically big things: armoires, sideboards, bedsteads, works of art. You get caught with a couple of hot Louis XVI vitrines or a forged Gainesborough in your possession, you—not your goods—have to be what vanishes, and I'm just not that fit. And Owen's remark at our first luncheon at Cliveden about how stolen or forged decorative arts were not a priority of the government? Well, that's true in America, but in England, France, and Italy? The preser-

212 MARNE DAVIS KELLOGG

vation and conservation of antiquities are very high priorities, indeed. They prosecute to the full extent of the law. The thought of perpetrating fraud on the sheer physical scale of Owen and Gil's operation was completely out of the question—it scared me to death. I would be at the mercy of their competence, which I believed to be minimal. I'd sooner quit—take my marbles and scoot.

"I understand," he said, but I wasn't sure if he did or not. I still didn't know him well enough, mentally, to be able to tell what he was thinking. "Don't worry about it. Frankly, I think Gil would just as soon handle it himself."

Gil's willingness to have a conversation with me on the subject, which hadn't been that great to start with, had diminished. Sometimes it even bordered on hostile. Possibly he was jealous of my growing relationship with Owen.

"Now." He opened a folder on this desk. "Back to business. Would you get this guy on the phone for me?" He handed me a slip of paper with one word: Hiller. "I think he lives in Vermont."

"Is this his company?"

"No, that's his name. John Hiller. He's a hacker."

"You mean a computer hacker?"

"Best there is."

I put my hands over my ears. "Don't tell me. I don't want to know."

Owen was laughing as I closed the door.

The elevator chimed discreetly, the door whispered open, and the most beautiful, elegant woman I've ever seen in my life stepped into our reception area. I recognized her immediately. It was Odessa Niandros. She was a bigger celebrity than Princess Diana had been. Odessa was famous for a number of things: Her beauty—she had China doll, square-bobbed hair—so jet-black glossy it was blue;

wide-set, electric blue eyes, almost Asian in shape; and a tall, lithe, athletic body that moved like a ballerina's. She only wore white. She was very, very rich. She was very, very philanthropic. She was also said to be very, very nice. When she got her way, which was most of the time. And—this was the tire kicker: She controlled her late sister's, Princess Arianna's, estate. Odessa Niandros was major-league, and she was looking for someone to do her bidding, auction her goods. The competition for her attention among the top three houses had heated up to a state of free-for-all. Any of us would do anything to get her.

She glided toward my desk like an angel from heaven.

I put a smile on my face.

"Welcome to Ballantine & Company, Miss Niandros," I smiled. "Such as it is at the moment."

"What a tragedy. I'm so sorry for your losses." Her voice was low, throaty, full of cigarettes and what sounded like late nights. Her accent was thick, and honey-coated. "Mr. Brace is expecting me."

"I'll let him know you're here. Excuse me." I closed Owen's office door behind me. He had his regular phone to one ear and his cell phone to the other. "Did you know Odessa Niandros was coming today?"

"What?"

"Odessa Niandros. She's here. She said you're expecting her."

Owen made a face and shook his head. "What does she want?"

"Who cares what she wants? Put on your jacket and fix your tie. Do you want me to call David? Have him sit in?"

Since the bombing, David de Menuil attended practically every meeting and listened in on almost every conversation because our world had become a locus for anybody even tangentially associated with the legal profession. Because of the influence and financial resources of the customers who'd been injured in the explosion, our case was coming close to setting records for litigiousness in Great

Britain. Lawsuits had come instantly and in an avalanche, changing our business overnight from auctioneers to defendants.

David informed Owen that this was just the beginning. "The bigger suits are in the works, and they'll blow all the rest out of the water," he'd warned. "The best legal minds in the world are working for the injured parties."

"Bring 'em on," Owen said. "They don't scare me. We're as injured as they are."

"Not exactly. You still have all your eyes, ears, skin, arms, legs, fingers, and toes."

Owen considered whether or not to include David. "Let's see what Miss Niandros wants first."

Once I'd fixed them up with beverages—hot tea for her and black coffee for him—I returned to my office and crossed my fingers.

". . . so?" I said, when Odessa left twenty minutes later.

Owen shrugged his shoulders. "I don't want to get my hopes up, but she's going to award the collections individually, so we're definitely in the running, especially with the jewelry. Thanks to the Russians, we're the ones with the Big Mo in that department. We'll see."

"She reminds me of Kublai Khan."

"What do you mean by that?"

"Well, not only does she look a little Mongolian, she also looks like she might be a little bit into pain, if you know what I mean."

"Whose? Hers or mine?" He smiled lecherously.

"Definitely yours."

"I think you're nuts."

"Yes? Well, watch your flanks. I think she could tie you up and rip your heart out and eat it before you even knew you'd been kissed."

"You know what?" Owen put his arms around me and ground himself into my thigh.

"What?"

"I only have eyes for you."

"Baloney." But then he kissed me and fondled me and pulled my jacket and bra off in one smooth motion, and so I believed him.

A few minutes later he asked me to get Gil on the phone. "I got the info," he said without preamble. "And I've got the strategy. She'll never know what hit her."

Kublai Khan meets Godzilla. Poor Odessa.

FORTY-SEVEN

Owen and I grew increasingly besotted with each other. The Fraud. The Bomb. The Jewels. Everything was more, more, more. It was like being rock stars. Wherever we went, Green's or Wilton's or Le Caprice or Mark's or for martinis in the tiny bar at the Dukes, or on weekends at Cliveden, which became our weekend retreat, people would come up to Owen and ask him about the bomb and the Russian jewelry and speculate about what huge security measures he'd be forced to take in the future. He basked in the recognition, his ego was fed. I basked in his reflection, which I kept telling myself was close enough to the flame for me.

The sex became more and more passionate and satisfying. I received the benefit of Owen's years of womanizing. He laid me out. He petted me. He pushed me to levels of ecstasy I'd never imagined existed. He worshipped me. He adored me.

"I love you, Kick," he said.

We were at "our" table at Caprice, which had become "our" restaurant. It was my birthday. The waiter had just cleared our first course of oysters on the half shell and refilled our glasses with the last of a bottle of champagne.

"What?"

"I said, I love you."

"Don't be ridiculous."

"What are you so afraid of?"

"I'm not afraid of anything."

"Why can't you see how right we are together?"

"It's too long a story, Owen. Let's just leave things alone."

"Here's how things are: I am in love with you. But"—he held up his hands—"I'm not saying you have to love me. But I'll tell you what, one of these days you will love me back, because when I want something, I keep after it until I get it, and I know that sooner or later, you'll surrender to my charms."

"You are something else." I laughed.

Dinner was an appetizer of braised white asparagus, followed by lamb shanks, so tender they fell from the bone at the slightest touch, with buttered spinach and garlic-roasted potatoes. Owen even ordered the wines himself: a Louis Bovard Sauvignon Villette 1998—"I know it's Swiss," he informed me, "but it's perfect with asparagus." (He was right.) And a 1983 Guigal Côte-Rotie Brune et Blonde, a great Rhone from a great year.

"Nicely done," I said.

"I'm trying."

We talked about wine and food, and business, not love. Owen talked in detail about his plans for Ballantine, how he could picture it as a billion-dollar company within five years, a mega–cash machine. It still annoyed me that he had no passion for the business itself. He'd invested a lot of money, expertise, and hope, but nothing visceral. Ballantine & Company was simply a means to an end. For me, as the silent owner of 15 percent of the firm, his lack of personal commitment didn't bode well for its success in the long run.

"A billion dollars in five years? That puts a lot of pressure on Bertram," I said.

Owen shrugged. "If he can't take the heat, he'll have to get out of the kitchen."

"Oh, baloney. If you didn't have Bertram's relationship-building ability with the clients, you would have been out of business six months ago, and you know it. Face it, Owen, when it comes to personal relationships, one-on-one stuff, you're hopeless."

"Except where it counts."

"True." I lifted my glass.

Chocolate soufflés arrived. And more champagne. Followed by the maître d' with a large package wrapped in silver paper and tied with green satin ribbon.

"Happy birthday," Owen said.

Inside was a set of six, early-eighteenth-century, Chinese export plates painted with the Keswick coat of arms—my very, very, very, distant ancestral family, although I still had never been able to figure out how or why anyone with the honorable Scottish name of Keswick ended up in Oklahoma.

"That's the Keswick family crest," Owen announced proudly.

"I know." I was almost speechless. The plates were rare and extremely valuable. "Where did you get them?"

"It wasn't easy, especially without asking for your help."

"I can't believe it. I've never gotten such a thoughtful gift."

"And I've never given one. Believe me. How's that for relationship building?"

I laughed. "Touché."

He raised his glass. "Here's to us."

"To us," I answered with less reluctance than I wanted to feel.

He began to give me other gifts as well, none of them from companies he owned. He gave me thoughtful, authentic, appropriate gifts—old books, rare vintages—and I found myself being pulled into a vortex of pleasure and happiness that I struggled against. Half-heartedly. Futilely. I was accustomed to luxury, but receiving pleasure was a new experience. Love was knocking at my door. There is no "us," I kept telling myself, and him.

I felt the dangerous truths about myself struggling to get to the surface, an almost overpowering need to share them. A number of times I felt the words filling my mouth to tell Owen everything, to admit I was a juvenile delinquent from Oklahoma, a jewel thief—one of the best, and most notorious, in the world—a forger, a

Provencale farmer. That I had a driver's license and owned not one, but *two*, cars! Sometimes the words packed themselves into my mouth as if I'd taken a bite of a sparkler and I had to swallow them whole and make them go away. I had to bat them away from the inside of my head like a swarm of bees. "Can't you see?" I wanted to scream sometimes. "Don't you get it? *I'm Raskolnikov's sister.*" I was living proof of Dostoyevsky's *Crime and Punishment*. My past was looming, and I had to run harder and harder to stay ahead of it.

Owen and I didn't spend every evening together—sometimes he had meetings, or I was just plain too tired. On those nights, I'd pick up curried chicken and rice from the Indian restaurant in Cadogan Square where the curry was so hot, it almost set my hair on fire (Owen hated curry. I adored it. The hotter the better.), and stay home and eat as much as I wanted, letting the fiery spices and burning chutney swell my eyes shut and make my nose run.

I packed up boxes of books—my disguised library of jewels, jewelry, faceting, and cutting—and shipped them to a post office box in St. Rémy in care of my caretaker Pierre's sister, Helene. I restocked the shelves with leather-bound volumes that were about what they said they were about. Why was I doing this? I wasn't too sure. Was it because I still planned to take off, or was it because I didn't want to risk that Owen would start to notice them and get curious? And then what? Not love me anymore? Was I loving him? Oh, God, I hope not. I wanted to love someone better than I was, not someone worse. I needed someone to lift me up, raise my sights, make me a better person, not appeal to my baser and more nefarious instincts.

Sometimes, I'd take the Queen's Pet out of the safe, clasp it on my wrist, and lie in a hot bubble bath listening to a symphony, trying to reclaim my equilibrium, trying to find happiness in the hard, fast, tangible elements that had provided it to me before.

FORTY-EIGHT

Owen and Bertram sent letters, flowers, and gifts to Odessa Niandros, and got nothing but silence in return. Then one morning, three weeks after her visit, she called.

"Good morning, Mr. Brace's office," I answered.

"Odessa here."

"Good morning, Miss Niandros. I imagine you're looking for Mr. Brace."

"Yes, would you put him on?"

"I'm sorry, but he's out of the office. I expect to hear from him soon. Where can we reach you?"

"Let me tell you what I want, dear. Would you arrange for him, and Bertram, and . . . what's your jewelry man's name?"

"Andrew Gardner?"

"Yes, him. Arrange for them to come to my London house at four o'clock a week from next Thursday. I will have all the princess's jewelry here at that time, and they can see about making a proposal for me."

"They'll be there. Also, Miss Niandros, do you have a time line?"

"Time line? What do you mean, 'time line'?"

"Yes, well." I felt myself getting a little flustered. "When do you want to have the jewelry auctioned?"

"May first."

It was March.

"Perfect. I'll let Mr. Brace know. They'll see you at four o'clock next Thursday."

Click. She didn't even say good-bye. I didn't think that was so nice for someone who everybody says is.

When I told Owen, he didn't bat an eye at the timetable. Neither did Bertram.

"This falls right in line with your plan," Owen said. Both of them were smiling, and Bertram nodded enthusiastically. The only visible trace of his wounds were the pinkish lines of fresh scars on his face and the backs of his hands, but they were already falling into the natural folds of his skin and would soon be invisible.

"Delicious, isn't it?" Bertram beamed.

"What plan is that?" I asked.

"While I was lying in hospital," Bertram told me, "it gave me the opportunity to do a full assessment not only of our industry, but also of where we fit in it. And the reality is, no matter how much money Brace pours in, we'll never be able to grow fast enough or capture a sufficient percentage of market share to compete squarely with Sotheby's or Christie's—they're too entrenched. Too powerful. So I looked at the big picture and realized we could either keep bashing our collective head against the wall, making a little progress here and there, but never a deep enough cut to inflict a real wound on the competition, much less a mortal blow, or we could reinvent ourselves. Get off their playing field and make our own."

"Such as?"

"Such as become specialists."

"Specialists?" I forced myself not to get alarmed or paranoid that a plan to change the direction of the company had been developed without my knowledge.

Bertram nodded. "Instead of accepting any item that comes our way, whether it's Roman antiquities, twelfth-century manuscripts, or early-twentieth-century American furniture, we're going to put all our energy behind becoming the world's leading auctioneers of only three categories: furniture, specifically nineteenth- and twentieth-century English, French, Italian, and American; paintings, European, American, and South American nineteenth- and twentieth-century only; and jewelry."

"What about the Carstairs estate?" I shot a glance at Owen—he couldn't send all that stuff down the drain. He'd already invested hundreds of thousands of dollars in those reproductions. "It's primarily eighteenth."

"This isn't going to happen overnight," Bertram, who was still ignorant of the scam, replied. "And because the Carstairs goods will be our last major auction of eighteenth-century furniture and paintings, the competition will be keen. Buyers will think we're desperate to sell. We'll hold a secondary auction to clear out our warehouse. It will be fabulous. People will go wild. Well?" He looked at me. "What do you think?"

"I think it's thrilling."

"Wait till you see what it does to our bottom line." Owen beamed at Bertrand. "By limiting our areas of expertise, we can reduce our staff by about 50 percent—no more suit-of-armor, or Staffordshire, or Gobelin tapestry brainiacs. However, there is one possible roadblock."

Bertram raised his eyebrows. "Such as?"

"Got to get the Ballantine board to approve it."

"Why wouldn't they?"

"I've got that 15 percent wildcard: the KDK Trust and that tight-assed bank officer who votes the shares. I wish to hell whoever controls that goddamned thing would listen to sense and sell out. It'd sure make my life a lot easier."

I didn't tell him not to worry about the KDK Trust officer—he'd approve because I'd tell him to. The plan was as adroit as Bertram. He was the only one who loved and understood the business and Ballantine's as much as I did. His passion and genius would save the house in the long run, not Owen's greed, and certainly not his fake furniture scheme.

On the other hand, I was more than a little ripped that Owen hadn't put me in the loop on this plan sooner. "Well, you're right," I said. "Whoever it is could sabotage the whole idea. That would be too bad."

The phone rang, and I answered from Owen's desk. "One moment, sir, I'll let him know you're on the line." I punched the hold button. "Lord Spaulding."

"Lord Spaulding?" Owen looked blank.

"You know," I said. "Lord Richard Spaulding, eighth Earl of Lincolnshire, as in Spaulding Air, the Spaulding Group. Spaulding Scotch Whiskey. Hello? Any bells yet?"

Bertram shook his head and laughed.

"Right." Owen smiled. "I'm with you." He took the receiver. "Lord Spaulding, what a pleasant surprise to hear from you. How may I be of service?"

Owen was learning fast. He listened. Nodded a couple of times, kept listening, and finally said, "I'd love to, thanks. See you then." He hung up. "I'm going away next weekend."

"Oh?"

"I'm going fishing in Scotland."

"That's terrific," I said.

"No big deal."

It was a very big deal, and it was exactly the sort of affirmation Owen had been seeking. This was his first invitation into the inner sanctum of that upper-class, private world, where people had hunting and fishing lodges on gigantic private acreages, and art and sword and suit-of-armor collections that had been in their families for generations, for all the good that would do us now, once we put Bertram's specialization plan into effect.

"Their retrievers and spaniels have better pedigrees than most of the aristocracy," Bertram commented. "Well done, Owen. This is a landmark. Invitations to Richard Spaulding's castle—Lord Richard's anything for that matter—are hard to come by. I've only been there a few times myself." He couldn't help preening. "Better get yourself over to Hardy's."

"Hardy's?"

"You know, man. The House of Hardy. The fishing store down around the corner. You've got to get properly suited up. This will be a crowd that takes their fishing seriously."

"Right."

"Funny. I've heard the sport up there is for more warm-blooded prey," I said, unable to keep an unfortunate cryptic sneer out of my voice.

"What do you mean?"

"That it's like the Playboy Mansion of Scotland."

"Rubbish!" Bertram barked. "That's those bloody tabloids for you, always just short of libelous. It's nothing of the sort."

"Oh," Owen looked disappointed. "Too bad. I'd much rather fuck than fish."

"OWEN BRACE!"

"Sorry, Kick." His face was instantly red. "I'm kidding. Sorry, Bertram."

"One step forward, ten steps back," Bertram muttered as he left the room.

FORTY-NINE

"Will you be okay on your own this weekend?" It was Thursday noon, and Owen was leaving in an hour. "I know we'd talked about going to the country."

"Of course. I'll be fine." My tone was more abrupt than I wanted it to be.

Deep down, I was disappointed he was going away without me, although I never would let him see it. I was really getting to like being with Owen, counting on it, getting the hang of this love thing. He made everything a challenge, kept me constantly on my toes, always ready to thrust and parry. He forced me to go in directions that had never appealed to me, such as listening to rock and roll—I kept telling myself that the headaches were getting smaller, but I swear to God, most of the time I felt like pulling out a gun and shooting the radio. Or eating a late dinner—he was a night person. I was not. I'd stopped cooking. I don't think he even realized I knew how, but who wants to start putting dinner on the table at nine o'clock at night? And then clean it up? Not I. There was nothing peaceful or relaxing about our relationship, which I regretted in one corner of my mind because I loved peace, quiet, stability, the simple repetition of my day-to-day patterns. I didn't like always being on guard, but I'd done enough reading to know that is the sort of thing that keeps one mentally agile, even better than crossword puzzles, which I also hadn't had time to do. In the other corner of my mind, of course, was the fact that we kept each other in an almost constant state of mental and sexual stimulation and anticipation. I reminded myself regularly not to confuse this with love; but it was getting harder and harder not to, especially because he talked about it all the time.

I told myself I was relieved he was going away for the weekend. I hadn't been to France for over a month, and I was longing to get to my little farmhouse and just be me. Quiet, peaceful, predictable, stable me. Catch my breath. Make an omelette. Roast a chicken. Okay, that's a bunch of bull. I was jealous. I didn't want Owen to go to Richard Spaulding's castle, I'd read too much about it. Even if it was rumor mongering about the parties and the girls—every lie holds a kernel of truth.

"I promise I'll make it up to you."

"Look out for those Spaulding flight attendants," I said. "I've heard it gets pretty wild up there."

"This is men only. Besides, I've already lived that life. You know that, Kick." He traced his finger down my cheek. "If I wanted some mindless chimp of a calendar girl, I wouldn't have to go to Scotland to find her." It was true. Just because he'd taken himself off the market—our picture had already been in the *Seen About Town* column twice! Okay, let me tell the truth: Owen's picture had been in the column with a partial me in the vicinity. My face was never really seen and my name was never mentioned, but I knew it was me—*I* was the one there with Owen, not some bimbo, and I knew it and he knew it. But the demand for him by the girls never abated. They still called up all day long.

"I'm all yours." He put his arms around me and kissed me. "Seriously, what are you going to do?"

"Work in my little roof garden, put away my winter clothes. Get some uninterrupted sleep."

I went home and started packing.

FIFTY

I'd just started the dishwasher and was almost out the back door for Heathrow and the ten o'clock flight to Marseilles, when the downstairs buzzer rang. I must have jumped ten feet in the air. What on earth? Owen was in Scotland, he'd flown up on Lord Richard's private jet. I knew they'd taken off and landed because I'd checked, and Owen had called me when he arrived. He'd lugged along twenty thousand dollars worth of brand-new, salmon-fishing gear and clothing, the finest available on earth. 'Why don't we own this company?' he'd asked me. 'It would fit right in with our other lines.' 'You need a fishing-gear company like you need a hole in the head,' I told him.

"Yes?" I answered the buzzer.

"Good evening, Kick. Commander Thomas Curtis, here. Have you got a moment?"

Oh, brother.

"Of course, Thomas. Just give me a minute. I was just getting into the tub." As I dashed into my bedroom, ripping off my wig and glasses, pulling off my clothes and throwing them into the closet, a million things went through my mind. He'd become a fixture of sorts around the office, but why would he come to my house, unexpectedly? It didn't seem possible that there were any questions left unasked. He'd drilled us all, researched every possibility, for weeks. Was it possible he was onto me as the Shamrock Burglar? No! No way. My mouth went dry. I pawed through my closet and slipped on a deep turquoise, heavy Chinese silk robe with coral silk lining and gold frog closures, silk slippers, sprayed on a little scent, and buzzed him in. What else could I do?

My carry-on suitcase was sitting in the back hall at the door to the service entrance. My purse and gloves resting on top. I darted into the kitchen, opened the utility closet, and shoved them inside, remembering suddenly I still had brown contact lenses in my eyes. I dropped the second one in my pocket just as he reached the landing.

"Please," I said. "Come in."

I could smell tobacco, and a vague tinge of Trumper's lime cologne. "What's wrong?" He sounded concerned. "Do you have something in your eye?"

"No. Just an eyelash or something. It's gone now. May I take your coat?"

He shook his head no and dug his hands in his pockets. "I apologize for dropping in unannounced. I hope I'm not interrupting." His eyes took me and my flat in at a glance.

"No." I shrugged. "Just wrapping up the day. Would you like a cup of coffee? Or how about a whiskey?"

"Actually, a light whiskey would be much appreciated."

"Wonderful. I was just going to have one myself." I selected a bottle of hundred-year-old, single malt from my well-stocked drinks table and a cut-crystal tumbler.

"This is a first-rate painting," he said. "It's not a *real* van Gogh, is it?"

I shook my head. "School of."

"I wonder where it was painted, it's beautiful. Provence, I imagine. Have you ever been there?"

"Once. On a vacation with friends. It is beautiful."

"I'd love to live there when I retire."

"Who wouldn't. Ice?" My head started to ache, a big sharp throb behind my left eye.

"No. Neat is fine. It would be a sin to dilute that," he said.

"I agree." Thank God. I didn't want to have to go into the kitchen.

He might have followed me. Even though Owen thought my out-door pots of shamrocks were sprouts, I was certain Thomas Curtis would not be so easily fooled.

I poured us each a good one-inch wallop. "Please, sit down." I handed him his glass and settled in my favorite red-and-gold silk damask wing chair. Between the robe and the chair, I was amazed he didn't have to squint to look at me. "This is a pleasant surprise. Salut."

He scanned the room as he drank. "You've done well for a juvenile delinquent from Oklahoma."

"There's little mystery if you know the story." I placed my glass on the table.

"It's none of my business, Kick. That's not why I'm here."

"I was Sir Cramner's executive aide and confidante for twenty-five years. I was also his mistress. He settled me well."

There it was again: the Truth. The sparklers in my mouth. What was it about Thomas that made me want him to know about me? He knew more truth from our few meetings than Owen did from a few months, a few very intimate months. Owen knew my body more intimately than anyone ever had, but when it came to me, person-ally? He still knew basically zero. He took what I said at face value. He was completely uninterested. I'd pretty much come to grips with the trite, but true, fact that Owen was a male caricature, interested in three things: sex, business, and fast cars. The order was random, and equally satisfying for limited periods of time at every stage.

"Anything else you'd like to know? You seem to have a way of going to the heart of my secrets." I liked the way Thomas looked—comfortable, intelligent. Maybe not smarter than Owen, but defi-nitely more cerebral. Accessible. Okay, let me put it this way: Thomas and Owen were probably the same age, but Thomas was, as he'd already pointed out, a grown-up man, substantial. Owen was an overgrown brat. Thomas was like Bertram and Sir Cramner—if only I'd met him earlier.

My hand drifted absentmindedly to my neck and began playing

with the thin chain that was attached to the *Pasha*, twisting it around my fingers, slowly pulling the stone into sight, like a bucket of sparkling water being drawn from a dark well into the sun.

Thomas's mouth opened and closed a couple of times. He scratched his ear and struggled to keep his eyes on my face. "No." He grinned and his cheeks reddened. "But I will say Sir Cramner was a lucky man."

"Yes, well, I looked pretty good when I was younger."

"You're still so beautiful, I don't think my heart could have taken a younger version."

Our eyes met, and we both looked away quickly.

"Sorry. That's not why I'm here, either." Thomas twirled the whiskey in his glass. "We're close to concluding the investigation around the bombing—at least to clearing all the Ballantine employees of any involvement."

"That's good news. Not unexpected, though. We're a pretty honest group." I smiled at him, and he grinned back.

"Yes. The fact is, during this period, some other elements—unrelated to the bombing—have emerged, and I was thinking that possibly you could shed some light on them."

"Other elements?" I crossed my legs and smoothed the silk robe. "You mean besides Gil Garrett's missing past?"

Thomas nodded slowly. Portentously.

My mouth filled with cotton. The air in the room became thick as molasses, weighted down with danger—as though a giant safe or atom bomb was approaching from above at a high rate of speed and at the next second would crash through the ceiling and flatten us into pancakes or blow us to smithereens.

The *Pasha* swung from my fingers like a hypnotist's charm.

Thomas cleared his throat and rolled the glass between his hands. Then he looked into my eyes. Then at the stone. It was taking him too long to speak, and the longer it took, the more my head ached. I began to prepare myself, mentally, for a rout. To assess and try to identify what I'd done wrong. Except for overstaying my time in

Lady Melody's dressing room, I hadn't gotten sloppy, and I hadn't taken any chances. There hadn't been any complaints at the company about inferior stones or suspicious pieces. While Thomas seemed to be girding himself for something, I took advantage of the silence to sort through the last few heists. I couldn't see a crack anywhere in my operation, but maybe I was wrong. Maybe I'd left a calling card other than shamrocks and a lump on some stranger's head at Mrs. Winthrop's. Maybe I'd left clues somewhere big enough to drive a truck through.

How stupid of me not to follow my instincts and bail out for France months ago. I would be safe there by now.

Oh, hell. Why doesn't he say something? He looked like he was a million miles away.

Is this how it will conclude, my brilliant career as one of the most brilliant jewel thieves in history? This easily, in my own living room, without scramble or bloodshed or fancy gunplay? Were there police in riot gear lined up outside my door waiting to take me into custody? Or shoot me if I put up a fight? My mind skipped down a list of solicitors.

Would Owen come to my aid? Don't be silly. Not a chance.

I was on my own.

FIFTY-ONE

"Thomas," I said. I couldn't take it anymore. Whatever it was, I wanted it over with. "Have you fallen asleep? *What* other elements?"

His eyes looked glazed. "Sorry. It's that damned diamond or whatever that thing is. I can't take my eyes off it."

My hand caught the pendant midswing and held it tight. "It's the *Pasha of St. Petersburg.* A gift from Sir Cramner. Thirty-five carats. I'll put it away." The stone vanished down my front as quickly as a shooting star, causing his head to jerk slightly and his vision to clear. I gave him a big smile. "You were saying something about other elements of the investigation?"

Thomas took a swig of whiskey. "Right. Just how much do you know about Owen Brace?"

"What?" Stay cool. Stay cool. I could not let my relief show. He didn't want to know about *me*. It was *Owen*. Talk about a break. "What do you mean, how much do I know about Owen Brace? You mean about his business life, his personal life. What?"

Thomas smiled guilelessly. "You're right, it is a rather broad question. Let me put it to you differently. During the course of the investigation, we've uncovered some questions about his background, and I was hoping you could possibly help answer them."

"I'll do what I can to help. I don't know him all that well."

He looked me straight in the eye. "I wouldn't go that far, Kick." At least he had the class not to make a crack about *droit de seigneur* or my being company property, and for that, I was grateful and impressed.

"You know what I mean," I said.

"Yes. I do. The fact is, I suspect you don't know him well at all. An unusual string of coincidences has emerged, completely unrelated to the bombing."

"Such as?"

"Has he ever talked to you about his first wife?"

"His first wife? Let me think." I worked to recall what he'd said. "I think he said they lived in New Jersey and she was killed in a car accident."

"Anything else?"

"Not that I remember, but I really didn't pay that much attention. If you must know, we don't spend a lot of time talking about his ex-wives."

"No, I don't suppose you do. But if you'll indulge me . . . what about his second wife? Has he told you anything about her?"

I frowned. This was getting a little weird. "What exactly are you after, Thomas? You're making me uncomfortable."

"I'm not sure what I'm after. Probably nothing. Just some rumors, bits of stories floating around. That sort of thing."

"All right. Let me make this quick." I didn't attempt to hide the impatience in my voice. "Here's everything I know about his wives: The first one died in a car wreck. He said he loved his second one. I don't think he said what happened to her, just that she's dead. Then his marriage with Tina hit the skids, and he says he'll never get married again, because he has such bad luck."

"When did he tell you all this?"

"The night he filed for divorce from Tina."

"Who then died. That night."

"Oh, give me a break. You've been watching too much television. She committed suicide." I got up and poured more scotch in our glasses. I didn't want to appear to be rushing him, but I was thinking that if he left within ten minutes, I could still make my plane. "Besides, why aren't you asking him these questions?"

"I have."

Funny, I thought. Owen didn't tell me he'd had such a conversation with Thomas. But then, I didn't tell him about mine, either.

"He said the same thing you said, that the first was killed in a car accident in New Jersey—the car went off a bridge and fell hundreds of feet into a river. However, when I contacted the New Jersey State Police, their records revealed they suspected foul play but never had been able to determine, definitively, what happened. Now as to the second Mrs. Brace, according to Brace himself, she was killed in a fall in the Grand Canyon when they were on their honeymoon—he was living in Las Vegas at that time." Thomas's tone was pejorative.

"There's nothing wrong with living in Las Vegas," I jumped to Owen's defense.

"It's a very different place now than it was fifteen years ago. He lived on the fringe of the law, he skirted the edges of the rackets, wanted admittance, but never really got it. I'm sure you know by now his whole empire was built on stolen auto parts and rigged, secondhand gaming devices, but his parent corporation is incorporated in Luxembourg and the New Jersey statute of limitations for theft on those goods has expired."

"No, I didn't know that."

"Surely you suspected."

I nodded. I didn't add that I wasn't surprised.

"And when I spoke to the United States Park Service in Arizona, they said the investigation into his wife's death was never satisfactorily concluded. Did she fall or was she pushed? We'll never know. Too many question marks." He tossed off his drink and placed it on the table. "Well, as I said, I'm just following up, trying to cover the bases and close out a few loose ends."

"I'm sorry I can't shed any new light. But Thomas, for whatever it's worth, whatever Owen was like ten or fifteen years ago—he's not like that now. He might have a few rough edges . . ."

Thomas's eyebrows shot up.

"Okay, a number of rough edges, but Brace International operates solidly within the law. And, you can rest assured Owen hasn't been going around murdering his wives—he's just not the type."

"You'd be surprised what the 'type' is. The man's bad news."

"Want to know what I think? I think you're going to all this trouble to try to discredit Owen so I'll dump him and go out with you."

Thomas laughed. "One of the things I like best about you is your lack of ego. You're so self-effacing."

"I think you need a vacation."

"You're right about that. Fortunately, I'm due to retire soon, and this case will become someone else's problem. I won't take any more of your time. Thanks for the drink." He paused at the door. "You're a very special person, Kick. I'd hate to see you get into a situation you can't handle. Be careful of this man—many things about him and Mr. Garrett don't add up." He pulled a business card from his pocket and scribbled on it. "Here are my home and cell phone numbers if you ever need to reach me. Take care of yourself."

"I will. Thanks, Thomas." I examined the card and slipped it into my pocket.

"Do you mind if I give you a call from time to time? Just in case you do see the light and get rid of Mr. Brace and find you're free for dinner?"

"I'd like that." I offered my hand. "May I ask you a question?"

"By all means."

"Is there by any chance a Mrs. Curtis?"

"Not so far. Being married to a police officer doesn't appeal to the kind of lady that appeals to me. The job's too unpredictable, too dangerous, too many hours away from home. But I'm always optimistic. Have a good weekend."

I turned the lights out in the sitting room and stood in the darkened window for fifteen minutes to make sure he'd gone for good. His warning only reconfirmed the conclusion I'd reached about Owen long ago—he was even more of a criminal than I. But I wanted to go straight, clean up my act. He wanted to stay dirty, get dirtier. He couldn't help himself. He was born dirty. And, oh my, how I liked it.

I went to my bedroom and completely repacked. I wouldn't be back. This party was over.

F I F T Y - T W O

I switched on the day/night timer for the lamps, redisguised myself, and left through the service entrance, rushing down the back stairs in the dark. Once I'd satisfied myself the mews were empty, I crossed through to a passageway that cut to the street beyond and caught the Underground for Heathrow.

The train car was almost empty. I looked at my reflection in the window: I could have been anybody's grandmother, traveling to see her family. My size, instead of being a voluptuous asset clad in well-made clothes, cut to flatter, was crammed into a seemingly too-small, old wool suit that unbecomingly hugged my stomach, back, and hips like plaid wallpaper. What looked like rolls of fat mounded up between my shoulders and hips like a stack of thick bicycle tires were in fact rolls and rolls of thickly padded diamonds. A short, curly, grayish brown wig covered my blond hair; I'd removed my nail polish; and a nondescript pair of bifocals camouflaged my eyes, which bore no makeup. I'd put the brown lenses back in and added a smear of bright pink lipstick in a girlish attempt to appear done up. I was a baby boomer gone to seed. A woman who spent all her extra funds on gifts for her grandchildren instead of a face-lift for herself. I was the reality of myself if I hadn't had any money.

I wasn't feeling particularly anxious, but the train couldn't go quite fast enough to suit me.

My disguise was so effective, a businessman helped me get my suitcase onto the escalator when we arrived at the airport, and it wasn't because he wanted to hit on me. "I'd want someone to do the same for my mum," he said.

"Thank you, dear."

The line at the Air France counter was nothing compared to what it would be later in the spring and throughout the summer—the demand for weekend travel to the south of France on Thursday night hadn't started yet. Even so, there were about twenty people waiting to check in, most of them looking much smarter than I, which was just the way I wanted it. I was invisible. At one point I thought I saw Thomas Curtis talking to one of the armed guards that patrol the airport, and my heart stopped. My grip tightened on my purse. Steady on, steady on, I warned myself. He's not looking for anyone who looks like you, but nevertheless, I couldn't control the shaking in my legs. The look-alike turned out to be an older gentleman evidently asking directions.

By the time I reached the head of the line, I'd regained my poise. My hands and legs were solid. I handed my Swiss passport and credit card over the counter to the agent.

"*Merci*, Mme. Chaise." She returned my documents and boarding pass without a second look. "The flight starts boarding in twenty minutes. You just have time."

I dashed to security as quickly as I could.

Get me out of here.

Security to gain access to the concourses at Heathrow is always extremely tight—teams of guards with submachine guns and attack dogs scrutinize every action. And tonight, even though all the metal detectors and high-speed scanners were operating, the line was gigantic, as though there'd been some sort of scare or alert, and the guards were being particularly conscientious. I checked my watch, only thirty minutes till my flight left. I could possibly make it. The cache of stones I'd crammed into my specially constructed jacket and padded bra dug into my torso and breasts. The guards were body searching all the passengers, which they always did, but to-night each search seemed to be taking more time. A small trickle of sweat rolled down my back. Minutes kept disappearing on the over-head flight monitor.

Finally, it was my turn. I placed my suitcase and purse onto the conveyor and passed through. The female guard was thorough, pat-ting up and down my sides, her hands circled my breasts intimately and then ran up and down my legs, inside and out.

She passed me through, as I knew she would. My smuggler's cos-tume wasn't bulletproof but it was definitely grope-proof.

I raced to the gate. They were just closing the doors that lead to the ramp down to the last bus.

"Oh, *merci Dieu*," I said to the girl as I ran onto the half-full con-veyance. She examined my passport and boarding card, and returned them without comment. The bus doors slid shut with a quiet swoosh and we rumbled our way through the maze of road-ways painted on the tarmac, stopping and starting in the middle of nowhere at invisible, empty intersections. Two minutes later I was climbing the stairs onto the plane, and a couple of minutes after that we left the ground and quickly disappeared into the heavy cloud cover. Outside, the plane's strong lights turned everything white until we broke through into a moonlit, starry night and sailed along—a little rocket speeding over a silver carpet.

I put my head back and closed my eyes and said a prayer of thanks. After that, I didn't know what to think about first. Deceit. Sex. Bold moves. Or Owen with some lilting, little Scottish stew-ardess in some silly little kilt and tartan underwear. I thought about murdering him.

"Aperitif, Madame?" The flight attendant placed a small linen napkin and a ramekin of cashews on the console between the seats.

I opened my eyes. "Johnny Walker Black, please. Double. No ice."

I thought about Thomas Curtis's ideas about Owen and decided he was nuts.

I thought about if I really was falling in love with Owen.

I thought about if I would go back or not, or if this was really it. Was I really gone? My life in London over?

I thought about Lady Melody alone in there with Owen. And dead. I thought about the secret door from the street to Owen's office, and I pictured Tina on the sofa. Dead. Could I really believe that Owen would inject her between her toes with a killer dose of heroin? No! Kill two women in one day? It was way too crude. Too tawdry. Too melodramatic.

I thought about his and Gil's furniture scam. And the bomb.

I had another drink.

How glad I was to be on this plane on my way home and wondered if there were any dinner party invitations waiting for me.

I thought again about Owen in Scotland at Lord Spaulding's castle and how Owen had insisted it was going to be men only and how, no matter how much I tried to, I didn't believe him. In spite of trying to drown it with scotch, the green worm of envy was having a field day in my stomach—turning, twisting, digging in.

I thought about Owen's trio of dead wives and decided although the deaths might have been odd, or oddly convenient, they weren't suspicious. I knew Owen too well—I think I probably knew him better than any woman he'd ever known, except possibly his mother. I would know if he was lying, whether it was about murder or other women. I wondered how many other women had thought the same thing: That they knew him better than anyone but his mother.

I wondered if he'd miss me.

I thought about how complicated everything had gotten. I wanted it all to be peaceful again, the way it used to be.

I thought about Owen's hands on my body and I shifted in my seat. I let the alarm bells that clanged in my head drift away, buried completely by feelings of pleasure and longing and intense desire.

FIFTY-THREE

After an hour and a half in the air, we plunged back into the clouds and touched down in Marseilles.

Rain fell in sheets—pelting everything mercilessly. It was a deluge. But it was also surprisingly warm for so early in the year, and the air was fresh, ocean-filled, not the damp, frigid, exhaust-drenched city air of London. I wouldn't have cared if it'd been a blizzard or a typhoon; I couldn't even believe how glad I was to be there.

I buttoned up my raincoat, popped open my umbrella, and strode the distance to the long-term parking lot, its overhead lights muddled by the rain. The lot was full of cars, but, at this late hour, it was empty of people except for a handful from my flight. I watched where each one of them went and waited until they were on their way to the exit before going to my own car. When I pushed the remote on my key, the lights on my black Mercedes station wagon winked. I smiled hugely and got in. The stones in my jacket and bra even stopped hurting. I yanked my wig off. Then I pulled the pins out of my hair and ran my fingers through it, massaging my scalp. I unbuttoned my jacket. Removed the glasses and contact lenses, put on lipstick and blusher, lit a cigarette, slipped the car into gear, paid the man, and turned onto the Autoroute du Soleil.

The highway was almost empty—and after the big interchange at Salon-de-Provence there was little traffic, mostly trucks. It was just me speeding along over the rolling hills in the rain. I made reasonably good time to my exit at Senas, and onto the smaller route to

Orgon, where I turned left onto a country road. My country road that ran through *les plaines*, the flat-bottomed land at the foot of Les Alpilles. It was pitch-black out. The avenue of budding platane trees, their awning of craggy branches lit up eerily by my headlights, waved above as I drove slowly through the ferocious storm. Rain pounded deafeningly on the car. Just before I reached the town of Èygalières, I turned right, crossed the Canal des Alpilles, and drove through a nondescript gate, my nondescript gate, onto a rocky dirt lane banked with olive trees that wound through fields newly planted with sunflowers. I rounded a stand of trees and there it was. A single light burned in the front-room window of my little yellow farmhouse with its hyacinth blue shutters.

Welcome home, Kick.

Ahh. I can breathe.

I dashed through the rain into the kitchen, a good-sized, brightly tiled room with a professional, eight-burner range, three ovens, and a long oak refectory table, upon which sat a large bowl of fresh fruit. A note from Pierre, my farm manager, lay on top of the stack of mail:

Welcome, Madame. Helene has stocked the refrigerator with a few necessities. She will be available tomorrow if you have need of anything. The mail is on the counter. I have to visit the doctor in St. Rémy in the morning but will be on the property in the afternoon—we must discuss your garden. I hope your trip was satisfactory. Pierre.

The mail consisted of bills and notices, and a couple of invitations. I poured myself a scotch and took it into the darkened living room and stood by the window which, in daylight, looked across the valley to the mountains. I don't know how long I stood there, thinking about nothing but how incredibly lucky, and happy, I was. I smoked a cigarette and watched my reflection in the dark glass. I looked more comfortable and relaxed than I'd looked in months. I hated being energized and on-point. I smiled and started laughing. Oh, my God, I was happy.

Shortly, I rinsed out my glass, put it in the dishwasher, straightened everything up, turned off the lights and went into the bedroom— everything pale yellow and white, serene and luscious. I lit the fire in the fireplace, tossing in some dried rosemary branches, and turned on the steamer in the shower. While it heated up, I undressed and put on my old, pink terry-cloth robe. Then, I got down on my hands and knees and removed a two-foot-square section of pale yellow, ceramic-tile bathroom floor and opened my safe.

I hadn't brought a lot of stones with me, only my finest ones, ranging in size from one to twenty-five carats, mostly perfect diamonds, for which the market was always strong, and the Kashmirs, of course. The Velcro sealing the compartments in my jacket and bra separated with a satisfying rip, exposing the dozens of individual, glittering pockets. I sorted them back into their proper order, put them into their *briefkes*, and laid them in the safe, along with the Queen's Pet, and my Léonie Chaise passport and paperwork. I withdrew other documents: my French driver's license, insurance and health cards.

I was home. My own name, my own house, my own town, my own life.

I lay down on the hot tiles of the bench in the steam bath and didn't think about anything. I brushed my teeth, cleaned my face, and went to bed, and slept like I was dead, lulled by the rain.

I have no idea when the storm stopped, but when I woke up at nine-forty-five, there was no sound of the storm, only birdsong. I pushed the shutters open and there before me was a perfect, warm day. Sunlight sparkled off the washed lawn and trees with their tiny lime green, still-furled leaves. A thin misty veil, sensed more than seen, covered the fields and chalky white rock hillsides of Les Alpilles, and made the ancient ruins of Église Sacre Coeur de Marie on a nearby hilltop seem illuminated by flocks of whirling angels.

I pulled on my robe and walked through the house and out the kitchen door into the kitchen garden. This particular garden was my bailiwick—Pierre couldn't touch it no matter how much he wanted to, which, by the looks of it, I imagined was pretty desperately, as his note implied. It did need a lot of work. Rosemary, basil, tarragon, parsley, enormous bushes of lavender—no shamrocks—all fought for space with spiny winterkill and hardy weeds. The gravel path crunched under my slippers as I assessed my project. There was much to do—weeding, restaking, replanting. There was no rush.

Pierre had come by earlier and left a fresh baguette lying on the counter along with a paper sack of two fresh croissants and today's *International Herald Tribune*. I started a pot of coffee and set the table in the kitchen window with my best Limoges breakfast china—sweet pink rosebuds on a glazed white field—with linens to match, a thick slice of butter and a pot of golden Mirabelle preserves. I whipped up a cheese and fines herbes omelette.

The air was so rich with its own sounds, I didn't even put on any music. Not a note of rock and roll to be heard anywhere. Ever again.

FIFTY-FOUR

"*Bonjour*, Madame Keswick," the girl in the cheese shop said. "It's getting to be that time of year again isn't it? All of our good friends come back. I'm very happy to see you."

"I'm very, very happy to be home. Now, let me see . . ." I made my selections and proceeded into the patisserie next door and into the charcuterie next to that, then the vegetable stall, and finally into the wineshop. I loaded everything into the "backseat" of my Panther Madrigan—the groceries filled it completely—and cut through the old town center to the Café des Alpilles for lunch; cassoulet and a glass of Burgundy. I took out my book, *Rule Britannia,* a Daphne du Maurier I'd discovered in a used book shop in London.

Outside on the tree-lined street, traffic buzzed past, friends greeted each other, plump women in dresses carried net bags of groceries, workmen in blue overalls tore up a section of sidewalk. At the newsstand across the way, tourists in rainproof anoraks basked in the sunny morning and studied a spinning rack of postcards.

I couldn't concentrate on the book—I kept thinking about Owen. I tried to picture this idyllic life—idyllic to me anyhow—through his eyes.

He would be interested for two or three hours—tour the town, lovely lunch that he would pretend to appreciate, followed by lovely, passionate, lovemaking. But then the break would be over. He'd need to be on the phone, or we'd be talking business, finance, angles, projects.

On the other hand, I could picture someone like Thomas Curtis or Bertram sitting through a long lunch, the longer the better, talking, talking, savoring the wine, appreciating the food, having a big walk, sticking his head into one or two antiques shops, then taking a long nap. Or reading a book. It occurred to me I'd never seen Owen read a book. We'd never even talked about books.

Okay, what about sex? Well, I just couldn't picture it with Thomas or Bertram, but it used to be that I couldn't picture it with anyone, so who knew. Besides, they both make me laugh, and sometimes laughter is better than sex. At least that's what I *used* to think.

I started laughing and buried my head in my book. What am I going to do?

"Kick!" Flaminia Balfour dashed through the traffic, her hand waving. I was about halfway through lunch. "When did you get back?"

"Late last night."

"Isn't it glorious? A little break from the rains."

"So beautiful I can hardly stand it. Do you want a coffee?"

"No, thanks. No time. What are you doing tonight? Can you come to dinner? There's a man I'd like you to meet—at least I think he's going to be in town this weekend."

We both laughed. This was an old joke between us—she was always promising to fix me up with some great fellow or other, but somehow he never materialized.

"Sure. I'd love to."

"Eight o'clock."

"I'll be there."

Flaminia and Bill Balfour's farm—Ferme de la Bonne Franquette— was in the hills outside of St. Rémy near the village of Les Baux-de-Provence, only about twenty minutes from my place, and my Madrigan V-12 made quick work of the distance. La Bonne Franquette had a big, old, tile-roofed, stone farmhouse that rambled along the top of a hill with a spectacular view of the surrounding countryside. Vineyards and olive groves carpeted the hillside. Flaminia had filled the house with comfortable furniture and works of art. The Balfours prided themselves on their hospitality and were known for throwing the most beautiful parties. They lived in Brussels, and we'd known each other for years. I'm not sure what Bill did—importing and exporting, or something. And Flaminia—a part-French, part-Italian, part-Iranian, art and antiquities expert, and as mysterious and languid as an Abyssinian cat—occupied herself with making sure everything they acquired was the finest available.

It didn't make any difference what they did. In St. Rémy, everyone came to escape business, and we only talked about what we'd done that day or planned to do tomorrow. Unless we had to leave tomorrow, then we'd talk about what we planned to do when we got back. Or we talked about vacations, a subject I couldn't really contribute to, but I was a great listener.

With the sun gone, it was too cold for cocktails outside. Eleven of us gathered around the fire in the living room.

"Bad news," Flaminia said. She'd knotted her black hair into a ball and tucked a couple of shocking pink rhododendron blossoms into it to match her silk pant suit. "Our friend isn't here this weekend. Maybe next time."

I followed her into the dining room and watched as she put out the place cards. "Give it up, Flaminia. I'm happy with things the way they are."

"I will not give it up. One of these days, some straight, rich bachelor is going to walk through my door, and I'm going to wrestle him to the ground and hold him there until you get here. And the two of you will look at each other and fall in love. And we'll all dance at your wedding. Speaking of weddings"—she held up one of the place cards—"did you meet Harry Conroy's new wife?"

I shook my head. "I don't think I've met the Conroys before."

Flaminia shook her head. "You know, it's kind of sad, but so many of these trophy wives are interchangeable. Hostesses never even have to change the place cards—this is the same card from a year ago. Mrs. X is Mrs. X. Their first names don't make any difference."

"That's pretty brutal."

"I know, but it's reality—the women get left behind. Sometimes you have to choose. Harry and Carol were married a long time, maybe thirty years, and he took up with this new girl—oh, goodness, I've forgotten her name—and Carol decided to make an issue out of it. So now she's back there in Greenwich all by her middle-aged self, and this new girl's in France—the new Mrs. Conroy—with all of Carol's old summertime friends, entertaining them in Carol's old summertime house. She should have just kept her mouth shut and it all would have blown over."

"I think that would be hard to do. It'd be hard to trust someone again after that."

Flaminia shrugged. "It all depends on how old you are and what you want." She straightened a flower in the centerpiece. "If Carol had ridden it out, she'd be here tonight, not this silly, overdeveloped girl. It's just so shortsighted. So . . . *American*."

I followed her back into the living room.

"Here, have one of these teeny squabs. Dip it in the Chinese mustard."

I popped the grilled, minibird into my mouth and crunched it up. "How do you suppose they get the feathers off these things, they're so little? Who has fingers little enough to pluck them?"

"I don't know. Children, maybe?" She shrugged, Gallicly unconcerned at possible child-labor issues. "Bill," she called to her husband. "Kick needs another scotch."

The dinner was very fun—a table of new and old friends—even the new Mrs. Conroy was funny. Every now and then I'd think about

Owen and wonder how the fishing had gone today, and what he was doing for dinner, and try to picture him here at this delightful table. Would he fit in? No. He couldn't have a social conversation if his life depended on it. And friends? Other than Gil, he didn't have any. I don't think he believed in them. He couldn't afford them. And when we were together? We didn't need them. We didn't need anybody.

FIFTY-FIVE

By the time I left to go home the rains had moved in again, and on Saturday morning, it was still pouring buckets. I lit fires in every room. Well, even though I say "every" room, as though there were dozens, all there are are four: kitchen, living room, my bedroom, and a guest room. I tossed dried lavender on the burning logs, and the little house heated up quickly and smelled like a relaxing spa.

Pierre had left the paper and fresh croissants, and so I sat down and read the news of which, thankfully, there was little—except a small delightful blurb about a Caravaggio turning up in the Victoria Embankment Gardens substation of the London Police Department. Breakfast was sublime: the most delicious Israeli melon I'd ever had. It had an unusual, beautiful, burnt orange sort of color and with a little squeeze of lime became so succulent and sweet-tart that I had seconds. The *pain au chocolat* was still warm from the bakery, the chocolate all gooey and melted into the buttery pastry.

After breakfast, I poured myself one last cup of coffee and went into the living room, shoved aside a pile of books and magazines, and made room for my laptop on a table that had a postcard view of the fields and mountains. I pulled up a chair. I hadn't checked my personal e-mail for three weeks. I couldn't believe it. I'd completely forgotten. What if I had a message? What if someone needed me?

No one did.

I sat and stared out the window. Maybe I should just give it up, this adoption connection deal. All I was doing was torturing myself—constantly pulling the scab off a wound that would never heal, no matter how long I lived.

Sadness settled on my shoulders like the clouds that had settled in the fields. Muffled and isolating. I cleaned up the kitchen, took a shower, put on my makeup, stuck my book in the pocket of my slicker, and left for a walk.

I was the only one on the mossy towpath along the canal. Rain had made the trail spongy and weighted down the branches, turning it into a green tunnel. A few times I had to crouch to navigate through. At one point, I pushed and patted my way past a small herd of milk cows huddled under the leafy awning. They were soft, warm, gentle, unperturbed by my presence. The whole time, my mind churned, weighing the pros and cons of returning to London.

Reasons *in favor of* going back to London:

1. Owen. Not only the sex—I knew that had a limited shelf life, or so I'd heard. But because he loved me. And he needed me. And I just possibly loved him. I owed it to both of us, to myself especially, to find out, see if this affair was really going to go somewhere.

2. Business. The Romanov Collection—the auction would be spectacular. And the Arianna Collection—I knew we'd get it, she'd be nuts to award it to anyone but us. And beyond that, Ballantine & Company was on the verge of a whole new era of prosperity, thanks to Bertram's brilliant plan. I didn't want to miss it.

3. Thomas. How did he get into this?

Reasons *not* to go back to London:

1. The Carstairs forgeries and the chance of being caught and prosecuted and incarcerated and never being here in Provence again.

2. Owen. The deep-down, actual mature knowledge that I was one of dozens and dozens, maybe hundreds, of affairs, and anytime I thought for one second I was different from the others, I would be fooling myself. To go back for him would be pathetic. There's no fool like an old fool, I reminded myself.

3. Business. I'd committed my last theft and had more than enough cash and stones in my Swiss and French bank accounts to live in extreme comfort for about two hundred more years.

I sat down on a bench and smoked a cigarette and watched my watch and kept mulling over the choices. Finally, it was time for lunch. I walked another half mile into Éygalières and took a window table in the bistro and ordered grilled turbot and a bottle of Montrachet. I drank the whole thing—not sure if I was trying to drown my demons or myself. The only thing I knew for sure was for the first time in my life, I was lonely. And miserable. And okay, my body was practically paralyzed with desire. I had to have him. Have It.

The next morning I returned to London.

FIFTY-SIX

"Do you want to grab an early dinner?" Owen said.

"Sure." The moment I heard his voice, a huge weight lifted off my chest. I'd called Signature Aviation at Woolwich Field, the close-in military airfield that the Queen, and others fortunate enough to have private jets and royal permission, uses. Lord Richard's plane had landed at three. It was four-thirty—he'd been on the ground for an hour and a half. I'd been trying not to get paranoid or ticked. "Let's go to Quentin's," I said. "They're open on Sunday night."

"I'll pick you up at six. I can't wait to see you."

"Me too. I think I might have missed you a little bit."

"I'd call that progress," Owen said. "I missed you a lot."

"So." I took my first sip of an ice-cold martini. "Tell me. Was it great?"

"Unreal. I wish you could have seen it." His face was ruddy with windburn, and his eyes sparkled. "It was so cold I thought I would freeze to death, and Bertram was right, this group takes its fishing very seriously. It was like going to Outward Bound."

I grinned, trying to look interested. Fishing has never been a big turn-on for me. Mostly I was thinking about what we would be doing after dinner. I ate a handful of sesame sticks.

"He's got a couple of helicopters—these things are so cool—little Hueys, go like bastards."

Hmmm. Guess I'm not much interested in helicopters, either. He went on, and on. I watched his lips move around the words, his white teeth, his tongue. The shadow of his beard.

"They dropped each one of us miles from each other, in different spots along the river at six-thirty in the morning." He jabbed his fingers onto the tabletop indicating the river's course and the spots along it. I studied his hands—they were so absolute, so decisive. "Out in the middle of nowhere, and let me tell you, this river was wild, out of its banks."

Kiss me. Kiss me. Kiss me, I thought. Can't you tell how much I want you?

"We each got an emergency kit with a bottle of water, a decanter of scotch, a couple of cookies, a compass, and a map with two Xs, one for where we were being let out, and one for the lodge, in case we had to walk back. No phones allowed."

"This sounds absolutely horrible." I finished my drink and signaled for another round.

"Well, it was definitely a guy thing. But, at least they came and got us for lunch . . ."

I continued to watch but stopped listening and thought instead about later. I imagined Owen's lips on my breasts and his strong hands caressing me, teasing out the dampness between my legs. His hungry kisses. Him, hard inside me. I could feel him moving, slowly at first and then faster, and faster. I could feel myself surrendering to him, my breath coming in quicker and quicker bursts, my throat tightening.

". . . and then we went out again in the afternoon. And the other guys couldn't wait to get back out there. I've never been so goddamned cold in my life. And I don't happen to know a damned thing about fishing, either. But who the hell knew? Or cared? I was by myself, and Dickie . . ."

"Dickie?"

"You know, Lord Richard."

"Ah. Good old Dickie." I licked my lips and cleared my throat and ran my hands down across my front as though I were arranging my blouse. Felt good.

". . . wants it all to be catch and release, so no one knew the difference if I'd caught fifty of the damned things or spent three hours trying to get my line untangled from a tree branch."

Felt great actually. I did it again and recrossed my legs for the tenth time. My God, aren't you ever going to stop talking? Let's just forget the dinner. I've got some eggs and cheese at my house. We'll eat afterward. Don't you appreciate that I've come back from France for you? Put myself in jeopardy for you. Made some sort of decision in your favor. Let's just shut up and do it.

"After dinner, we played bridge for a couple of hours, then hit the sack. I'm glad I got invited, but I'm not sure I'd like to go again."

"Who else was there?"

"Two other great guys—an American, Sam Tucker, runs Drake Industries; and Ian MacGregor, an old friend of Dickie's. President of the Bank of Scotland."

"No stewardesses?"

Owen laughed. "No. No stewardesses."

He was lying.

I froze.

FIFTY-SEVEN

"Wasn't *that* worth waiting a couple of days for," Owen murmured into my shoulder.

I studied my ceiling, my beautiful champagne-and-pink paisley pleats, my beautiful Baccarat chandelier. "Ummm." It had been okay. Not great. He didn't know that, of course—I'd had experience faking ecstasy with Sir Cramner, who'd almost held his own pretty darned well right up to the end.

"Are you all right?"

"Yes." I kissed his cheek. "Why?"

"You seem a little off."

"I do? I'm not. I'm a little tired—I worked hard over the weekend."

"I thought a lot about you this weekend, Kick. A lot about us."

"Owen, we've talked about this. Let's not ruin a good thing." I was feeling pretty stupid. I'd made a big mistake by coming back. What on earth made me think that he would be faithful to me? Even the sex that I had been so breathless for, the desire that had carried me back across the ocean, was empty. I was trying to remember what time the next flight left for Marseilles, if there was one late-Sunday night.

"I think there should be more."

I pushed him away from me by his shoulders, up far enough that I could look into his eyes. "No." I shook my head.

"While I was out there freezing my nuts off, all I could think about was being here with you. I love you so much, Kick. You're so beautiful, so refined. You're everything I'm not—you're everything I want in my life, by my side. But I can't take your lack of commitment anymore. You have to make up your mind. I want you to marry me."

I studied his eyes. Was he dissembling, or was I wrong? Did I only *want* to think there'd been other women in Scotland because I wanted to protect myself in case there *had* been? "Oh, Owen, I . . . , I . . . , I . . ." I what? I thought.

"Just say yes. Don't work it to death. I know you love me, too. I love you." He kissed me. "I love you. I love you. Please say yes." He reached over to the bed table and scrabbled around with something and came up with an enormous diamond engagement ring.

I felt champagne bubbles fizz all the way through me, and I heard that deafening, irresistible, Angel of Death roaring sound. It blanketed me, cosseting all my senses, and, more to the point: Neutralizing all my sense. What the hell, Kick. Just hold your breath and jump off the high board into the deep end of the pool. Live a little, for a change—this is what you came back to find out. Of all the girls in the world, this beautiful man picked you out of the lineup to be Mrs. Owen Brace. Goddammit.

"Yes."

That was it. I was committed. My die was cast. I surrendered. I took my idyllic existence as a single woman in Provence and spit in its eye.

Because Owen and I were not kids, we liked our privacy and our independence. We respected each other's separate patterns of going to sleep and getting up. And even though he was a regular visitor to my flat, he always went home, no matter what time it was.

So now, for the first time, Owen spent the night, and it was unbelievably strange. I slept fitfully, thinking the whole time: I've just said I'll spend the rest of my life sleeping with this man. But when he wakened Monday morning, he went out of his way to make me feel secure, beautiful, loved. We made love sleepily, slowly, deliciously. And when we climaxed it was as though we'd been practicing for that single moment our whole lives—it was so fulfilling, so satisfying, so melded, I could not tell where he ended and I began, and this was the way it was going to be, now and evermore.

As I've mentioned before: Once I'm set, I'm set. There isn't anybody more rapt than I. And once my mind's made up, that's it. Well, usually. I know I've been equivocating about France, but that turned out for the good, didn't it? I was in this deal with both feet and I drank in and evaluated and analyzed every single moment and feeling. Was this what love was? Was this what I'd been resisting all my life? (Should there be more? Did I feel a little disappointed? No! Absolutely not.)

And how did I feel about his being in my shower? Making himself at home in my bathroom? I tried to be generous with my feelings, but I really didn't like it much. In my opinion, there are just certain things that should not be shared. Or seen in bright lights. I used the guest bath.

I glanced down at my finger and the twelve-carat, flawless, D Colorless, square-cut diamond ring. It was very close to what I would have selected for myself. He did a pretty good job. I would have preferred a brilliant cut because I think when stones get this large, and are this good, a brilliant cut shows them off best. But for someone who didn't appreciate the niceties, went for surface area instead of perfect proportion, he did all right.

But then again, on the plus side, once we were dressed, we rode to work together for the first time. I felt like a princess. I felt like Grace Kelly with Cary Grant. I felt every silly, schoolgirl emotion—pretty: the prettiest girl in the world, and special: the girl all the others envied. And smug. Just as smug as the cat who swallowed the canary.

It was one of the most beautiful spring days I'd ever seen in London. Maybe ever, anywhere, in my life. Flowers seemed to burst from everywhere—daffodils blanketed Green Park like a bright yellow carpet. The carriage horses had little bouquets tied to their harnesses. Window boxes bloomed before my eyes. I had turned into a cornball.

The top was down on the car, and the bright morning sun bathed our faces. The radio blared—Pink Floyd.

Owen said something and patted my hand.

"What?" I yelled back.

Whatever it was, he said it again.

"I'm sorry," I yelled, "I can't hear you over the radio."

Thank God he turned it down.

"I said I'm happier than I've ever been, because you're mine."

"Get over yourself, Owen. It's just a beautiful day, okay?"

"You are such a grouch."

He took the long way, down Constitution Hill to the Queen Victoria Memorial in front of Buckingham Palace. We circled the roundabout three times.

"I swear to God, Kick, I feel like such a kid, if there were a drive-in movie around here, we'd be at it and I'd be trying to feel you up. I feel bigger than Elvis."

Okay, I was thinking Grace Kelly and Cary Grant. But I could be Grace Kelly with Elvis. I'm sure I could. I can. I will. I *am*.

We zipped all the way up the Mall to Trafalgar Square, over to Pall Mall, and back down past St. James's Place to a little private garage behind the hotel. He rented the space from a broke aristocrat.

I had to get out before he put the car in, the space was so tight. "You could save the world for the insane amount of money you pay this guy," I said, watching him tug the garage doors closed and attach a formidable padlock. "At least he could put in an automatic opener."

"I don't care how much it costs—no one touches my car but me, and there aren't any other cars on either side of it that can ding my doors."

"You are so neurotic."

"Come on, babe." He put his arm around my shoulder and squeezed. "Let's get some breakfast."

Babe.

I grinned.

Babe. Wow.

FIFTY-EIGHT

While he changed out of his casual weekend clothes into regular business attire, I studied the room service menu. His two-bedroom penthouse suite at the Dukes felt more like a country house. There were windows on three sides of the sitting room, faded-chintz-covered sofas and comfortable chairs, a wall of bookshelves packed with first editions dating from the 1940s, a working fireplace, and a small terrace, the door to which was open, letting in the crisp morning air upon which floated a bit of ocean.

"What do you want?" I called into his bedroom. "Orange juice? Eggs? Muffins? French toast? Sausages?"

"You know what I like—something high-protein, low-fat. Order for me. Why don't you get us some protein shakes?"

I felt at sea, as though I'd never met him before. I knew what he liked for breakfast at Cliveden, and at the office, but this was a different Owen. What if he liked something else at home? This sounds crazy, I know, especially at my age, but the fact is, this was the first time I'd ever been in a man's private quarters. I'd been in hotel rooms with Sir Cramner—even after he'd bought me the Eaton Square flat, he still liked to spend a night or two, every now and then, at Claridge's.

"I think we need a little Pink Champagne Holiday, Kick," he'd say. "You've been working too hard." And off we'd go for a jolly little escape.

Owen and I had stayed numerous times at Cliveden. But here's the deal: Hotel rooms are neutral ground. They are their own, independent reality.

So now I find myself in Owen's rooms, with him dressing and talking on the phone, and me wandering around his living room, not too sure what to do with myself. It all seemed incredibly *intimate*. Opposite from the physical and romantic intimacy earlier that morning, this made me feel far away. I noticed little personal, private touches of Owen—a few photographs: him on a ski lift, him on a yacht, him lying nude on a snow-white beach next to an emerald ocean. A different girl was with him in each picture and in all of them, he was the same: laughing, smiling, having a ball. There were no pictures of me, or us. Yet. There was a stack of personal letters that hadn't come via the office. I made a point of giving them a wide berth, just in case anyone was watching; one of his sweaters lay tossed casually across the arm of a chair; his well-used running shoes sat behind a door. I felt like an intruder.

I picked up the phone to call room service a couple of times but put it back without dialing. I was acting like a simpleminded fool, a teenage girl doing something naughty. Finally, I placed the order.

His cell phone rang, and for a moment I wasn't sure what to do about that either. Was this business time or personal time? If I answered, would I be doing my job or prying? There was no caller ID.

"Owen Brace's line," I answered.

Whoever it was hung up.

He talked on conference calls throughout breakfast, which was fine with me. I read the paper and returned a couple of personal calls, including one from Howard Beauchamp, my trust officer at the Private Bank of London.

"Miss Keswick, I'm so glad you rang me back. This is strictly a formality, no need to worry, but by law we're required to inform our clients when something irregular has happened."

"Irregular?"

"Yes. Nothing to affect you, but over the weekend, our computer was invaded, second time in six months. It's all been related to the UBS/Barkley's takeover—someone trying to find out the size of the UBS war chest. But I am obliged to let you know, in case you may wish to move your trust elsewhere, since we cannot guarantee total anonymity at the moment. Naturally, we hope you'll choose to remain with us, after all we've looked after you for many, many years, and hopefully have earned your trust."

"Completely, sir," I said. "I wouldn't consider moving." Mr. Beauchamp was the man who represented me at the Ballantine board meetings. His strict formality toward me, even after so long, gave me a sense of continuity and confidence, as though Sir Cramner were sitting at his desk watching over me.

"Very well. I'll await your further direction."

"Thank you for calling."

"Who was that?" Owen said when I'd hung up.

"A realtor. Everyone's always trying to buy my flat."

"I don't blame them. It's in a class by itself. You might want to reconsider, though, once we're married. We'll need to have something bigger."

The thought gave me a start. Me? Give up my flat? But by the time we walked down the street to work, back into terra cognita, I had settled down. I was so glad I'd come back from France—I could now see it would have been a mistake to stay and not see this through. If I was ever going to get anywhere in terms of a relationship, I needed to learn to trust. Owen would teach me.

When exactly I intended to start this business of trusting eluded me. My entire life lay like the proverbial dead elephant in the middle of the floor, with me tiptoeing around it pretending it wasn't there. My separate life in France. My safe-cracking, cat-burgling, stone-switching métier. The KDK Trust. I realized I hadn't been truthful with Owen about anything. Not even once. These issues weren't going to go away. If I really were going to marry him, I needed to start my new life with a clean slate. But it was a conundrum: What if he didn't want to be married to a professional jewel thief and a consummate liar, no matter how elegant she was? Then what would I do with all my hiding places revealed?

I decided I'd only show him one piece at a time, then, if that felt right, I'd show him another. Which one should I start with?

Clearly, Monday morning wasn't the time to start with all this truth stuff—the second he walked into his office he was on the phone again, and he was in a lousy mood all day. We quarreled over everything.

Hell.

He slept in his bed that night, and I slept in mine.

FIFTY-NINE

Next morning, hearts and minds refreshed, attitudes adjusted, bodies rejuvenated, and ready to begin again, we sat comfortably ensconced in the Bentley's backseat, Michael at the wheel, cruising down the highway for a meeting at the Panther plant.

"I'm starting to think about getting a helicopter," Owen said. "It would save one hell of a lot of time."

There was always something bigger. Something more to want. Part of Owen's success was because nothing was ever enough, but it interfered with his business judgment, something I had in spades. A sign, it seemed, that our partnership would be a strong one.

"Ummm," I said. "I'd put that right up there with the fishing gear store on the list of things you need to invest in at the moment."

"Are you going to argue with everything I say? Have you heard one good idea I've had, or are you just going to nix everything unilaterally? Don't you have any vision?"

"Well, I . . ."

"Know how you get places? You imagine the possibilities, then you head in that direction. Know what's wrong with you, Kick? You're acting your age. You're really turning into an old fuddy-duddy."

I opened and closed my mouth. Tears stung my eyes.

After a moment or two, he reached over and took my hand. "I'm sorry," he said. "I didn't mean that."

"Look, all we've done is fight for the last twenty-four hours. It's not worth it."

He shook his head. "It's nothing to do with you. Sometimes the pressure gets to me."

"I understand." That was the truth, and I tried not to let my voice betray the hurt I felt from his attack. I know I'm getting older, but I'm not exactly old, except compared to the girls he was used to hanging around with. And what's wrong with acting one's age? That's the point, isn't it? To grow up. If you haven't grown and learned, you can't get anywhere, can't make anything happen. I worked to keep my emotions under control.

Okay. This is not about me. This is about him and his own strengths and weaknesses. I could never withstand the pressures he carried, and so what if he had to blow off a little steam every now and then and I was the closest target. I could take it. For better or for worse, wasn't that one of the promises? I could take it.

Owen stared quietly out the window and toyed with my fingers, lacing them absentmindedly in and out of his. "You haven't asked much about Project Caruso. Aren't you even a little curious?"

"I guess what I don't know can't hurt me."

"You really think it's going to bomb?"

"No." I answered carefully. "I'm sure it will be a huge success, but I'm not a big risk-taker. I'm a big chicken. Maybe it's because I'm acting my age." I jammed my elbow into his side. Hard. As hard as I could. "Maybe you should try it sometime."

"Ouch! God, I'm so sorry I said that. I take it back."

"Good. You should. The fact is, I've been giving the project a wide berth because I had a dream a few days after you showed me what you and Gil were up to, and it was about my trial."

Owen laughed.

"Not *your* trial and not *Gil's* trial. *My* trial. And no one was there speaking for me, but me."

"That's terrible. I'd never leave you in the lurch—if you go on trial, I'll come every day."

"Gee, thanks. You're a heck of a guy, Owen. A real gentleman."

We smiled at each other. The storm seemed past.

268 MARNE DAVIS KELLOGG

"I'd like to go by the workshop and take a look after we wrap up out here, if you don't mind. I hear it looks like Carstairs Manor."

"Not at all." The mention of Lady Melody Carstairs agitated me all over again. I could see her clearly, first welcoming him and Bertram at the door, lively and gay, and then, an hour later, sitting bolt upright on her sofa, a frightful look on her face, dead. I glanced at Owen.

"What?"

"Nothing." I smiled. "I was just thinking about Lady Melody. I'm sorry she's gone. I loved her books so much."

"Happens to all of us."

I nodded. The question is not if, but when. And how. Thomas's notions had firmly embedded themselves in my mind. I knew they were bogus, but they were also persistent, popping up at inappropriate moments. It was right at the tip of my tongue to ask Owen exactly how she'd died, ask him to tell the story again, about how he'd turned around long enough to pop the cork and pour the champagne and when he turned back, she was dead. But I didn't do it because I didn't want us to get into another squabble. It wasn't worth the brain damage. She was dead, and that was that. Case closed.

Okay, how about this one: *A wife can't be made to testify against her husband.*

"Oh my God!" I blurted out of the blue.

"What?" Owen jumped.

"Nothing. Sorry. I just had a little pain in my side. A little crick or something."

"Are you all right?"

"Fine. Fine. It's gone now." Oh, Commander Thomas Curtis, I could kill you for this seed you planted in my head.

I shoved Thomas and his congenial demeanor out of my mind with all my strength.

Comfort was for fogies, fuddy-duddies.

Comfort was not for me.

I was hip. I was a hottie.

I defended my love for Owen to Thomas as though I were already on the stand. Our relationship was difficult, but intoxicating and honest. Edgy. That was good though, wasn't it? Yes. It kept me on my toes. Our differences were our strengths. I never liked Elvis, much. Not at all, actually. But I could. I would. I would change myself, because Owen was melting me like an iceberg, my heart would open like a flower. I would hold his hand and jump off the cliff. Just look at how he had unlocked my body, bringing me pleasures I couldn't have imagined. I'd struggled not to confuse sex with love, but now I knew love and sex were the same thing after all, if they were with the right person. A meeting of the minds and hearts would follow. How could they not, when the bodies were so in tune? So addicted to each other. It was inevitable. I would change a little, he would change a little. We would become one. I would bury my independent self, along with all of my past, and, for better or for worse, become Mrs. Owen Brace. Number four. Out of left field, Flaminia Balfour's remarks about the new Mrs. Conroy drifted in: "It's kind of sad, but these wives are interchangeable. Hostesses never even have to change the place cards. Mrs. X is Mrs. X. Their first names don't make any difference." And then she also said, "It all depends on what you want out of a marriage."

A wife can't be made to testify against her husband.

Oh, shut up.

S I X T Y

That afternoon, when we arrived back in the city, I was greeted with a bouquet of three dozen long-stemmed ivory roses. The arrangement almost took over my desk, and their fragrance filled the landing and reception area.

"Please forgive me," the card read. "I love you, Owen."

"What are these for?" I followed him into his office. "Forgive you for what?"

"For calling you an old fogey."

"Fuddy-duddy."

"Okay. Whatever it was, I'm sorry. I hurt you, and I didn't mean to."

"I know." When I looked at him, I still couldn't believe he was mine. And, God forgive me for saying this, but, deep down, even if he was mine, I still wasn't sure I wanted him.

Twenty minutes later he stuck his head out his office door. "Kick, I left last night's Credit Suisse faxes at the hotel. Do you mind getting them? They're on the coffee table—I don't want anyone else to see them."

"Absolutely. I'll be right back."

I greeted the front desk staff, took the lift to the fifth floor, and let myself into Owen's suite. The coffee table was piled with correspondence and beneath the stack was a personal computer, a small titanium Portegé, like mine. I didn't know Owen had one. I couldn't resist. His passwords were predictable and within seconds I was into his e-mail—dozens of communications between him and Gil about the state of the corporation detailing the looming likelihood of bankruptcy and new rescue schemes. Then suddenly I found myself looking at a months-old message from Mr. Hiller, the hacker in Vermont. The subject was Query and the message read:

"The sole beneficiary of the KDK Trust is Kathleen Day Keswick." It went on to give my London address and phone number and a staggering amount of personal information—social security number, medical records, beauty shop appointments, even my grocery purchases. Everything I'd ever charged on a credit card. Trips using my American passport. There was nothing about France.

I wasn't sure exactly what to do. I stared at the message, dumbfounded. It was dated the day he took me to the Panther plant and then to Cliveden for lunch. The day this all began. The phone rang and startled me back to earth.

"Mr. Brace's office," I said automatically.

"Where in the hell are you?" It was Owen. "You've been gone for ten minutes."

"I'm sorry," I said. "The papers weren't where you said, but I've got them. I'm on my way."

He hung up without comment.

I carefully closed the computer and slid it back under the papers where I'd found it, tucked the confidential faxes into my briefcase, and then went into the bathroom and threw up. Afterward, when my legs could support me, I splashed cold water on my face. But I couldn't bear to look at myself in the mirror. I couldn't stand to see the marks of betrayal and humiliation I knew were there.

The phone rang again. I didn't answer it.

I really didn't know what to do, how to act, how to proceed. All I knew for sure was that until I decided how I was going to handle this, I had to move forward as though everything were fine, and Owen, being the sort of man he was, would never be able to tell the difference, which was one of the greatest differences between us. He was self-consumed. I was wary and aware.

I had self-control. He did not. That's the difference between grown-ups and adolescents.

"Where do you want to have dinner tonight?"

"I think I'm going to go home and go to bed. I feel like I'm getting a cold."

"Let's just go out and grab a quick bite. You have to eat something."

What I wanted to do was go home and pull the covers over my head, but I needed to protect my position. Okay, Kick, do you have the fortitude for this or not? I studied his face. How could someone who looked so good be so bad?

He stroked his finger down my cheek. "Come on. Let's just go over to Caprice and I'll buy you a martini and a bowl of soup."

I nodded. It was the best I could do at the moment.

SIXTY-ONE

The next morning was beautiful. It was Odessa Day, when we would get our first look at the Princess Arianna Collection. I dressed with particular care—brand-new navy Chanel suit with black trim and several strings of pearls. My bus bumped its way through the neighborhood along its familiar route. The coffee and cruller were probably as delicious as ever, but my mind was swamped with this terrible mess. It had kept me awake most of the night with a variety of choices, plans, and schemes about how to deal with it, ranging from murder to retribution to revenge to simple vanishment.

Did I feel as though I were in danger? That he'd kill me for the company stock? No. I felt as though I'd entered a whole new dimension, as though I were observing my life from a distant spot. I felt in complete control. In fact, I was in complete control, not only of myself, but of him.

Last night at dinner, we tried to reach a consensus on where we'd live once we were married—he wanted to stay at the Dukes, just take over the suite next door, but the hotel management was balking, which was fine with me. I just kept going through the motions.

"It's a great hotel, Owen, but I think we need our own furniture."

"Yeah. I suppose you're right."

I suggested that we keep my town house, maybe take over the one next door, but Owen nixed that idea: The neighborhood was too stuffy and stodgy. Housing became another bone of contention, and so we'd just set it aside.

The sex was the usual deal, except I'd never been so disengaged. I sent him home at nine-thirty.

"I'm sorry," I said. "I just feel lousy. I think I need a good night's sleep."

His reluctance to leave was hollow. Maybe it had been that way all along, but now that the gauze had been removed from my eyes, I saw everything about him in high definition.

"I have an idea," I said when he got to work. "It sounds crazy, but maybe we should just continue to live in our own places."

"Don't be ridiculous," Owen snapped. "Find us something." He was in a rotten, petulant mood—irritable and argumentative.

"You know, I'm beginning to think this being engaged deal is not that great," I said to get a reaction, give him a little heartburn.

"What do you mean by that?"

"Well, if you want to know the truth, you're in such an awful mood all the time, being married to you is starting to sound absolutely horrible. You should know that I'm really having some serious second thoughts."

"Come over here," he ordered, and wrapped his arms around me. "If it weren't for you—I think I'd probably come unglued. You are my whole life, Kick. I promise I'll make it up to you." And then he gave me one of those kisses and that made him think that I thought everything was going to be all right.

At three-thirty, our team was ready. Andrew, Bertram, Owen, and I.

"I'd feel a lot better if you'd stay at the office and keep things under control," Owen said.

"And miss seeing this collection?" I said. "Not on your life."

"Let's go away for the weekend."

"Not unless you get one hell of a lot nicer between now and then."

"You have my word."

Owen talked on the phone for the whole ride to Odessa's palatial Kensington town house, so the three of us sat silently, which I didn't mind, but I could tell that it rankled Bertram. There had been some friction between him and Owen lately. Although I didn't know specifically why, I suspect it was because Owen kept the pressure on him, and he didn't like it. It wasn't good for the company in the long run. "You've got to stop looking at this as a short-term, fast-cash business," I'd overheard Bertram saying. "We need to invest more in relationship building." "Just do what I tell you," Owen had responded.

A liveried butler opened the door, showed us into a grand reception room, and offered us tea. We all accepted, and fiddled around, making small talk. But then, as the delay stretched first to ten minutes, then fifteen, then twenty, the four of us settled into a silence we willed ourselves not to let turn insolent or angry. This was the opportunity of a lifetime, and we would make it happen. I watched it all from a perch somewhere up near the ceiling as I wandered around admiring the furniture and fabrics, works of art and bibelots.

"I'm going to ask Odessa who her decorator is," I said to Owen. "I think we should get a place like this."

"I think it's a little grand, don't you?"

"No. I think it's just right. We'll be entertaining so much, we'll need this much room."

Finally, almost forty-five minutes later, a set of French doors opened and in she swept like the Queen of the Nile, all in floaty white chiffon, her cleavage sparkling like sugar-sprinkled café au lait.

"Owen." She took his hand and kissed his cheek. "I'm so glad you could come."

It should have hit me like a punch in the stomach. A bucket of cold water over my head. A smack in the face with a big, cold, slimy fish. A big, cold, slimy, Scottish salmon, for instance. But it didn't. Unfortunately, I wasn't even a little surprised. You son of a bitch. I saw it all. Odessa had been in Scotland with Owen. It hadn't been a stewardess. And it hadn't been a fishing trip. It had been Odessa Niandros.

My God, I thought, how much more tawdry can this get?

"You know my team," Owen said. "Bertram, Andrew, and my fiancée, Miss Keswick."

I almost laughed out loud. Oh, Owen, you were making this so, so easy. And you didn't even know it. You idiot.

Odessa tucked her arm through Owen's and led us through the door. "I've set the pieces out in the dining room, I think the light is best in there."

He turned and winked at me.

I winked back.

SIXTY-TWO

I fixed myself a strong drink, turned on the music, and got into the bathtub. I looked at my body and started to laugh. Absolutely nothing was where it used to be. It was all still there, but lower. And there was so much of everything. And while I didn't mind that—I mean, age is age, and unless you want to spend thousands of dollars and endure weeks of excruciating pain having it all hoisted and anchored back into place—what on earth ever made me think that a man like Owen would be interested in a woman like me, I'll never know.

I'd been tricked, twice! In two days! With my eyes wide-open. The story was as old as time. Of course people were astonished by our engagement—all they had to do was look at him and look at me. The power of sex had deluded me into believing everything he told me. Now that I could see all the pieces, it was so obvious. No wonder he hadn't wanted a prenuptial agreement. Star power had never been important to me before—but Owen had turned those beams on high and I was caught in their blaze.

Oh Kick. You've been used. You've been had.

Well, that was simply not true. I'd *almost* been used. *Almost* been had. Sheer good fortune had kept me from being totally fooled. There are no accidents.

The phone rang and rang.

———

I opened a bottle of Chianti, fixed myself a light dinner of capellini tossed with garlic, olive oil, fresh chopped tomatoes and basil, and quite a lot of cheese, watched television, and gathered myself together. My guardian angels had helped me dodge a veritable hail of bullets. Or, as Owen had so succinctly put it the day the Romanov Collection arrived on our doorstep: I'd just escaped what could have turned into my own personal—excuse my French—shitstorm of the century.

By the time I got to dessert, a blueberry trifle I'd made the day before, I was feeling much more together. And I knew exactly what I was going to do.

I put on some Schubert—no more rock and roll for me, and by God, this time I mean it—fixed myself a mug of hot cocoa with a fat plop of thick cream and a scoop of brown sugar, put on my nightgown and robe, snuggled into the living room sofa, and picked up my sketchpad.

SIXTY-THREE

The next morning, the phone rang at ten o'clock.

"Odessa here. May I speak to Owen."

"One moment, please, Miss Niandros."

With that call, she officially awarded us the Princess Arianna Jewelry Collection—it would be the biggest sale anywhere of the springtime, international magnificent jewelry auction season, which was imminent. It would blow Sotheby's and Christie's out of the water. Bertram was so happy he was ten feet off the ground.

I gave him a hug and kiss. "I'm delighted for you, Bertram. Congratulations."

"I love this business." He beamed. "There's just nothing like it."

"You're so right." I laughed. "I can see Sir Cramner smiling—Ballantine & Company is lucky to have you. We're in good hands."

I kept my own counsel around Owen, never letting him get the slightest inkling that I knew what he was up to. I tolerated his affair and continued to sleep with him, although I did allude to having some sort of "condition" which cooled his ardor basically completely. He stayed predictable and true to form: Once the contracts were signed with Odessa, and the collection delivered and safely stored in our vaults, once the publicity was launched and the catalogue in the works, the bloom fell quickly from the rose. He was getting tired of her.

"She's so goddamned boring—always talking about Lord this and Lady that. Who gives a shit?"

But here was the rub: She wasn't getting bored with Owen. She was *liking* him, lots, and he was trapped. "She's so fucking dull. And I don't think she's very bright, either."

"I'm so sorry, darling," I sympathized. "But, don't worry, it won't be for much longer."

The nights he wasn't at some function or other, I was usually too tired to do much more than go to dinner.

"What are you so tired from all the time?"

"Planning our wedding. It's exhausting."

"Why don't we just go to a magistrate and get it done?"

I frowned. "Don't be silly. I've never been married before. I want it to be special."

I'd made—and paid cash for with his money—excessive nonrefundable arrangements. Not only did I intend to keep putting it to him in every subtle way I could think of, but also, I'd taken it upon myself to give a fairy-tale wedding on behalf of all us girls who never would have one. Everything any one of us had ever dreamed about, I was planning.

Although I never actually contacted the church, I told Owen the ceremony would be at the Chapel Royal at St. James's Palace, where Holbein painted the ceiling and where the Queen's own rector conducted regular services. Owen would be expected to make a significant gift to the Queen's Purse.

And then, we had to have the horses and carriages to get the wedding party and all our guests up to the reception. That required a large deposit because the carriages were so in demand this time of year.

The reception would be at the Ritz and I'd met with them. Big time. We would take over the main dining room, a privilege granted to the few who could afford to underwrite the famous room's entire Saturday night business in addition to the cost of the party itself. We would have an eight-course, seated dinner for two hundred, as well as a block of fifty rooms and suites for our out-of-town guests. Cases upon cases of wines and champagne had been purchased, and the wedding cake had twelve tiers and was refulgent with icing ribbons, flowers and doves, all gilded with gold leaf and sparkling sugar. All of this, of course, had to be paid for in full, up front. I'd also made a hundred-thousand-pound deposit with the florist.

"I'm stunned," Owen said, "at how much all this is costing."

"Well, you have an image to keep up. I know cash flow-wise, it's not especially good at the moment, but in the long run, it's worth the investment."

"What in the hell do we need a thirty-piece orchestra for?"

"Dancing. It'll be fun. I have a fitting for my dress this afternoon. Do you want to come?"

"No. How much is that?"

"I'm not really sure yet." I shrugged.

Creditors in addition to Credit Suisse were closing in, and he still couldn't totally control the maneuvers because of that one burr under his saddle: the KDK Trust. He had no idea how close he'd come to getting it—if he knew, it would kill him.

Office life became exactly that: office life.

I uprooted all my shamrock plants, chopped the greenery into a lovely zesty pesto, threw away the dirt, and stacked their pots neatly in the corner of the garden.

Bertram came and went on his regular schedule. He was kind, humorous, and respectful, in spite of the fact that he was under severe pressure from a number of fronts. Not only was the Arianna Auction quickly approaching, but there was much to be done to get the house ready for the grand reopening. He carried it all in good stride, like a man who had come fully into his own: His years of experience had culminated into this well-deserved, highly acclaimed, moment in his career.

I loved seeing it all come together. The house hummed with the same kind of energy it had in its heyday with Sir Cramner.

SIXTY-FOUR

The Monday before Friday's gala auction, we moved back into our St. James's Square headquarters. The workmen had done such a meticulous job, it looked better than brand-new—the black enamel on the window frames gleamed and the brass rails shone. All the decades of city soot, smoke, and exhaust had been steamed and scrubbed from the limestone.

I'd thought I'd be glad to be back at my command post. But it felt very different. Everything looked the same, but it was all changed. Alcott wasn't there anymore—he'd retired. As had Roger, our chief guard. Even the dopey X-ray machine girl had gone on to greener pastures.

When the doors opened to the Arianna Exhibition, throngs of people poured in. Because of the massive interest in the sale, Ballantine's instituted an admission charge as well as a "reservations only" policy to help control the crowd. Security was very tight and would remain that way indefinitely.

"Isn't it lovely?" Bertram stood by my desk beaming down the stairs. "Just look at them. Every single one of them has paid forty pounds just to walk through the door, and almost every hand is holding a twenty-pound catalogue. We're going to make more off the admissions and catalogue sales than we've made off many of our auctions."

Wednesday evening, just as I was getting ready to walk out the door and head home, the phone rang.

"Kick?" A familiar voice said.

"Yes."

"Thomas Curtis here."

"Thomas! What a surprise."

"Just checking in as I said I would. Are you free for dinner tomorrow?"

"I'd love it."

"Seriously. You're free for dinner tomorrow night? You're not joking?"

"No." I laughed.

"There's a great little Indian restaurant in your neighborhood with the hottest curry in London."

"Know it well."

"Seven o'clock, then?"

"See you there."

Who says there are no second chances? If something is meant to be, it comes in its own time . . .

I went to the restaurant the next evening. Seven o'clock came and went, as did seven-fifteen. I ordered another scotch and a bowl of shrimp curry. At about seven-twenty-five, my cell phone rang, and I stepped outside to answer.

It was Thomas. "I'm sorry, Kick. I've been called out, a particularly gruesome case, and it's going to be a couple of hours before I can get away. Is there any chance for Friday? We could go to the symphony. It's Schubert."

I could now fully appreciate how lucky I'd been not to have been more involved with men during my lifetime. They simply were not worth the effort.

"I'm sorry, Thomas, but I'm busy Friday night. It's our grand reopening when we start the Princess Arianna jewelry auction. You should come."

"No thanks. Can I call you next week?"

"Sure. Absolutely."

Whatever.

. . . and if something is not meant to be, no matter what you do, there's nothing you can do to make it right.

SIXTY-FIVE

Friday.

Ballantine & Company was massed with flowers. The new floors and windows gleamed in anticipation of tonight's grand affair. All day, crowds continued to pass through the exhibition rooms looking at Princess Arianna's jewelry.

I gathered up a couple of files, knocked on Bertram's office door, and stepped inside, closing it behind me. He looked up.

"Excuse me, Bertram. Do you have a moment?"

"Of course. Have a seat."

"There's something I want to talk to you about and give to you." I felt nervous. "In strictest confidence. Do I have your word?"

"You do."

"When I was a young woman, Sir Cramner never wanted me to have to worry about my future. He knew how much I loved Ballantine & Company. He gave me a 15 percent ownership."

Bertram's mouth opened slightly. "You?"

I nodded and smiled. "Me. I'm KDK Trust."

Bertram burst out laughing. "Does he . . ."

"He knows. But he doesn't know I know. That's why he's pretended to be in love with me and asked me to marry him."

"Oh, this is rich."

"Very." I looked down, and my hands were shaking slightly.

"What a bastard that man is."

"He wrote the book. But the reason I'm telling you this, Bertram, is because you love the business and the house as much as I do. You've put your heart and soul into her, and you're bringing her back from the dead. What you don't know is that Owen's empire is crumbling, and he won't be able to maintain the façade much longer. He's about to be forced into bankruptcy."

Bertram looked stunned.

"And that's not all." I proceeded to tell him about the Carstairs forgeries, replicas, and reproductions.

"You can't be serious."

"I'm completely serious. You can't imagine how shaky and shady things are. These men are desperate. But at least Ballantine & Company hasn't been involved in any illegal activity, yet. So far, you're not in any jeopardy. But as you can see, it's just a matter of time, very little time."

"This explains a lot," Bertram said.

"Doesn't it, though?" I answered. "At any rate, thanks to Sir Cramner and some good investment advice, I'm very secure, financially. I don't need to depend on the KDK holding." I opened one of the file folders and withdrew a bundle of papers. "I'm drawing this out terribly. I apologize, I know how busy you are. So I'll cut it as short as possible. I'm giving you my shares, Bertram. You've earned them, and I know I can trust you to do the right thing. To continue and improve Sir Cramner's vision. As soon as this is signed and notarized, you will become the sole trustee and beneficiary of KDK Trust."

"I don't know what to say."

"You don't have to say anything. It'll be up to you to let him know—or not—you're the 15 percent owner."

"Why are you doing this?"

"I've already told you why, and with the opening upon us in a few hours, it's time to hand over the reins, and for me to step aside. Starting tonight, you will put your personal stamp on Ballantine & Company—it's a whole new place, literally and figuratively." I felt a great burden being lifted from my shoulders. "Sir Cramner is dead, long live Sir Bertram. I want you to walk into that auction room with a whole new sense of power. And propriety."

"Are you absolutely sure you want to do this?"

"More sure than you can imagine. It's making me as happy as it's making you."

"I admire your subtlety, Kick. It's exquisite. There's no way I can ever thank you enough."

"You don't have to. Let's get your clerk in here and wrap this up, we all have a lot to do."

Once Bertram and I had each signed, and the clerk had notarized the papers and been instructed to deliver the file immediately to Mr. Beauchamp at the bank, I stood up and offered my hand. "Congratulations."

Bertram was too overcome to speak. And me? I felt wonderful. I'd done the right thing all round. Ballantine & Company was in the hands it should be in, and as a bonus, while I know the saying goes: Living well is the best revenge, well, the fact is, revenge itself can also be the best revenge.

The doors closed to the public at three o'clock in the afternoon to give the staff time to complete preparations for the evening's VIP cocktail reception and first night of the two-day sale. We all changed into our formal evening wear, which we'd brought from home. I put on the same black gown I'd worn to all our openings for ten years—tailored, classic, unobtrusive. I was staff. Wallpaper.

"You look gorgeous," Owen said, and kissed me. He was almost as skillful a liar as I was. He did look gorgeous in his black tie.

Arianna floated in at five o'clock like a goddess. Black kohl surrounded her scathing blue eyes. Her bright white Hervé Leger dress clung like mummy wrappings. We greeted each other with something like gracious condescension—she was sorry for me because she'd stolen my boyfriend. I was sorry for her because she had him.

At five-forty-five, Bertram stepped into the foyer and clapped his hands. The staff—experts, associates, auction assistants, cooks, and waiters—lined up, a well-dressed army, ready for inspection.

Was there a different bounce to his step? Oh yes.

At six o'clock the front door was opened and at eight o'clock sharp, Bertram gaveled the sale to life.

I returned to the showroom to help the Jewelry ladies break down the exhibit. All the safes were open as we worked busily, laughing and talking, transferring the pieces from glass display cases into the velvet-lined drawers of the rolling safes. I wandered around, visiting with them. Lending a hand. Unobtrusively switching the pieces I'd copied. Out of one pocket of my gown, into the other. Now you see them, now you don't.

Bertram was about a quarter of the way into the sale, and so far, had tripled the estimate on every piece. I asked the doorman to call a taxi.

"Where are you going?" Owen materialized out of nowhere.

"I think I have food poisoning."

"Do you want Michael to take you?"

I shook my head. "Not necessary. The taxi's here. You go back in— call me in the morning." I kissed his cheek.

"What about the reception?"

"Go and have a good time. You've earned it."

"I'll miss having you there."

"Me too. Behave yourself." I joked.

Owen closed the taxi door and gave the driver my address. We pulled away from the curb.

"Change of plan," I said.

"Oh? Where to, miss?"

"Liverpool Street Station, please." I never looked back.

Half an hour later we pulled up at the chaotic railroad terminal that serves as the connecting point for trains north to Norwich and Gatwick.

"Are you needing a porter, miss?"

"No thanks. I can handle it."

I entered the terminal, found a ladies' room, changed back into my business clothes, and left my suitcase, a brand-new one with no identification, in a temporary storage locker. Then I took the escalator down two flights to the Underground station and caught the next train back into town.

The post-sale reception at the Savoy would just be starting.

SIXTY-SIX

By the time I got to Heathrow that night, the last flight to the Côte d'Azur was long gone. I got a good night's sleep at the airport Marriott, and caught the first flight out Saturday morning. Before leaving, I placed two calls on a brand-new British cell phone bought specifically for this purpose, and when I got to the airport in Marseilles, I placed a third call from a pay phone using an untraceable card. Then, in the parking lot, I laid the cell phone under the front tire of my wagon and drove back and forth over it until it was crushed into an unrecognizable pancake of black plastic and little shiny silver things which I scattered across the lot with a couple of good soccer-style kicks.

That was that.

I drove as fast as I dared to the farm and immediately turned on the TV set. Since the explosion, television crews had become a fact of life at Ballantine & Company, and I knew today would be particularly busy with the second day of the auction.

I made a pot of coffee. It was just starting to come undone.

"Scotland Yard . . ." the pert young woman explained from in front of our building. It was Allison Porter, one of the SkyWord reporters. ". . . received an anonymous call early this morning from someone claiming that certain pieces of the Princess Arianna Jewelry Collection were missing. We have here with us Mr. Andrew Gardner, the director of jewelry for Ballantine & Company. Good morning, Mr. Gardner, welcome to SkyWord."

"Thank you, Miss Porter." Andrew was paler than usual, and his pointed, long upper lip was locked over the lower one, like a turtle's.

"Is it true? Has there been a robbery?"

"I'm sorry to report yes. From what we've been able to determine, approximately a dozen pieces have been switched with replicas—very fine replicas, incidentally. Which is not to imply that we wouldn't have caught them whether we'd received the call or not. We examine and reconfirm everything completely before and after every showing."

"How much were they worth?"

"Their evaluations were in excess of 25 million pounds—that's what we estimate they would have brought at auction, minimally. In reality, the bidding could have been double or triple that."

"You mean they could be worth as much as 75 million pounds?"

Andrew nodded. "It's possible. Most of them were pieces with colored diamonds, very rare."

Thank you, Mrs. Fullerton, for all your colored stones, especially all those oversize pink and yellow and green and pale, pale blue sapphires which your jeweler told you were colored diamonds and for which he no doubt charged you accordingly.

"What are you going to do? Will the auction be canceled?"

Andrew shook his head with as much conviction as he was capable of. "No. No. Nothing that drastic is required—this doesn't affect the entire collection. Obviously, the counterfeit pieces have been pulled, and all the rest, as I've already said, are being carefully examined and recertified by our experts."

"So the auction will proceed as scheduled?"

"Absolutely. Eight o'clock tonight."

"Excuse me, one minute, Mr. Gardner." She held up her hand and listened to a voice speaking into her earpiece. "I have some breaking news. Yes . . . Yes. . . ." She looked brightly into the camera. "I've just received word that the jewels have been recovered."

Andrew's eyebrows shot up. "What good news."

"We're going now to my colleague Mark Hallifax. Mark, are you there?"

"Yes, Allison, I'm here at the Dukes Hotel in St. James's Place—just blocks from the Ballantine & Company auction rooms." He was hard against the wall of the tight little courtyard at the hotel's main entrance. Two police cars sat behind him, their blue lights spinning. Uniformed police officers stood at the front door controlling access. "There is another remarkable twist in this already intriguing story— we have it on very good word that Scotland Yard has just arrested Mr. Owen Brace, the chairman of the board of Brace Industries, which owns Ballantine & Company, among many other luxury goods companies, including the Panther Automobile Company here in England. Mr. Brace lives here at the Dukes, and they should be bringing him out any minute."

I saw David de Menuil dart past the reporter, have a quick conversation with the bobbies, show his identification, and pass through the front door.

This was too good for coffee. I opened a bottle of Mumm's Cordon Rouge 1995 and poured myself a glass, and then, although it was a perfect spring day, I built a fire in the kitchen. Once it was burning just right, I tossed all my fake papers and identifications into it.

"Do you know why Mr. Brace is being arrested?" Allison asked.

"The rumor, and keep in mind this is just a rumor, is that the stolen jewelry has been found in Mr. Brace's car, a Panther Madrigan that he keeps in a private garage behind the hotel. According to our source, the jewels were rolled in a hotel towel and stashed in the trunk, beneath the spare tire, where the repair kit sits."

"It sounds as though that could be done by anybody."

"It's my understanding that the garage is kept padlocked and only Mr. Brace has a key. Naturally, I'd assume he keeps the car itself locked as well. So it's highly unlikely it could have been anyone else."

"Sorry to break in," said Allison, "but I'm just getting word that we have a crew at the Panther plant in Henley where Scotland Yard detectives have uncovered a warehouse of furniture pieces that are said to be copies? Something to do with Lady Melody Carstairs? Am I getting that right?"

"You are, Allison," answered a reporter stationed in front of the shed that housed the phony Lady Melody collection. Police officers and detectives swarmed in the background. "From best I can gather, Scotland Yard received a call early this morning and the individual said they would find a warehouse on the distant grounds of the Panther factory, packed with identical copies of Lady Melody Carstairs's furniture. Her estate is scheduled to be auctioned by Ballantine & Company in the next few weeks and according to the caller, these pieces were intended to be passed off as the real thing. If it's true, that the entire estate has been copied with an intention to defraud, this would be an extremely serious offense."

While I stirred the papers around in the fire, I watched Owen and David leave the hotel, escorted by Chief Inspector Thomas Curtis. Owen looked aggravated as hell. He got into the backseat of one of the police cars, and I knew David was telling him he was following directly.

By the time they'd left and the courtyard was empty, my past was ashes.

SIXTY-SEVEN

"Kick," Flaminia said. "Can you come this evening? Six o'clock? It's just cocktails—it's too hard to do dinner on Sunday night, everyone's leaving for Paris, and it's the cook's night off."

"Sure, I'd love to."

"I've got a great man."

"Un-huh."

"No, really, I do."

"Whatever."

"Get done up."

"I'm always done up."

"Well, you know what I mean. Tonight's dressy."

"Right."

I arrived at Flaminia's a little after six and, as usual, there was no new man. But I hadn't been expecting one. There'd been a few lame attempts over the summer to fix me up, but I'd learned my lesson: I was off men. Forever. I'd had enough men, sex, romance, whatever, to last me a lifetime.

Was I sorry for the fling with Owen? Not a bit. And now I saw it as a fling, nothing more. Would I fall into that "Is it love or is it sex?" trap again? The thought was laughable.

"You look exquisite," Flaminia said. "That bracelet is magnificent."

It was the Queen's Pet, the only souvenir of my life of crime, other than my safe full of perfect diamonds. It seemed the ideal accessory for a cool autumn evening with black silk pajamas, a black cashmere shawl, and several strings of pearls.

"Thanks. You said to get done up."

"Well, you certainly did. Have you ever seen a more spectacular fall?" Flaminia said. "This is without a doubt the most perfect October on record."

The evenings had turned crisp, and the fields were moist and earthy, waiting for their next crops to be planted, and the sun had tilted in the sky so the light hit everything a little more cleanly.

I followed Flaminia into the kitchen and watched as she arranged a cheese platter. "I hope you like this new fellow. Can you believe it, I've completely forgotten his name." She shuffled a stack of papers on the counter. "What did I do with my list? Bill must have it. Anyway, he's a retired law professor or something. We just met him last week—totally charming. He's just retired and moved here from England or Scotland or Ireland, somewhere like that. English-speaking at any rate. He's staying up at Beau Manoir until he finds a place to buy. He's very well-fixed."

"I'd say so, if he's living at Beau Manoir. Where's his wife?"

Flaminia shrugged. "Dead. Gone. Who knows. No longer in the picture, at any rate."

Bill Balfour came in. "A couple of guests have arrived—and I don't know them."

"Just tell them hello, darling. Offer them a drink."

"You come. You're much better at that."

"I'll be right there." Flaminia shook her head. "Men are so hopeless. Do you mind finishing up? There are just a couple left to add." She handed me the spatula. "And you're so much more talented at this than I am anyway."

"No problem."

A man from England or Scotland or Ireland. I thought of Thomas. I'd thought a lot about him over the summer as I distilled my experience with Owen down to its earthy, physical, forgettable, essence. If

I'd actually been looking for a man, a real man that I could share my life with, he'd been right there in front of me. But the fact is, I stopped looking once Owen walked in and took me over, lock, stock, and barrel. But if I'd been paying attention to my world from the waist up, I would have seen Thomas. We'd had so much in common—music, books, paintings, love of food and wine, early mornings. He was nice, and so was I. Boy, I really screwed that one up, didn't I?

I mounded the olives and apple slices here and there artistically among the cheeses.

I was as happy as I'd always expected I would be. Everything was as I wanted it. I'd gotten a puppy. A beautiful, fluffy, little snow-white Westie. I named her Jewel. I took her everywhere with me. I helped out four mornings a week at the library in St. Rémy, and gave English lessons in the afternoons. I frequently met friends for dinner and had been invited to take a trip to Turkey in November.

My old ways had served their purpose and no longer held any attraction.

SIXTY-EIGHT

By the time I got back out to the terrace, a number of guests had arrived. The evening was chilly, and a fire roared in the outdoor fireplace. It was twilight, and the flames danced on our faces, giving us all a healthy, golden glow. Lights flickered here and there across the valley. Flaminia motioned me over.

"Kick, come here. I want you to meet someone."

The man turned to greet me and held out his hand. It was Thomas.

I stared at him, unable to believe my eyes.

"Thomas," I said at the same time he said, "Kick."

"You know each other?" Flaminia said. "I can't even believe it."

"What are you doing here?" I asked.

"I tracked you down."

"Excuse me, I have other guests to attend to," Flaminia said, but we ignored her.

Oh, no. Please don't let this be happening. "How?" My mouth was so dry I could scarcely get the word out.

"I was a detective, you know. A commander." His blue, blue eyes studied mine, but I could not read what they were saying. They looked kind and gentle as I remembered, but perhaps they always had that sorrowful glow, even when he was making arrests. "Aren't you going to say anything?"

A huge pain shot through my eye. I tried to speak, but no words would come out. I put my hand over my mouth and took a deep

breath. I was sure I was about to have a stroke. My thoughts rico-
cheted: Here I was at a friend's house, about to be arrested. All the
years of secrecy, all the effort, everything, for naught. Who would
take care of my puppy? I knew I was about to cry and decided to ask
Thomas to take me discreetly, escort me to the parking lot to make
the arrest, not do it here during Flaminia's beautiful soirée. Not
humiliate her and Bill. And me. "Thomas . . . ," I began.

"I wanted to thank you," he said.

"Thank me?"

"The collapse of the House of Brace could only have been orchestrated by you—it was masterful and elegant. The style with which
you did it made me admire you even more. Not to mention the fact
that it let me leave my career on a very high note."

I licked my lips. "Oh? Good, I'm glad." Could I be wrong? Is it
really possible he doesn't know? That he's not here to take me back
to stand trial?

"So I set about finding you."

"Oh? And how did you do that?" I was making what felt like a
superhuman effort to be bright and gay, but the edges of hysteria
welled up in me, choking off my breath and threatening to make me
sob out loud with fear. I decided to see if I could take a sip of my
drink without spilling it. The swallow of undiluted scotch went
down like a spine-stiffening tonic. I took another and my pulse
began to slow.

"After I traced you to Liverpool Street Station, where you literally
disappeared from the face of the earth, I only had one unsolved clue:
the painting in your living room, you know, the one from the School
of van Gogh."

"I know the one you mean."

"Well, I recalled that during that brief discussion we had about
Provence, your eyes took on a sort of special shine, then you
changed the subject immediately, which is a dead giveaway when
somebody's trying to hide something."

"It is?"

"Yes. So I was quite confident I'd find you in Provence. I knew I was going to retire here anyhow, so when I got here, I pulled some strings with the local gendarmes and eventually, some dozens of towns later, I found you. It's a matter of volume."

"You didn't want to find me for any other reason than to thank me?"

Thomas shook his head. "Yes and no. I wanted to find you because I wanted to see you again. I was upset when I discovered you'd vanished, Kick. I didn't like the way it ended between us, with me standing you up for dinner. Are you all right? You look like you've seen a ghost."

"Well, it is kind of a shock that you're here, Thomas. I guess it is a little like seeing a ghost—I really never expected to see you again."

"Are you sorry?"

"No." I started to laugh. "Actually, I'm so delighted, I just can't seem to comprehend it. Are you the man Flaminia was talking about who's staying at the Beau Manoir?"

Thomas nodded and held a match for my cigarette and then lit his own.

"Detective work must pay better than I thought. That's one of the most expensive hotels in France."

"I have other resources."

"Evidently. How long have you known Flaminia and Bill?"

"I met them last week when they were at the hotel having lunch. When Flaminia heard I was single, she practically held my neck to the ground with her foot until I said I'd come this evening. I knew you'd be here."

"How did you know?"

"She told me."

"That's not really very good detective work, is it? Just to have it all handed to you like that. Flaminia says you're a retired law professor." I was feeling more comfortable.

"True. Among other things. I've had a number of incarnations—law professor, barrister, magistrate, detective—but they were in the first half of my life. I have other pursuits in the second half—I plan to become a gourmet cook, a wine connoisseur, and a porcelain expert."

"I can't believe how happy I am to see you." I held up my glass. "I'm so glad you persevered."

"You look even more beautiful than I remember," Thomas said. "And that bracelet is amazing. Where did you get it?"

This was it. This was where my rubber hit the road, wasn't it? The moment upon which the rest of my life would hinge. I had to make a choice, and the decision was that I wasn't going to live in or with any more lies, no matter the consequences. "Thank you," I said. I put my hand on my wrist and fingered the clasp with its diamond melee and secret portrait of Prince Albert. "It is beautiful, isn't it. I stole it. I used to be the Shamrock Burglar."

"Right." Thomas laughed. "And I used to be the Samaritan."

I had told the truth. It was up to him to believe it or not.

"Do you want me to give you a lift home?" It was almost eight, and guests were starting to depart.

"I know it's out of your way, but I sent the driver back."

"Come with me."

I took him to my house, instead.

"Do you want something for dessert?" I asked, after taking him on a quick tour. "I have some fresh apples. I could make a Tarte Tatin."

"I can't think of anything I'd like more. I saw a bottle of '71 Château d'Yquem in your cellar. It'll go perfectly."

Of course. He knew without my having to tell him.

I peeled and sliced the apples and put them on to simmer in a cast-iron skillet with a huge amount of butter and sugar. While they caramelized, I went to work rolling out the pastry. Thomas poured us each a small glass of the exquisite dessert wine, which filled our mouths with bouquets of rich, sweet fruit.

"I'll be right back. I brought you a gift. I left it in the car." He was back moments later. "Come here."

I put down my rolling pin, picked up my glass, and followed him into the living room. "What?" I looked around and didn't see anything.

"Over the mantel," he said.

It was the Renoir *Polonaise Blanche,* stolen from Sheiglah Fullerton's bedroom.

I turned to face him. "You?" I said, incredulously. "The Samaritan Burglar?"

He nodded and put his hands on my shoulders. "Yes, and I've been meaning to speak to you about it. You didn't need to give me that mighty a whack—it took almost a week to get over the headache."

"I promise I'll never do it again."

"Good. To us, Kick. To our new lives."

"To us, Thomas."

We clinked our glasses, put on the music, ate the whole tarte, and laughed all night.

EPILOGUE

Owen Brace—Owen was charged with grand theft, grand larceny, fraud, and conspiracy, but David de Menuil got him out of jail that afternoon on bail, and thanks to David's expert legal maneuvering, all the charges eventually were dropped. It hadn't amounted to much more than a tempest in a teapot, but at least I caused Owen a little final humiliation and heartburn of his own. Christie's and Sotheby's protested that the whole thing had been a publicity stunt. The auction was a huge success.

I'd left a gigantic clue for Owen to demonstrate his innocence in the theft in case he needed it: a bouquet of shamrocks on his bed pillow. But I knew he'd never make the connection—he'd just think it was a new addition to the hotel's turn-down service and throw them away. I was right.

I'd also left a note on his bed table along with the engagement ring, telling him I couldn't go through with the wedding and had gone to Palm Beach to stay with friends indefinitely. He was unaccustomed to being jilted, so it's possible this added to his humiliation.

Brace International declared bankruptcy, Panther Automobile Company and Ballantine & Company were sold, at sizable losses. Owen moved to New York, and, within months, he and Gil became partners in a luxury cruise company (not associated with the Niandros Lines).

No investigation was ever made into whether or not Owen had murdered all his wives and Lady Melody, although Thomas continued to contend he had. Looking back on it, I think if they had been murdered, Gil was probably the one who did the dirty work.

Those responsible for planting the bomb that blew up Dimitri Rush's car have not yet been apprehended, although various factions continue to emerge and claim rightful ownership of the jewels which, to my knowledge, remain the property of Mr. Rush's family and are still stored in the Ballantine & Company cellar.

Thomas insists that Owen planted the bomb as a publicity stunt, but admits the chances of bringing him to justice are zero.

The replicas of Lady Melody's furniture and paintings were destroyed.

Bertram Taylor—Thanks to his grubstake, Bertram had no trouble putting together a limited partnership to buy Ballantine & Company. If I were to have any regrets, which I don't, it would be that I would have liked to have been able to see Owen's face when he learned Bertram held the KDK Trust. That would be a moment.

Bertram's idea of making Ballantine & Company a specialty auction firm was successful, and today the company dominates its fields of expertise, especially jewelry. The Arianna Auction guaranteed Ballantine's spot as the most powerful jewelry auctioneer in the world.

Thomas and I—We got married and are living happily ever after in Provence. We read books, have lunch, take walks, listen to music, teach English at the library and school, drink wine, cook, and make love. But the fact is, some things really are better than sex. We are unbelievably happy.

Every Saturday morning, I still check my e-mail for a message from my lost child. No word yet.